W9-CAA-462

A FARM AT SHAWNDO

Southern Minnesota
Mid-Nineteen Eighties

by
Jean Samuel McConnell

Northfield Public Library
210 Washington St.
Northfield, MN 55057

97-1107

A Farm at Shawndo
by
Jean Samuel McConnell

Published
by
Lone Oak Press.
304 11th Avenue Southeast
Rochester, Minnesota 55904
507-280-6557

Copyright © 1993
by
Lone Oak Press
NO PORTION OF THIS PUBLICATION MAY BE USED WITHOUT
WRITTEN PERMISSION FROM THE PUBLISHER

ISBN Number 0-9627860-7-1
Library of Congress Catalog Number
93 – 077295

PHOTOGRAPHY BY RAY HOWE

To:

Debby, Kathy, Diane, Terri.

My Daughters... My Friends

...betwixt the bridge and the brook,
the knife and the throat... who knows
how he may be tempted? It is his
case, it may be thine...

Robert Burton... 1621

Forward

The storm had been gathering for many years. Rich farm land that sold for seven hundred dollars an acre in the Sixties rocketed, in the Seventies to three thousand dollars or more.

Then, in the early Eighties, the bottom dropped out. Values were cut in half. Or worse. Mortgages, written to the inflated values, could not be sustained: the value was gone.

Thousands of family farmers were trapped in this situation. Some had only themselves to blame, others were innocent victims of events and economic factors beyond their control.

Out of this evolved a new grassroots organization. This is the story of Harvest.

Part One

The Prodigal

CHAPTER ONE

Marta found the body at four in the afternoon. She had dreamed often, imagined, feared the discovery for so long that the event had lost the primal power of shock. All that remained for her was a sadness so immense that her breath was stilled, her body near to a mirror image of the lifeless, ashen form before her. She did not cry out, the tears were wellsprings within that would need another time for release. Now Marta dwelt, for unmeasured moments, in a bleak land where time stood still and the sun was blotted. There was no haste within her, all frantic rush was forever in the past. Marta's being held only one feeling, a gray shroud of sorrow encompassed her. The final act had been played, as she had always felt it would, while she was away, in town. Now, time was as trivial as space and light or animal warmth in the big barn. Minutes passed, how many she would never know, before Marta moved to the tool room for a sickle blade, stumbled back to the barn and cut the body down.

The task was not simple. Mike, knowing ropes and how the fibers can stretch, had taken no chances on an ignominious spectacle of feet dragging on the hay-littered concrete floor. He had snugged up to the beam, fully twenty inches of space was beneath his boots...the hay bale had been kicked aside. The body, given the perversity of hemp strands, did not hang still but twisted, almost imperceptibly, a half turn, first one way then the other. Old timbers gently creaked and the cows turned soft eyes to watch, with indifference, the human comedy. Marta forked loose alfalfa beneath the corpse. Then she dragged two bales of hay together, threw a third one crossways on top of the others and mounted the bales like steps. She sawed at the rope, which moved constantly away from the sickle blade action. Somewhere in an alien world clocks ticked, shadows lengthened. Marta's hands reddened from the strain, from the vise-like grip. An instinct prodded that she should have gone to the house for a better tool, perhaps a butcher knife.

But the gap in the rope widened, fibers sprang apart, slowly, then with a twisting rush. The body dropped into the piled hay. One final tenderness had been enacted.

The body lay crumpled. The woman tugged at the limbs, first the legs. She pulled them straight and together, grasping the worn leather boots with her reddened hands. Then she arranged the arms at the sides; the first shudder gripped her as she felt the cold hands. Marta paused. His look was much too rigid, formal. She took each hand in turn and lay them across the midsection, one upon the other as Mike had often done in meditation. Then the eyes, which were

3

neither closed or open but crinkled in that farmer's squint that measures the elements, that contemplates the odds. Marta used her thumb and forefinger to close the crease of the lids.

Mike lay in dignity on the hay. The black and white faces of the animals regarded him with bovine mildness. Placid jaws worked the cuds in ancient rhythm, a metronome of slow contentment. Mike might have been asleep, there was a hint of healing slumber in the stocky figure and the stubbled face. Only the mottled purple, now near to black, on the neckline marred the portrait of peace. For the first time Marta glanced at her watch, a reflex. The barn windows were beginning to darken. There was so much to do, the cows would soon turn restless. Fresh hay must be pushed down the chute from the hay loft and distributed to the animals, both the milk cows and the young stock. The calves were quartered in the old horse stalls, unused for a generation by the transition to mechanical power. All horses had long departed the rural scene, except of course for the Amish. She must precede the alfalfa with a ration of ground feed, heavily fortified with additives. And then the hay. Silage could wait until tomorrow morning. The routine was as natural as breathing. She set about her work and the still figure, his last breath drawn hours before, lay without fear or failure or pain on the soft alfalfa hay.

A time, a place – a duty. The outside world filtered into Marta's sealed brain. This call must be made, this fact reported. A blizzard of questions, interviews, forms, depositions across her horizon. All in good time. There was a finality in death. But cows must be milked, twice daily, at the appointed time. The rhythm of lactation was no different from the measured beat of planting, cultivation, harvesting – even the rise and fall of jaws on the chewing cuds. Marta set the tools in place, the Surge milkers, the cans, the warm soapy water to wash the udders and cleanse the teats. Her body moved as effortlessly as hands on an assembly line or fingers at a keyboard. Thirty cows, ninety minutes to transfer the foaming milk from the herd to the stainless steel tank in the milkhouse.

The whole ritual, feeding, milking the cows, storing the milk, fresh bedding for the animals, tending the young stock, took well over two hours. Marta moved through the familiar chores like a sleepwalker and her husband's body rested on its cushioned bed, the hands folded in benediction, the eyes closed, the unshaven face serene. "Sleep," whispered Marta. "You've tossed and turned for months, known no peace."

She sat on a bale beside him. Many of the cows' heads were lower now, the animals had lain down on the fresh straw. The gentle eyes were unchanged, the hay and ground feed had been cleaned up and the cuds regurgitated to the slow measure of chewing. Marta's voice, a whisper, went on. "Don't worry, Mike, I've taken care of the work." She touched his cold face, caressing the stubble. "Tomorrow I'll face what we must go through. Not tonight. This is the day of our parting. I won't clutter this day with the concerns of others."

Marta left the warm barn. Billows of steam followed her out the door as she crossed once more to the tool room, a wooden lean-to against the bulk of the corrugated steel machine shed. From a shelf she pulled down a stiff, folded tarpaulin, one of several canvases used to cover outdoor ricks of hay when the barn was full. The tarp was rigid with cold, nearly impossible to carry. But it was wrapped with several strands of twine and she could use the twine as a handle to wrest the canvas a few inches off the floor. By tough stages Marta moved her burden through the shed door and into the barn, lowering the tarp to the snow every few feet as her strength gave out. Inside the barn she brushed the snow away and unwrapped the canvas. She viewed the stiff, unyielding folds with weary disdain.

She spoke aloud. "Marta, for Christ sake, get hold of yourself. The tarp simply won't do." She sat once more on the bale and thought of messages, slender threads back to us from the other side. Mike had been taciturn, he had always had trouble speaking. She remembered weeks during harvesting with no more that a dozen words a day. Still, she did not wish for others to make the discovery.

Marta reached inside the left hand pocket of the still figure's red mackinaw. Some nails, washers, an envelope. The letter was addressed to both of them, the crest on the upper left hand corner was Growers State Bank, Shawndo, Minn. Marta hesitated, then pushed the letter into her own pocket. In the right hand pocket of the mackinaw was more paper, a page from a lined pencil tablet, folded neatly. She unfolded the note, and read the message. Then she folded the paper to a smaller size and slipped it into her shirt pocket and buttoned the flap.

For moments the woman was disoriented. The gulf she had pushed back, kept at arms length for hours, suddenly yawned, black as night, airless as a tomb. She fought for breath and wondered idly why she was crouched, motionless, on a hay bale when the chores were completed, yet so much else to do. She had not formed, consciously, a plan. Yet, priorities enclosed her, the weak moment passed.

On the tarpaulin she had used poor judgment, more likely blind reaction, thought Marta. Of course the canvas was too unwieldy. She rose and walked to the house. In the bedroom closet she found an extra blanket, soft blue and woolen. She walked back to the barn and wrapped the body with care, working the edges safely under the

5

trunk and legs. She covered Mike's face and the swollen, discolored neck and tucked the remaining folds into a soft pillow beneath the head. This will guard him from the scurrying mice, even the probing curiosity of the barn cats. The sleek, fat mousers had not been too ambitious of late, overfed with milk.

Marta left the barn, leaving the lights burning. She closed the double dutch doors but did not lock them. She walked to the house, locked the door behind her and picked up the kitchen telephone and dialed a number. She did not consult the directory.

A deputy answered. Marta asked to speak to the sheriff.

"Sheriff Adams is at home, Ma'am. Can I be of help?"

"Thank you, Mr. Snyder, but I have to speak to the sheriff. There's been a death."

"I see. An accident?"

Marta could barely breathe. She shook her head. Only words, she thought. Only words.

"No, certainly not an accident. Please – I must speak to the sheriff." Her voice was flat.

"Well, O.K., I'll buzz him." In a few minutes she heard the deep voice.

"Sheriff Adams. Can I help you?"

"This is Mrs. Crawford. Mrs. Mike Crawford."

"Marta!" The deep voice was pleased. "Haven't seen you in ages. What's up?"

"Mike is dead. He hanged himself."

Silence. Then, an audible sigh, near to a groan.

"Oh God. Marta, I'm sorry."

"Yes. Well, you must come and take the body, and, whatever you do. Call the coroner I suppose. Whatever the procedure..."

Marta's voice trailed into vagueness.

"Certainly. We'll get right on it." The voice was brisk but still soft.

"The body – the body, Mike, he's in the barn. I'm going to bed. I need the rest. The morning chores ..."

"Please, Marta. I know how tough this is. You might doubt that, but I really do know." Sheriff Adams nearly said "This will pass", a natural reflection of counsel, but long experience choked back the words. Now the deep tones held authority. "Marta, I'm devastated by this. But there are the regs. We have to know ..."

"I understand, Bill. Regulations. A statement, a full description of the events, probable cause, all that bullshit. Yes, I understand that. The body is safely covered, in the cow barn. The lights are on, the door is unlocked. I'm going to bed. I am going to bed or I will not survive. I'll talk to you, and the others, tomorrow."

"Marta! Don't make this tough on us." A struggle was in the man's voice. "You know we can't come in after you. We could, sure but we won't. But please, change your mind. Help us."

"Good night, Sheriff."

"Was there... a note?"

"Yes. A personal one. I burned it." She put down the telephone, there were two more calls to make.

She phoned Duluth, direct, and spoke to Steven first, then to Karen. She could hear, in the background, the bubbling voices of her grandchildren, being hushed by Steven. Marta spoke for a few minutes with Karen, then said good night. Next, she dialed a number in Brenton, Pennsylvania. There was no answer. Marta waited, tried twice more, then phoned Western Union and dictated a message.

She stood for moments, gathering her thoughts, then turned off the lights and went upstairs to her bedroom. In the darkness she removed her boots and jacket, loosened her shirt and slipped beneath the bedspread.

She stared at the shadowed ceiling and did not stir when the ambulance and the official cars gathered in the hard packed snow near the barn. She heard muted voices but she could not make out the words... they might have been in a foreign tongue, the visitors from a country she would never know.

CHAPTER TWO

At five the alarm clock awakened Marta to a world of blackness, the window a faint gray shadow, ghostly against the wall. Somewhere past midnight she had found sleep and now that discipline which had dissolved to mere formlessness on the previous day took hold. She undressed and showered. Marta had always found clarity in the enveloping shroud of warm water. She had slept in her clothes, now she lavished the white soap.

I am blessed, she murmured, while the fragrant steam billowed about her full body. I am blessed and cursed at the same time. How many women, and men, have faced arrows clothed in armor like mine? The rivulets flowed around her shoulders and neck, down and between the round breasts, across the sturdy belly. If the avenging angel had caught me unawares I'd be lying, side by side, with Mike today. And perhaps that's my place. But Karen, yes, and Garth, they must not be dealt a double blow. My sense of fairness — is such a thing possible today? — does not permit it. The angel has met his match because I was forewarned. She fumbled for shampoo and drenched her hair, the flattened strands, trimmed short, did not reach beyond the nape of her neck. If I had not, secretly, read the books on death and dying... Mike paid little attention to what I read... the literature on grief and recovery, I could never face today and all the tomorrows. But I'm prepared, I know all the stages... thank you Kubler-Ross. I'll march through those fashioned stages one by one. She stepped from the shower and briskly toweled.

But first, I must milk the cows. I will fork the silage and feed the calves. Yes, and number seventeen, I must watch her closely.

By nine o'clock, the work was completed and a warm breakfast inside her, Marta was in the county seat, Prairie City, a town of four thousand. She drove the fifteen miles in weather near to zero, by-passing her "home town" Shawndo on the way. In the flat country each town was visible to the next one. Steeples from the churches of "Divine Indifference", the grain elevators, stood massive in each community, seeming to shrink the miles in between. There were few wood lots or wisps of forest, only sentinel rows of windbreaks, mostly spruce and willow, some cottonwood, guarding each farmstead from the north and west. The corn and soybean fields, harvested too late for fall plowing, rested under the deep snow. Few animals were in sight, milk cows and hogs all safely housed. Only the occasional group of beef cattle could be seen, straggling around a feeding rack or hunched in three-sided shelters, open to the south.

She drove her pickup down the main street. The cafes, meeting places for the morning crowd, showed lively atmospheres but the stores seemed barren of traffic. Printed neon signs, "For Rent", on several store fronts were like bandages on old wounds. She had known all the proprietors.

Sheriff Bill Adams was a living montage of sorrow, compassion and anger. He offered condolence with a slight frown.

Sheriff is an elective position. An awkward embrace was gently parried into a hand clasp by Marta. But Adams raged at the disregard involved, the non-compliance on the statutes regarding sudden death. The stipulations on prompt·reporting, cooperation with authorities, tests, prompt autopsy, pathology findings... the list went on. Marta had violated nearly every code.

"Here's the thing, Marta... Mrs. Crawford. You know the facts on this case. And I think I do, too. But that doesn't satisfy the law."

She stared directly at the flushed face. She said nothing. The yellow walls of the Sheriff's office gave the room an oppressive dullness. The four adults clustered about an old wooden desk.

Adams went on. "This is one case only. We can't deviate. I shouldn't have to tell you, at a time like this, all kinds of purported suicides are used as a cover for foul play, all kinds of shenanigans. The law is the law, don't matter how brutal that sounds to the family members involved. Now, here's the three of us, me, Roger and Doctor Charlie." The sheriff indicated, with a gesture, the solemn faces of the county attorney and the coroner. "All of us, up to our ass in regs and a case that could drag through the courts and probate for years." Sheriff Adams paused for breath, his face held a look of real discouragement. The Sheriff was a kind man, he hated what he was doing.

But he had set the tone. Marta, shielded within her own thoughts, was not concerned. All this was programmed by the system, she would have expected thoroughness for a neighbor's death as well. The coroner, Charlie West, had little to say. He was a local physician, harried by work and a Medicare blizzard of papers he would never understand. His unpaid accounts were staggering, each year piled up more un-collectables.

But the county attorney, Roger Carlson, was all business. He made the obligatory remarks of condolence, rubbing his hands together, rising to pace the Sheriff's small office. Then he sat, scowling, looking beyond the window.

"Do you understand criminal law, Mrs. Crawford?"

I should let that pass, thought Marta. Then, "No, does anyone? I mean, outside the profession?"

"Most people understand about accomplices. You help in any manner, overt or covert, in a criminal matter you become an accomplice."

"Are we talking crime, or suicide?"

"Suicide, Mrs. Crawford. Or so I assume. In this case, little doubt."

"Then?"

"Then?" The attorney's balding head turned full face, the dark eyes slitted in severity. "Well then, if there is foul play, an accident, a homicide, by one or more, collusion of other minds or interests. You can see that, I know you can."

Marta was bewildered. "I don't follow."

The attorney slapped the desk. The paper bounced.

"The time element. A suicide scene, like a murder scene, it has to be sealed. Otherwise, well, clues are lost, the trail grows cold. This is all impersonal, Mrs. Crawford. But you must see the implications. Not what happened at the farm, I'm sure. What could happen, why the rules are strict?"

Marta frowned, the protective shield was thin. But now she did begin to understand. She felt, dully, a small remorse, a feeling for Carlson. The man was in a bind. His was, also, an elective office, and there were oaths to uphold. The day's first weariness closed in.

She said softly, "Mr. Carlson, I do understand. I have made your position difficult. I think that, instinctively, I knew the rules or close enough."

"Then why did you wait, for several hours in fact, before notifying the authorities?"

I had to milk the cows, she thought. And feed the calves, and push bales down the chute. I had to get on with my life, or my life would cease. Mike was dead, there was so much work to do.

She said, "I'm not sure I can explain."

Sheriff Adams reached across the desk and flipped a switch. A recorder, she supposed, she didn't know. "Marta," the voice was gentle. "Please try. There has to be a statement for the record. We have to begin somewhere to close the books." His eyes pleaded. "Can you answer the question?"

"I felt my death."

Now she had voiced the feeling. The office walls loomed around her, over her, ready to pounce, to suffocate.

"Your death?" Carlson's voice was puzzled.

Marta scarcely heard him. "We were so close," she whispered. "Mike and I. What they say about farm couples, we were a team. I was drawn to his still figure, like a magnet. I felt his death, in my eyes, my ears. I could taste the sweetness of death. I knew that if I didn't carry on, right from that moment, that I'd join him."

"You were suicidal yourself?"

"That's just a word." Marta paused in wonder. Yes, that's all it was, a thing people said. "I survive. Not that I'm better or worse, survival is my nature." This was difficult but the others said nothing, they were watching, listening. She could hear, now, the faint hum of the tape.

Marta continued.

"It's just – I wanted to be with Mike. I couldn't bear a world other than the world he dwelled in... whatever that might be. And I also knew I had to carry on. Mike's work, you know. Here. The thread between worlds was too slender. I felt, truly, to face these questions, all the details, last night – I wouldn't have survived."

The men were still. Marta breathed. The walls pulled back. She could see a chipped spot, new paint was needed.

"Just the chores, the cows... all that. Just one night, to save my life. For what it's worth," a small mirthless laugh. "Just to survive one night. I felt I had no choice. I couldn't die, there was no one else left to run the farm."

In the yellow room the silence dragged. The coroner looked thoughtful, fingers steepled on his ample stomach. The forbidding attorney was pensive. Sheriff Adams made notations on a yellow pad. Is this all? wondered Marta.

Perhaps from all this a statement will spew forth that I have to sign. The Sheriff looked up.

"You said something last night about a note."

"Perhaps. I think you asked me. Yes, I'm sure you did. I burned the note in the kitchen range." It seemed so effortless to lie.

The Sheriff winced. "You shouldn't have, Marta. That's destroying evidence."

"Was I supposed to know that regulation, too? The note wasn't evidence, it was a personal message to me – alone."

"Yes, of course." Adams glanced at the county attorney who gave a slight shrug.

"Then, this question. Can you give us, for the record, a motive?"

Marta was gripped by a sense of the unreal. She said, "I can't believe that question, Bill."

Again they sat in silence. It was obvious the interview was over. Marta rose and buttoned her parka.

"Thank you, gentlemen," she said. "You've been kind. I apologize for any distress I may have caused." She pushed open the office door.

As she was leaving, attorney Carlson had one last question. Marta had known she could not escape the one subject on all their minds.

"Can you rely on Harvest, for help today? I mean with the arrangements, the funeral?"

Marta smiled, almost fondly.

11

"They'll be there. Harvest is always there when there's a need. Mike knew that, and so do I."

Marta drove again through Main Street. There were a few more cars at the curbsides now, the time was approaching mid-forenoon. Still, the wide street held the languor of a Sunday afternoon, the bustle of years past, so well remembered, was nowhere in sight. Ten years past, even seven, the street had been a bazaar of commerce, especially in winter when the crops were safely stored. She looked with fondness on the furniture store, as boarded and forlorn as in a ghost town where silver had been king. Her bedroom furniture and the sofa had come from Peterson's & Son. Now, snow drifted around the double doors and a remnant of awning flapped in the wind. The women's apparel shop was closed, farm wives favored the rough clothing of work and shop girls used the catalogs or drove to bigger towns. A hardware store was closed and Jansen Feeds showed a lonesome tatter of Purina checkerboard through the cracked window.

She parked the pickup in front of the columned sweep of the Hanson Funeral Home entrance. Three neighbors, two middle aged women and a grizzled older man, were waiting on the brick steps, bundled up against the biting air. The women embraced her, the oldster gripped her mittened hands, and together they entered the cloistered stillness of the mortuary.

They were greeted by the owner who spoke to them in the calm, concerned tones of his profession. The words were a soothing sound in Marta's ears. She murmured appropriate responses to questions that did not penetrate her mind. Her eyes searched the muted interior for just one person. She was led to an inner room where Karen sat on a straight-backed chair, her eyes brooding and red rimmed. The daughter looked up and managed a small smile, then, silently, she embraced her mother, holding tight, clinging, like a drowning woman, to a life raft.

CHAPTER THREE

The old Crawford house was comfortable, braced against cold with bottle gas flame from the converted furnace in the basement. Yet they sat in the kitchen and drew warmth, as they had as children, from the black stove. The table, part of Marta's scant inheritance, was wooden, warped with the years. On the kitchen curtains black swallows soared on muslin. The coffee pot was squat, black-ringed enamel, the handle worn.

They sat together at the old table and remembered. When Marta was twelve and Garth eight they had plotted together, on a farm short miles from here, the ultimate Christmas gift for their father. They would rise early on that morning and do the milking before their father awakened. Merry Christmas, Pa, they would shout, stomping into the house. You can enjoy a lazy breakfast, slug down the eggnog, read a book, while Mom prepares the dinner.

None of the great plans had succeeded. The hay bales were too heavy, they forgot the ground corn. A temperamental Holstein had kicked off the milker. The foaming milk seeped into the gutter while the children scrambled to retrieve the machine from the muck and further damage.

Garth chuckled. "Milk in the cowshit. And the cats looking at us like we were criminals." He poured coffee refills and they smiled over third cups.

"Yeah," Garth continued. "We screwed up that deal royal. When Pa got to the barn we weren't half through milking. The cows were bellering for feed and the whole place was a steam bath 'cuz we hadn't remembered to turn on the fan."

"`Merry Christmas, Pa,' we yelled," said Marta. "What a present!"

"And what did Pa do," said Garth. It wasn't a question. They had sealed in their minds through the years what had happened.

"Pa just smiled," said Marta. He said, 'Thanks, kids', just as gentle as could be. God, he could be a terror, that man. `Specially if he'd been drinking. Then, Christmas morning, when he had a call to be mad at the mess we'd made, he was like a lamb."

"Well, Pa was mostly awful strict. Ma was too easy. I guess we had an even break."

"Thirty-six years ago, December." Marta's mind drifted through the intervening years. " A long time. Now here we are, just the orphan kids."

"And Mike gone."

"Yes, my Mike has left."

"What can I say? He was a good man."

13

She had been afraid that Garth would arrive too late for the funeral. He had missed the wake, her telegram had reached his house after he left for his night shift in the steel mill. Then, with dense fog, it became tough to get a flight. But he had made it to Minneapolis, and caught the bus to Prairie City.

Marta hadn't minded that he missed the wake. She didn't take much stock in wakes herself, although she had sat the long hours and recited the Hail Mary's for scores of friends through the years. She had discussed the whole business with Burt Hanson at the funeral home. Pro and con, full wake, simple service at the church, graveside ceremony. She had decided on a full wake, open casket. Marta felt that the Irish expected it. The Germans and Scandinavians were indifferent to the ancient custom but would pay full respects either way. But Marta had a reason, beyond religion and custom. Mike's name and memory must be preserved. A closed casket, she knew, and a phone call to Sheriff Adams confirmed, would spawn rumors. Rumors, over the years would become facts. Long tales would grow of mutilation, a neck broken beyond straightening, discoloration to the black of midnight. Marta faced the facts, rode the storm of emotion, and strove for normalcy.

Hanson had done well with the purple neck. With cosmetics and a high collar the neck appeared almost normal. Mike lay in repose, his face a mask of peace. Marta was content. She couldn't still the talk, she could only stem wild conjecture. The visitation, five until nine on the second evening became a vindication, a stamp of faith, the link of comradeship with a fallen friend. Six hundred people, a third of them Harvest members, filed in and out and touched the wife and daughter with hand clasps and kisses. Marta and Karen were engulfed in a sea of love. They managed the tough hours, stoic and smiling.

Then, this morning. Garth, just arrived, joined his sister and niece at the funeral home. They stood in silence, hands locked, while the casket was closed. At the church the religious service was brief. The minister, young and solemn, said little, he believed in the eloquence of the flock.

And, in their quiet, anguished ways, many spoke with an earthiness near to poetry. Neighbors, both men and women, eulogized the stocky, friendly, helping man who was always there when needed. A man, said George Rogers, who would work from dawn until well after dark, then visit the night away with a dying friend... or search the fields for a lost child. Another spoke, in a voice so choked he could not finish the thought, of a man who spent two weekends building a tree house for transient laborers he barely knew. There were others. Garth listened to the words and could not comprehend the meaning of such a life, such a death. The anomalies of love, of uncommon human concern... and suicide. I never reached this man in life, he faced the truth of his thought, how can I face him in death?... in these ceremonies of remembrance, these paeans of praise? All this seems to come together in a common theme, the cry of the survivor, `there but for the grace of God ...' Karen cried softly, head bowed. Marta stared, dry-eyed, at each speaker, her silent lips thanked each in turn.

One-half mile to the cemetery. The road was choked with cars. Some people walked the distance, the cold wind unremarked by the mourners. There was no room to park. All those who had visited the funeral home and hundreds more, from all corners of the state, and northern Iowa. They braved the frigid weather, they gathered later at the Legion Hall for lunch. Here the talk was informal, relaxed. Mike, for all his reticence, had been an easy man to know. Bumper stickers, in the lot and on the street and one huge banner on the wall of the Legion Hall spoke, with silence, the one word message of Harvest. Garth, an old union hand, scarred by labor wars in the steel mills, was caught by the power of the word. He thought, I have to learn more. There must be, here, below the surface, a hidden strength. Parnell came to mind, and O'Leary... `A terrible beauty is born'... Is this another such story?

"You're tough, Marty. At the church today, and the cemetery. Like a rock."

She stirred uneasily.

"Don't say that, Garth. Please. I'm no rock, it's just, well I was prepared. I saw this coming."

"How long?"

"Oh hell, I don't know. A thing like that... so gradual, creeping. But finally I knew. Like a train bearing down and you're roped to the tracks." Marta lighted a cigarette, her first in days.

"Garth, you have to know this. You think I'm tough. Mike was twice the person I am. The man was a fortress, when he was beside me I felt invincible." She sipped her coffee, now cold. The hands of the clock had crept past midnight.

Garth was puzzled.

"Seems to me, though, you had the stamina. I mean, well hell, you're here."

She touched his hand. "I knew you were thinking that. And you are so wrong. Every life is different. Don't consider tougher, softer... just different. Mike's death was a statement. His. My life, going on is another statement. I can't do what Mike did. He made the ultimate expression of our times... our problems."

Garth frowned. Half a lifetime removed from the land, he was learning the hard lessons of desperation.

"You saw how the people turned out. Hundreds that he didn't even know. You saw the love, Garth, you could feel it. Every farmer there has walked in Mike's shoes, or near enough, His pain was theirs. Maybe some of them envied Mike today."

Garth said, "I'm full of coffee. Makes me jumpy. Got any beer around here?"

"In the fridge. Bring me one while you're at it."

He flipped the tabs, pouring hers into a water glass and took his deep from the can.

"Marty, I've got to know the situation here. I didn't know Mike as well as I should have. Christ," he sighed, remembering, "haven't been around these parts. Broke up with Thelma ten years ago. Got drunk a lot after that. Had the support payments... when I was working... till the girls were grown. Lost all my roots, and, still, never put deep roots in P.A. Lost years, a wanderer."

"Garth, I know... I know. Not easy. I think it was beautiful you could make it this time, getting here on such short notice."

The brooding man waved this aside, there were things he had to know. Marta could not know that her brother stood, as Mike had stood, at a crossroads. "Can you tell me more, Marty? If it ain't too painful. Why you're here... and why Mike's gone.?"

She smiled, tenderly. "Look, Mike got out of high school in nineteen-fifty. Mike's folks were renters, had it rocky, his Dad's health went south. They just tossed in the towel. Mike worked on farms here and there and at factory jobs at night when he could. Just wanted to farm, that was his life. Well, mostly. Later on I was part of it, and then Karen. One kid, think of it. He'd have liked a dozen."

"Yeah, Karen. Christ, only got to talk to her for an hour. She's back in Duluth by now."

Marta glanced at the clock. "For sure, by now. And her and Steve and the kids, another tough row."

"This family is jinxed. Where the hell is all this prosperity I hear about? Sure as hell ain't in the steel business." Garth finished his beer and popped the tab on another.

"Nor here. Or Duluth. Anyway," she resumed her narrative. "Mike finally got some dough together, bought this place right, real tobacco road at the time, and together we gradually fixed it up, improved the stock. We had a good life, yeah, really good, Garth. But we never got out from under. Looked for a time like we'd make it, but there was always something. Short crop, big vet bills... whatever. Then a few years back, prices went to hell, taxes way up, we needed more machinery. Not to mention a building to house the gold-plated monsters." She shook her head. "Sixty thousand for one tractor – what got into us? And the price of a combine, corn picker? Mother of god!"

"Of course. And not just us. Practically everyone we knew. Seemed like we were just sailing, hardly a ripple on the sea. Then it all came down."

"You close to the edge?"

"Not close, Garth. Right _at_ the edge. Slipping over." She shrugged. "The old bromides. Misery loves company. Maybe so, but it's still misery."

"Want another beer?"

"I hate beer – but, yeah." He watched as he refilled her glass. For the first time, her eyes were moist.

"Mike and I were so alike. Yet, so different. About the land. Mike's life was in the soil, this special three-twenty was in his blood. Going back to how he scratched and fought to get a start. He felt... he never really said it, but I know... that if he couldn't save the farm it was like he'd never lived, like his name and record would be stricken from the rolls."

Garth asked, gently. "And you?"

"I felt the same, about the land." Marta struggled to make it plain. "But I got... I don't know, maybe a longer view of history than Mike had. Land can't be lost, not like a plane that crashes or a ship, the land will always be here, just different owners. The cycle is against the farmer now. Maybe the wheel will take a turn. Maybe some of us will lose our land and then get it back. But even if we don't, the land will be here. And I'll... we... will survive."

She sipped her beer. "Shit I sound like Ma Joad. A lousy script, this ain't Oklahoma."

"For sure. More like the Yukon. I'd damn near forgot how friggen cold it gets here."

"Well, old P.A. ain't a summer resort from what I've heard. Remember. Mike and I were only there once, in July I think. Hot and stinking in Pittsburgh."

Garth laughed. "The stink is down, the smoke is a lot less now. Some days you can see the sun."

Marta yawned.

"Sorry. I gotta crash, Garth. Milking time comes around too soon."

"For both of us. I'm pitching in tomorrow."

"You'd be lost, kid. No vending machines."

"Shit."

"There's still plenty of that."

"I can pitch hay, scrape out the gutters." For a moment he brooded, he, too, felt the weariness of the long day. "I ain't forgot everything, I know which end the milk comes from."

"Hey, great."

Garth hesitated. "I got no business asking this, Marty. But was there a note, anything you want to tell me?"

"Sure. Bill, the sheriff, asked the same thing. I lied to him, of course. Not to you." She opened the table drawer, unfolded the penciled note and handed it to her brother. She muttered, "Why am I drinking this? That six-pack sat there for a month. We just kept it for company." Marta crossed the room and poured the remainder of her second beer into the sink.

Garth read: "Marta, you can handle things better without me. I love you. Keep a close watch on NO. 17 she is due in a few days and always has trouble with the calving. You may have to help. Mike."

CHAPTER FOUR

Two days after the funeral Garth Kyllo walked into the Growers State Bank of Shawndo. He had driven into town in Marta's pickup. The morning was brilliant, snow sparkled like precious stones. The temperature had moderated, a brief respite.

Radio and television spoke, ominously, of threatening weather sweeping in from the Dakotas. Standard fare. Dakota and Nebraska storms, Alberta Clippers, ferocious jet streams. Just another February in Minnesota. "Theater of Seasons" as tourist bureaus named the state, was a standing joke on the windswept prairies. He parked the Chevy pickup, slant to the curb, on the barren street.

Garth approached a teller window and was directed to a desk at the edge of the lobby. A pleasant voice asked, "May I help you?"

Garth was slow to answer. His eyes, snow-glazed by the outdoor brilliance, swept leisurely over the woman... old force of habit. She was dark haired, possibly on the low side of thirty-five. Her wide smile was a bit lopsided, but friendly. Large eyes looked at him through horn-rimmed glasses, the frames spotted, decorously, with tiny sequins. Well, hey, what have we here, he wondered.

"I should speak a little louder, I guess," she acknowledged. "I don't believe you heard me."

Garth grinned and helped himself to the upholstered chair in front of the desk.

"Naw, my hearing is okay." His glance swept the bank's interior. Not one customer in sight, the women at two teller windows doing make work. They slouched at their posts. The drive-in window was servicing a customer in a battered dump truck. "But I can see why you keep it low, you might wake somebody up."

She laughed. "Come on, you're being a little rough on us. We have our busy times, Mr.... ?"

"Kyllo," he said. "Garth Kyllo." He liked her laugh. "I'd like to see the bank president. And aren't those glasses a little glitzy for a town like this?"

The remark was ignored. "The president, Mr. Kenseth, is very busy at the moment. A meeting of department heads. I might get you an appointment later in the forenoon." She consulted her pad. "Perhaps by eleven. Could you tell me why you want to see him?"

On the wall behind her desk was a discreet 'No Smoking' sign. Garth extracted a Marlboro and struck a light. He did not hurry, and he ignored the question.

"Department heads? In this toy store? I've been in popcorn stands bigger than this."

19

The woman glared. Garth laughed.

"Hey, lighten up. Besides, I told you my name, you didn't tell me yours."

A red nail pointed at a nameplate. "I assumed you could read," she snapped.

"Oh, yeah. Sorry." He peered. "Gail Samarro. Nice to know you, Gail. Don't mind me." He dragged on the cigarette and blew smoke in the direction of the sign. "I just want to talk to – Kenseth isn't it? – about my sister's loan."

"I see. And your sister is... ?"

"Crawford. Marta Crawford."

"Oh." The crisp poise, for a moment, left. "That's Mrs. Mike ?"

"It was Mrs. Mike." Garth's voice was deliberate.

"Yes. Well, Mr. Kyllo. I'll see. Please wait." The receptionist disappeared into an inner office. Garth stubbed his Marlboro and lit another. He glanced at one of the tellers, a chubby brunette of no more than twenty. She had been following the exchange. Garth smiled in friendly fashion. Quickly, she looked away.

Gail did not reappear for more than five minutes. Then she came back to the desk. Garth liked what he saw as she slipped into the chair opposite him. God, he thought, Shawndo! Maybe nine hundred people, and it has a specimen like this!

"The meeting is nearly over, Mr. Kyllo," she said. "He'll see you in just a minute." She returned to her work on the desk, frowning at the papers, flipping through her Rollodex. Garth lounged in comfort. The buzzer sounded.

"Right through that door, Mr. Kyllo." Her voice had warmed a bit. Well, shit, he thought, this is getting somewhere. As he rose he was struck with a dampening thought. Maybe he was hearing, not interest, only sympathy. In the private office a tall lean figure rose behind a walnut desk to offer a firm handshake.

Kenseth extended condolences. He had, he said, known the Crawfords for several years. Wonderful people. They parried, talking of the weather, the hope for a decent spring beyond a typical Minnesota winter. Kenseth was calm, in charge. He stood six-one, with rimless glasses and a high forehead. No banker formality, with grey slacks and a sleeveless white shirt. Cool, thought Garth. I'd expected fiftyish, florid, a paunch... this man is years younger than I am.

"Thanks for seeing me," said Garth. "I was a little pushy with the gal out front. She seems sharp. Is she just a receptionist?"

Kenseth smiled. "Also an assistant cashier. There are plenty of titles to go around in a small place."

"Well, even back east we heard of the Willmar Eight. Any influence from that scene?"

"Naw," the bank president was affable. He had heard the question too often about the Mid-State female bank employees, celebrated in documentaries, who walked a picket line for two years, winter and summer, for female employee rights. "We treat our people equally. We underpay all of them."

"Fair enough. Anyway, Mrs. Samarro... Miss Samarro, whatever... didn't know I had to catch a bus this afternoon to Minneapolis. I've got a plane to catch."

"I see." Kenseth did not pursue this.

The offhand manner of the bank official nearly unnerved the brash Garth. Still, he had a purpose, this was a visit he had planned since the night of the funeral.

"Marta wouldn't tell me very much about current matters, the pinch that drove Mike to throw in the towel. Just generalities, said she was on the brink, financially. No details."

Kenseth pulled a folder from his desk. He said nothing.

"Well, I ain't expecting details from you. I can't ask you to − what? Break a confidence?"

The banker's voice showed concern. "Of course not. If your sister wants privacy, I can't go much further."

"Yeah, I understand. But, look. All my life I've heard about the friendly small town banker." Garth's wide smile was innocent. "Hell, this ain't Chase Manhattan." The remark was greeted with a wintry smile. "It's just − Marta feels I have so many troubles of my own I shouldn't lose sleep over hers. I admire her for that. But maybe I can help. If I'm going to help I have to know."

"Know what?"

"What's needed to stave off foreclosure. That word, foreclosure, seems to be the common denominator around here. Marta wouldn't say. And, what she's been through, I couldn't press her."

"I see." Kenseth fingered through the worn file, his face a mask. He spoke carefully.

"I can't lay out details, Mr. Kyllo. We get into legal areas. I can say this..." He frowned. "I believe her main indebtedness is here, this institution. She may have other, smaller burdens, that she hasn't declared to us."

"Then, a guess. Two hundred thousand?"

"I wish. Lord, how I wish, after what has happened. But certainly well over twice that figure." Kenseth's voice was tired, he slumped in his chair.

Garth was stunned. He was entering a new world, unknown to his youth. Now the newspaper stories from the midwest, the T.V. docudramas took on a mantle of reality. This was beyond his experience.

21

"All due of course?"

The banker sighed. "Nothing in this part of the country is due. Merely due is a blessing. Far overdue, of course."

"What happens?"

"A year ago, a rather innocent question. Right now, with the politics of moratorium and negotiation, there's a breathing space, for some debtors. But foreclosure or not – and God knows I'm not enthusiastic about this bank owning farms – the interest goes on. It must be paid or the tally mounts. Beyond control, I might add. On the matter of interest the Crawfords have done badly."

Garth tried to assimilate the words. He felt empty. No wonder Marta had stonewalled the figures. He managed the next question.

"The interest then ...?"

"A year behind. At least forty thousand dollars. More than that will be due again this year."

"I see." But of course Garth did not see. John Kyllo, his father (and Marta's) had bought an entire farm, before Garth was born, for thirty thousand dollars. Not a large farm but with a good barn, a granary and chicken coop and a solid house. Now, forty thousand, a year past due, on interest alone! Through the office window the winter sunlight slanted across the carpet and the sounds of Main Street in the little town were muted. Garth felt a loneliness, as deep as he had felt in the snow covered cemetery. Mike was gone, that chapter had ended. Here was a continuing tragedy. Marta was only one of thousands. It was time to get back to the farm. He rose to leave.

He said, "Then what's to be done?"

The reply was ironic. "Why don't you tell me?"

"So much," Garth murmured. He stood in quicksand, there was no base. He asked, "What of this farm group I've heard of? Called what, Harvest?"

"Harvest!" Kenseth spat out the word. "My Lord, man. Harvest! The blind leading the maimed. What can they do, except hold meetings and mill about?"

"I got the idea they were well thought of around here."

"No doubt. Salt of the earth. Nice folks, good farmers. Good, busted farmers. They're not a joke. It's much too sad for that. Look, you think the farmers are united? Well, think again. Go to a foreclosure auction, you'll learn. The farmers will trample one another bidding for the pieces. Jackals scrapping over a corpse. Half of them have no thought for the victim. Individual survival comes first. That's part of it, the rest is that the law is involved in such sales."

Kenseth carefully placed the folder back in the desk drawer.

"Mr. Kyllo – Garth isn't it? Garth, do what you can for your sister. Maybe you can do nothing. But forget Harvest. There are no radical solutions."

"I suppose you're right." Garth paused a moment, then grinned. "It does look grim. But I'll think about it. Maybe I should rob a bank", he ventured. Who was that guy that said 'that's where the money is'?"

"Willie Sutton, I believe. But Willie spent an awful lot of time in prison."

"Not relatively."

"I don't understand..."

"Not as much time as Mike Crawford is going to spend dead. Now that is what I call a lot of time." Garth's voice was toneless.

Kenseth frowned. He leaned back in his swivel chair, eyes thoughtful. "This conversation, Mr. Kyllo, is taking a rather strange turn."

"Yeah? Well, it's jail house humor but what the hell?" Garth leaned across the desk and extended his hand. "Thanks for your time, Mr. president."

They shook hands, gravely. Garth left the office. He walked halfway to the front door, then stopped. He returned to the receptionist desk and the sequined glasses looked up at him.

"Hey," he said. "You can't work all the time for these slave drivers. Isn't is break time?"

Gail Samarro considered this. She glanced, unhurriedly, at her watch.

"Actually, yes. Why?"

"Well, actually, I was going to grab a coffee and sandwich at the world famous Crystal Cafe. I could use some company." He flashed his best smile, white teeth in a deerskin face. "How about it?"

To his great surprise she grinned. "Well, I am supposed to head up customer relations."

"That another department?"

"Of course." She reached for a heavy coat on the rack behind her. Garth caught a healthy glimpse of taut dress, upraised arms. "You are a customer, aren't you?"

"Um. Potential, you might say."

Gail zipped the lined coat and pulled a woolen cap over her black hair. "Potential. I see. Damn little potential around Shawndo these days."

They sat in a wooden booth. As they ordered coffee and grilled cheese Garth looked at her. The tiny sequins seemed to wink at him and he liked her fresh color, the tones of life.

"So, how long you been a financier?"

"Three years, close to four."

"Like it?"

"Sure. Look, it's no great job." She laughed. "Even Assistant Cashier. But what is there in Shawndo? Nothing. I like to stay close to my kids. They're used to the school here."

"Yeah?" His voice was a question.

"And before you ask where the father is, I'm not sure and getting so I don't really give a damn. He's in construction. Likes to work on foreign jobs."

"Saudi Arabia... like that?"

"He's been there. And South Yemen, even Iran in the old days. At the moment he is somewhere in the Sinai. The man is a gypsy. Sends a little dough now and then but he likes to stay long gone."

"You ditching him?"

"I suppose. I'll have to act sooner or later. See a lawyer I mean. Prairie City, we don't have one here."

Mostly I detest these personal histories, mused Garth. Self pity, always some slob of a guy done them dirt. The world isn't fair and so on. Not this one, tough luck and a twinkle behind those corny glasses. He lifted his cup.

"Cheers. And better luck next time."

"Christ, I hope." Her smile was radiant. Then she clinked cups and sipped her coffee. Garth consulted his watch.

"Tight schedule?"

"Not too close. Marta's driving me to meet the bus in Prairie. I'll be in Pittsburgh tonight."

"Pittsburgh?" She made a face. Garth laughed.

"Come on now. Anyway, I'm in Brenton, little place, twenty miles out from the big town."

"Like it there?"

"No."

"Then why are you there?"

An honest question. The weariness, the futility, the waste of the past years fell upon Garth. Good times, bad times, broken heads on the picket line. Big checks, unemployment checks, no checks. I'm forty-four, he thought, and I can't give a simple answer to a simple question. My daughters are grown. Pam is married, in Los Angeles. Connie is a nurse in Denver. They've left my life and they hardly notice the difference. I was only part time with them for a decade. In the homey cafe he felt drained. His body was a river, the tributaries were blood and salt. He smiled at the lovely woman opposite.

"I dunno. Really. I just drifted, like a chunk of wood in a stream. Ended up in the wrong place."

CHAPTER FIVE

The wind had freshened and the bright sunshine was gone when Garth caught the bus at one-thirty in Prairie City. Three days. A short visit, really. Now he felt he was leaving, not going, home. Marta hugged him. For the first time in twenty-five years the two had become close.

Marta had supplies to pick up in Prairie. Not shopping as she had once known the word. Shopping was a luxury long gone. Hardware and feed supplements and groceries... a different kind of buying. Her credit long used up, she paid cash at the feed store. So did everyone except the big corporation spreads. Fifteen bags of mix...she could have used at least thirty. Then she drove on toward home, stopping at the Crystal Cafe in Shawndo.

She savored the warm coffee. Oscar Thornstad eased his big frame onto a chair opposite. Marta always lunched at a table, there was usually someone to visit with. Oscar's brooding face was lined. He did not smile.

Marta's heart went out to her old friend. Oscar was eighty-two, a mountain of a man. He had always done two men's work, now he was down to one, the oak tree was bent. Well, I won't have crepe-hanging on my account, thought Marta. She laid her right hand on the sheepskin sleeve.

"Oscar, you old stallion," she said. "Why the long face?"

He mumbled, "Hi, Marty."

"If it's on my account, forget it. You know how Mike was. He always wanted his friends happy." She persisted. "Now, ain't that true."

He admitted it. "Yah, true." The quarried face was suddenly creased with a huge smile. The old man relaxed. Death was everywhere, but the woman would not give admittance here. Oscar, two farms down the road, had exchanged help with Mike in all the Crawford's married years.

"Your brother leave?"

"This afternoon. God, I miss him already."

"Seems like a nice guy."

"Garth? Aw, hell, Garth is a wise ass. Always had that cocky way about him, even as a kid." She marveled. "Now, even when he's beat down, he's still the same."

"Beat down. How's that?"

"A long story. He married a gal from Pittsburgh when he was no more'n a kid. Twenty, just out of the service. He moved there, went into the mills."

"Steel?"

"Shit no, Oscar. Diamond mills." Her laugh was musical in the busy cafe. Oscar grinned. "He did O.K. for awhile. Then, the same troubles that shut down northern Minnesota, the Range, about shut down the mills. Up and down since then, you know how it goes."

"Yah. Not a sure thing, like farming." The old man said this with the flat irony that had seen it all, the booms and depressions, wars, crop failures, and the scattering of his own flock. In two brief meetings he had been drawn to Garth. "Good looking fellow though."

"Yeah, I guess. Garth always had that nice tanned look. Little more weather beaten as he gets older. He's a nut about outdoors, always tried for outdoor jobs at the mills. But he's done his share of furnace time."

They were joined by others, all good neighbors. There were no strangers in the Crystal Cafe. Marta was especially fond of George Rogers, who had praised Mike in eulogy at the church. Helen Rogers and Marta had been pals for years, doing their own help exchange when George and Mike were deer hunting.

With Rogers, the absent Garth was again the subject. "Heard you mention that your brother left, Marty."

"Couple hours ago."

"Well, I'll be over to help you with the chores for the next few days. We don't have any dairy stock on our place now and I kinda miss it sometimes."

Marta blazed.

"George, you son of a bitch, you come over to my place I'll shoot you. By God, I will." She laughed at the shocked faces. "Now you and Helen come over some night to play cards, that's fine. But I'll do my own chores, long as I'm healthy." She relented further, George was like family. "Planting time I'll need more help. Then I'll hire a man if I can find one that doesn't think the liquor store is home plate. For the winter time, forget it. I'm just fine."

George Rogers blinked but didn't hide his admiration. "You always were tougher than a boiled owl." He hugged her. "But if you do come down with something, don't be a hero. Give us a ring."

"I will, George. I ain't no Ma Barker. You're a real friend. Mike would appreciate the offer."

"And tell me to go to hell, just like you." The men and women at the table roared approval.

They talked of milk prices, beef prices, a new cholera strain in hogs, the idiots in Congress. But, mostly, of foreclosure, real and threatened, and Harvest. Marta discovered her first normal feelings in the serious and bantering talk of her friends. She couldn't tear herself away. Despite her preparations for a death she had foreseen, a discipline near to self-hypnosis, the past three days had wound her tight. This was therapy no doctor could offer. She was washed in love, in unselfish concern. Jenny Peters, the cafe owner, turned on more lights as the windows grayed. Time to go.

"I've stayed too long," said Marta as she went out the door. The cold blast took her breath. As the pickup left Shawndo the storm was closing in. A little after four, still early, she turned on the headlights, low beam only. The swirling snow enclosed her in whorls of white and gusts of wind rocked the small truck as she hit the country road. An icy draft was on her neck, though the windows were rolled tight.

The four miles to the farm measured her mounting anger at herself for stalling at the cafe when she should've been smart enough to hit the road before the blizzard moved in. Marta swore at herself and thought of Mike and his knowledge of the elements. She knew the country, knew the untamed fury of blizzards, their savage suddenness. She had a lifetime of living in the area. The wheel wrenched in her mittens, the truck behaved like a balky horse. The wipers beat a smeared path on the windshield and she peered blindly into the maelstrom of white flakes.

Twice she barely evaded the ditch, braking at the last second, then backing up to the road's center. All previous tracks and snowplow edges had been eliminated, an impenetrable flatness was before her and the road and ditch and fence lines were one.

The pickup crawled, wheels occasionally spinning. She sat tense and braced. If there was a vehicle stalled ahead she was bound to hit it, the visibility near to zero. She was driving north, the wind quartering at her from the driver's side. Keep going... go, don't stop. The pickup inched the slow miles. Go... you could die right here, less than a mile from home. And you wouldn't be the first. Visions pressed in, of figures rigid in death, hands outstretched toward a house, a light, warmth they'd never feel again. Marta had lived through prairie storms before, always from the safety of buildings. She'd never been caught on the road.

She was shaking now and continued chewing herself out. Look hard, don't miss the driveway, you have no chance if you miss that, you could never turn around. Marta's eyes burned into the void, a hurricane of whiteness without break. She wanted to look at her watch but couldn't, didn't dare sneak a look. Her eyes were riveted ahead.

Then she saw it. Dimly, but it was there, the mailbox. In low gear she eased past the post. Ten feet, she calculated. Ten feet past the steel box, then the hard left should find the center of the long driveway.

Oh God, she sobbed, I've made it. I can't miss now, no matter what happens. The pickup worked along the driveway, creeping upon the gravel, the road bare in spots, piled high in others with two feet of drift. The old Chevy groaned and skidded. The tires needed replacing months before.

The garage was not attached to the farm house, but near enough. Marta clambered out of the cab. The wind, in sudden fury, whipped the cab door back against the hood and fender. She managed to raise the overhang door of the garage and climbed back in the truck. The cab door wouldn't close, the hinges warped by the blast of the wind. She held the door with one hand and nudged the pickup inside. Then she pulled down the overhang and, collar turned against the driving force of the storm, she eased out the side door and to the house, twenty feet away.

In the kitchen, Marta pushed back the parka hood and collar and threw her mittens on the table. She went to the kitchen sink and splashed warm water across her face to melt the snow from her eyes and cheeks, grateful for the banked heat of the kitchen range, aiding the warmth from the furnace.

"My God," she whispered in awe. "Must be a record breaker. That's a blizzard with the crack of a blacksnake whip." She hoped the others from the cafe had been savvy enough to stay in town. "And me, out in the middle of things, like a wetback that never saw a winter." Her color was bright from the cold, eyes sparkling. She remembered storms from the past, people going out in spite of official warnings, into a death trap. My stock is safely in the barn, that much to be thankful for. For animals, humans, caught out in this, a disaster... arctic death, swift and merciless.

She switched on the radio. Bulletins crackled from the speaker. The storm was worse, far worse that predicted. Drifts in the area were already mountainous. Cars and trucks were stranded but nothing could be done, the plows had already been taken off the roads. She switched stations. More of the same, announcers pleading for common sense to the stranded motorists. Stay put. Don't leave your vehicles, even if you think a farm house is near. Stay where you are, you can't possibly make it on foot.

Time was in flux, the minutes had run together in the past hours. Marta looked at the clock, expecting five and found it was near to six. Long past time to get to the barn; the metronome of milking and chores never ceased to tick. The Holsteins, accustomed to routine, would be getting restless.

From the basement, Marta gathered her wash line and hauled the heavy cord to the front door. All my life I've heard of this operation... mostly done in the Dakotas. Mike used to laugh at the stories but Mike had a compass inside him. He was never lost, his bearings were sound, no matter how tough the weather. Now, Mike isn't here. I'm lost, or I will be without the rope.

An anchor was easy; the porch rail. She looped the end of the wash line, twice, around the rail and tied it, carefully. Marta was not too sure on knots. She tied several for a margin of safety. Then she ducked back into the kitchen and pulled on her outer wear, finishing with a heavy scarf around her neck, over her face, nearly to the eyes. Then she tied the other end of the coiled line around her waist, securing this with a bow knot that she could easily loosen at the barn door.

The wind sighed and moaned in the soft maple and burr oak trees in the windbreak as she started the one hundred and fifty foot journey to the barn. The coiled line played out behind her, whipping in frigid gusts, as she struggled, boots heavy in the strangled steps of nightmare. The short distances seemed more like a mile but the line was a saving grace. She could never have dared the journey without it.

Even so, she missed the barn door, her target, by yards, barely finding the stone block corner of the foundation. Good enough. She worked sideways toward the red dutch doors. The frosted latch was tough to turn. The whole world was freezing into immobility. Marta was breathing heavily, each gasp was a cold knife into her lungs. Still, she managed the task, loosening the grip of the frost with blows from the heel of her hand. Inside the barn she was greeted with animal warmth, the steam and odor like a breath of spring.

Marta untied the line from around her waist, then tied a large knot in the end. She draped the line over a hay bale and plunged a pitchfork into the bale, securing the line fast for her return trip to the house. Rapidly, she set up the milking units and started the milking. She portioned out the ground feed to keep the restless animals quiet and cut the twine on bales of alfalfa, all the usual routine.

But number seventeen concerned her. The seven-year-old had finished her fourth lactation as top producer in the herd. Now the animal stood in obvious great pain in her stanchion. Marta put a halter on the cow and unfastened her from the locked stanchion. She led her to one of the empty stalls, next to the calf pen. The open box stall, the birthing area, was covered deeply with straw. Marta put the cow in the stall and removed the halter. All this between changes of the Surge milkers.

Again, two hours for all the work. The woman never paused, plodding through the work, her mind reaching back for things the veterinarian and Mike had taught her. The milk was stored in the steel tank, the young stock tended. Number seventeen was in great distress now, standing, legs splayed, hump backed and emitting strange guttural sounds. The other milk cows stirred uneasily in their stanchions and, outside, the wind howled, a crescendo of naked power, as the storm continued.

CHAPTER SIX

Marta felt marooned. The old red barn was an island, cut off from the heart beat of the world. She fought against loneliness, feelings of sadness engulfed her and the suffering of number seventeen mocked her helplessness. She was four miles from the vet in Shawndo, fifteen miles from the other vets in Prairie City. The distances loomed like a journey to the stars in the face of the storm that swept the plains.

Marta petted the black and white cow. She rubbed the animal's ears and crooned encouragement into the soft eyes. "A tough night, baby," she whispered. "I wish I could help. But I'm running blank, I can't remember the drill. I don't think we have the tools." She talked to the stricken animal as she always had. Mike had admired her way with the milk cows. They never panicked or shied away when she worked among them. The cows had shored up the fragile economy of the Crawford farmstead for years. They had helped, in the early eighties, to postpone final defeat. Many of the neighbors did not milk cows. The risks were enormous and never ending. There was an inverse ratio that almost seemed part of the business. The higher grade the animal, the more subject to physical ailments. Diseases and reproduction problems kept the vets busy. Breeding fees were high, milk prices always marginal. The dairyman prospered or went broke with his quality and the poor producers, the culls, went off to slaughter. Sickness was a blow, death a near catastrophe. Marta knew that number seventeen might die. No matter what she did or what she might have done, the loss of the best cow in the herd was a stark possibility. She must try to do what she could.

First, a telephone call. The lines might be out, but worth the attempt. Marta put on her outerwear, including the woolen scarf, removed the anchoring pitchfork from the bale and tied the line around her waist. She opened the double doors and faced a fury more violent than hours before. "I can't make it, I can't. This is beyond endurance," she thought. She shrank from the elements and closed the doors, the trailing clothes line not bulky enough to prevent the doors from latching. She unhitched the cord from her waist.

"God!" she gasped. "Like being set down in another world." She contemplated frozen spheroids in space, hurtling through endless ages where rays of the sun never warmed. She trembled from the thought, her resources dwindling. Her teeth chattered suddenly, tremors racked her body in a spasm of shuddering.

A few moments only. A sudden flight of fancy, then a conscious search for solidity brought Marta back from the edge. Mike's presence entered the warm barn, his voice calmed her. To Marta it seemed more true than life, an image as real as the sounds and smells and animal warmth around her. Marta grasped at the ghostly strength. She closed her eyes, the better to hear the words, the thought, the message. She held her breath, the tremors left her.

Marta heard no voice. Only the stirrings of the animals and the piercing sounds of the wind. But she had received the message.

She smiled gently and fastened the line around her waist once more. The message had soothed her. Relax, it's just a winter storm. Look, the lights are still on, the barn is operational. Somewhere, people are laughing and raising foamy mugs in salute. The line is safe, go to the house. She opened the doors once more and trudged into the void. Her mittened hands pulled, one over the other like a mountain climber, the one hundred and fifty feet back to the house. She stumbled and fell twice, some drifts were shoulder high and she clambered over them on hands and knees. But Marta kept, wrapped about her like an extra garment, the unhurried calm, the presence of Mike's reassurance. She reached the porch rail, her anchor, and stomped into the kitchen, snow from her boots and clothing spreading over the linoleum. She smiled, thinking she always was a lousy housekeeper, though Mike told her different, but that was just his way of being Mike. After all, Marta was the only wife the man ever had, he didn't have anyone to compare her with.

Marta picked up the phone, with little expectation. She was greeted with dead silence. But she went through the motions and dialed the familiar number. Nothing, not an echo, the lines were out. No help, no advice, the man who had tended thousands of animals would never know of her need. She was on her own, a oneness that obliterated friends and neighbors.

Marta knew she was pushing it a bit with herself. Fuel the machine, she thought, first rule of field work. She rummaged in the refrigerator and found ham, lettuce and mayo, diced fruit in a Tupperware container and milk. Two cans of Garth's beer stood, forlornly, on a lower shelf. She made coffee in the old enamel pot and fixed her sandwich and fruit. Then she sat at the kitchen table and considered options. The possibilities were limited.

Medicines. She didn't know animal medicines beyond teat inserts for the clotting of mastitis. She remembered, vaguely, hypodermic needles for afflicted hogs in the days when the Crawfords had been pork producers. No use, now. Marta sensed the mechanical aids were more essential than medicinal products in the crisis of strangled birth. She tried to visualize the tools of the vet. Powerful forceps, devices that spread the birth opening. Hooks to pull. The tough births had made Mike send her to the house. Now she wished she'd paid attention. She finished her lunch and felt refreshed. "I'm a blind fool in this matter," she thought. "But, what the hell, I can't any more than fail."

First, a hook and a chain. She searched the house and basement with a sinking heart. No luck. She knew that the only real possibility was the tool shed, fifty feet, at least, to the right on the trip back to the barn. She searched further but found nothing in the house that could serve her purpose.

"Well, I'm stronger now," she reasoned. "I was really famished before, weak as a kitten." She piled on the clothes once more, tied on the line and headed, at a different angle into the white maelstrom. The storm had lost no intensity. If anything, the wind was stronger and the temperature was still dipping. She had not chanced a look at the thermometer. She was too scared to want the truth.

The wallowing trip to the shed was not too tough. "I'm getting the hang of this," thought Marta. "I've gained confidence." Inside the tool shed she flipped the light switch. The piled tarps on a high shelf were reminders of her last trip to the tool shed when death was new.

She found the log chains, one with a grapple hook and one with a rounded running hook. She couldn't possibly carry both, she knew. The grapple hook looks best for the purpose. The chain was twenty feet in length. She could see no way of reducing the weight. She didn't have the strength to cut the links and wasn't certain which tool to use for the attempt. The chain weighed nearly forty pounds. Marta decided she could pull the chain easier than carrying it. She grasped the chain by the hook end, closed the shed door and, with safety line in place, worked her way toward the barn.

This was the toughest journey yet. The drifts were high in this part of the yard, the swirling snow blinded her and the weight of the chain was a dead pull on her mittened hand. Once, she dropped the hook and scrambled, in white blindness, to retrieve it.

She made the corner of the barn and, labored steps later, the dutch doors. She struggled inside and fell in a gasping heap upon the hay. The alfalfa had the sweet, wild odor of meadows mowed in full bloom, cured in the sun. Marta lay there for minutes, gathering her strength.

Number seventeen had gone down. The animal sprawled on its side in the deep straw. The birth, as Marta had feared, had barely begun. A trace of feet, placenta wrapped, was emerging. How simple it seems, most of the time, Marta remembered. She had led cows, too many to place in memory, from stanchion to the birthing stall. She and Mike had left them and resumed the milking. Often, within thirty minutes, they would return to find a wobbly, long legged calf, tottering on steeple legs, nuzzling at the extended udder while the mother calmly munched on the hay before her in the manger.

Now there was only agony. Quiet for the most part but with, still, some deep throated moans, the animal cried out with tortured eyes for help. Marta hauled the chain across the hay-littered floor and faced her impossible task.

She worked first with mittens but had to discard them, wet and blood soaked. She had no feel for the precision needed without bare hands. The grapple end of the chain was too large, a blunt instrument for a precise job. The hook turned and slipped in her hands.

She kept on. Her hands were wet and slimy, the metal still deep-cold from the unheated shed, stung her fingers. A half hour passed before she could work the hook around one small leg. The grapple hook caught behind the tiny hoof. She had a grasp on the calf within.

Then Marta backed away a few feet and searched her memory for the next step, looking for a hint, some special technique to aid the process. Nothing surfaced. Her mittens were soaked and slippery, useless. She looked around and found a feed sack and wrapped this around the cold chain, then looped the chain around her wrist. She pulled. Her feet slipped on the concrete floor. A brace! Marta dropped the chain and searched for solid footing. She found a piece of heavy plank that Mike had scrounged to repair a ceiling joist. She placed the plank flat on the floor, each end catching one side of the stall. Then she grasped the chain once again and pulled and her boots held, braced on the plank.

It was like trying to pull a gravel truck. Marta struggled with all her strength. Beads of perspiration stood out on her face and her muscles ached with a stabbing fatigue. She rested, then tried again. She thought that the tiny leg, peeking out from the birth canal, would surely tear. But the grapple held firm. The fetus did not budget. Outside the barn waves of wind beat through the trees and buildings. Marta could hear nothing and inside her clothing she was bathed in sweat.

For two hours the struggle continued. There was no progress. As she had in the pickup, Marta raged at herself, swore at her inability. "Am I so useless?" she savaged herself, "or just ignorant?" There must be other steps to take... don't know what they are. Is there a way to massage the animal's side? work through strong hands to push the calf along? Or surgery?... wouldn't know where to make the cuts, or how. It would be butchery. She looked at her watch. Past eleven... must make a decision... don't get some rest I'll be sick. Or worse.

She shook her head to clear the film. What to do? Or to do nothing more? She looked at her reddened hands, raw and bleeding... bad hands for the chores in the morning.

The decision formed... take a few hours, get some sleep. The storm was always there, a wolf trap, beyond the door. One false step, too great a weariness... no chance... think the cow's a goner. Mother Nature, ah, dear old mother of mine, I leave her to your tender mercy. The woman who had, in her lifetime, experienced much of what nature could provide, chuckled. Marta still had her balance. She unhooked the chain. "Good night, old girl," she whispered. "I gave it a shot. Maybe you can handle the job alone. If not ..." She gathered her clothing, cap and scarf and mittens, and once again fastened the clothes line around her waist.

The blizzard was the same, no better, but the drifts were higher, they had obliterated half the garage. Marta climbed the drifts, slipping and tumbling down the opposite sides. The driving snow pelted her eyes above the woolen scarf. She was beyond feeling the pain, a drowsiness was upon her that she fought with her waning strength. To rest on the way, to shut your eyes for an instant... Marta knew that, in the outdoors, complete exhaustion was the final trap. Again she managed to reach the porch rail and stumble into the kitchen.

She took off her parka and hung it on the wall. Her jacket was smeared with blood. Marta could not think clearly on the problem of the jacket and mittens. She threw them, together, into the sink. she'd try, somehow, to clean them up tomorrow. She thought "I've got other jackets and gloves, somewhere around here, for the morning chores. Now, a glass of milk, then to bed, five o'clock isn't that far away."

She climbed the stairs to the big bedroom she had shared with Mike for more than half her lifetime, undressed and fell into deep sleep. No dreams intruded.

She woke at the first sound of the alarm. In the shower the hot suds removed some of the ache, but her hands still pained her from the cutting pressure of the cold iron chain. She dressed and went to the kitchen and fixed hot cereal and scrambled eggs, washed them down with scalding coffee. Marta felt prepared for whatever the day might bring. The radio spoke of diminishing winds after the area's worst storm in twenty years.

Marta dressed for the trip to the barn. She stepped out on the porch to survey the elements and her breath was nearly stilled by the shock of minus twenty-five degrees. The wind still howled. The radio lies. She thought, "where's that announcer, in Miami?" She could take no chances, she must use the line again. But now there would be an extra burden. Marta went to the basement for the rifle.

The thirty-ought-six, nearly as old as the century, but Mike's only weapon, was taken down from the rack. She put two shells into her jacket pocket and carried the rifle back upstairs. Then she opened the door, wrapped the line around herself, shouldered the gun. She was grateful for the gun sling. Then she started, once again, her journey.

Inside the barn, all was peaceful on the dairy side and the calves scrambled to their feet in the big pens. Marta doffed her parka and walked to the birthing stall. Number seventeen lay as she had, hours before. There was just a faint trace of breath rising and falling. The calf had advanced only inches. Marta bent down and looked into the brown eyes. They were heavy lidded and seemed, to Marta, to speak a message. She put both shells into the magazine and pumped one into the chamber. Then she set the gun down and hauled silage in the big cart, from the silo to the feeding racks. She forked the silage to the animals, speaking in quiet, soothing tones to each one in turn.

"I'm going to startle you girls a bit," she murmured. "Sorry about that, but it can't be helped."

Then she walked back to the birthing stall and placed the muzzle of the gun twelve inches from number seventeen's face, aimed just between and slightly above the eyes, and pulled the trigger. The explosion cracked, like a bolt of lightning, in the quiet barn.

The cows startled in the stanchions, rearing back from the silage. In their pens, the calves raced about, slamming into the concrete walls and the wooden gates.

Marta could barely see. Tears blinded her eyes and her hands were shaking like leaves. She ejected the shell, slammed the other bullet home and fired the second shot into the dying beast's forehead. There was a sighing moan, the head fell flat, a trickle of white foam ran from one corner of the slack jaw.

Marta placed the gun in a corner near the dutch doors. "I must remember," she thought aloud, the action seemed important, "to return Mike's gun to the rack, he never liked it lying about." She said, "I used the blue blanket. Something must have told me I'd need the tarp." The tarpaulin had been in the barn for days, had lost some of its stiffness. She hauled it to the birthing stall, using the silage cart as a conveyance. Then she unrolled the tarp and covered the dead cow and the unborn calf. Marta had dried her eyes, the milk cows had settled down, the calves were now calmly eating the morning ration. The life cycle had returned to the red barn. Marta worked the tarp around the dead figures, just as she had worked the blue blanket, with tenderness, around the body of her husband.

CHAPTER SEVEN

Marta managed the rest of the morning chores. In the kitchen she had hot cakes and more coffee at eight-thirty then faced another intolerable task. The wind had finally died, the announcer had only jumped the gun a bit, or perhaps, thought Marta, I didn't note the station, he may well have been from a good distance west of here.

The great golden globe was back in the southeastern sky and the thermometer rose a few grudging degrees. There was a chance for zero by mid-afternoon. Marta gazed out her front window at a Sahara of snow drifts, swooping dunes that varied from bare ground to eight feet in height. One of the largest and most solid looking, the bright snow looked like white washed concrete, was stretched across the driveway, bellied up to the garage door. There's a snowmobile in there, she mused. It might just as well be hidden in a Swiss vault.

Too much to tackle at the moment. I'll rest an hour, she thought, switch back to normal. It will take an amazon to cut that mountain and reach the outside world. But it must be done. She thought of her C.B. in the pickup and wondered why she hadn't used that in her efforts to contact the vet. She dismissed the thought. The end result for the beautiful black and white cow could have turned out just the same. In a world of might-have-beens where the foundations of her life had crumbled, she could not afford the luxury of second guessing. But I will not use the C.B. for help now. If I can't handle my own snow drifts, how can I manage my own life? She moved to a deep chair in the living room and snuggled down. In minutes she was asleep, the punishment of the last eighteen hours had left her drained. She dreamed of Mike and Karen... the girl was in high school and had brought a girl friend home for the night and the two laughed and sang in the old kitchen.

She woke in an hour and drank more coffee to exorcise the lethargy that encased her. There was little strategy to consider, all that was needed was execution. Get at it, keep at it. She took her snow shovel from the porch and began.

Marta had no intention of shoveling a path all the way to the garage. She only wanted to dig an opening, deep enough to be able to open the side door. No easy task, the snow was solid as piled cement and half way to the eaves. She hacked and slashed with the aluminum shovel, being as careful as possible not to bend the blade.

The job was accomplished. She stood inside the garage, next to the Chevy pickup, and knew that much tougher work lay ahead. She scowled at the pickup's sprung left door. More expense... wonder if the insurance will cover it. With the deductible, I'm still going to be stuck. The pickup was indispensable, the door a hazard in its present condition. When, later in the week, she could get the vehicle to town, it was a job for a body and fender shop.

Marta was grateful that the snowblower was in good shape. She filled the tank and pushed the machine to the side door. The blower was just narrow enough to clear the jamb. She started the motor, pushed out the door into the cleared spot and began the job.

Three hours and two tanks of fuel later she collapsed at the kitchen table. Marta was utterly spent, her arms were lead weights, numb and heavy. But the bank in front of the overhead door had been cleared. Not far into the driveway but there was plenty of room for the snowmobile to clear. She had not imagined the job would be so taxing. But the drift was enormous and solid, the blower bite so small. She had felt like a Lilliputian.

Now the clock showed past one-thirty. She had time, and to spare if necessary. She tried the telephone again. Still dead, the issue was settled. Marta struggled into her sky-blue snow suit, took the big mittens and goggles and hoped the old Polaris would start. Only four miles to Shawndo. No matter what the conditions, a short trip. The snowplows might be out by now, but only on primary roads. Her own township road could not expect relief until the next day... at the earliest.

The Polaris roared to life. Marta bumped and swerved out the driveway. The township road was a wasteland, the whole countryside had become an unknown landscape. Across the flat land the effect was like looking at the sea on a gusty day. Waves of snow drifts stretched to the horizon, broken only by distant farm buildings and wind breaks. Fences could not be seen, all ditches were obliterated, there were no markers.

Marta kept, as near as she could judge, to the center of the road. Though the fences were lost to view she knew the danger of care-lessness. Riding double with Mike one winter, the extra weight a danger, they had hit a post top. Mike, on the handle bars, had hung on, Marta had been pitched into the snow and the snowmobile tread was badly damaged. Marta smiled, grimly, remembering. She had been unhurt by the fall, but shaken, the lessons of precaution had been driven home. Since then, in unknown wastes of snow, both she and Mike had driven cautiously. Now she kept the speed low, bobbing and twisting, like a cork, on the white desert. In forty minutes she reached Shawndo. She parked her machine among a dozen others in the street and walked into the Crystal Cafe. She was greeted with cries of friendly derision.

"Hey, here's the old lady," shouted one unkempt farmer. The man was unshaven, tired looking. He had, obviously, been caught in town overnight.

"Hey, is it spring already?" another asked, sourly. "Marta gets out, the snow must be gone."

Even old Oscar pitched in. "That Polaris still afloat, Marty?" The lined face was creased in a scowl. From another: "What a bucket, Marty. Get a new one. Nothing runs like a Deere."

The Crystal was nearly as old as the town. Through most of the century and a score of proprietors, the homespun eatery was the center of society in the community. If you didn't run into your friends at the Crystal, they simply were not in town. The Cafe was thirty feet wide and forty deep, plus the big kitchen in the rear. Six booths, several scarred tables and a counter with ten stools... room enough and more. Marta stood, hands on hips, her face scornful.

"What a bunch of city hot-shits!" She shook her head. "Why don't you guys move to Omaha, or Flagstaff? Some people have to work you know." Marta was relentless, her eyes glistened. "God, the pain, when the roads get cleared. Some of you cowboys might have to get home and help the missus."

Groans. More bantering from the rough men. Two women clapped loudly, agreeing, noisily, with the snow-suited woman.

Marta was ravenous. She ordered a hot beef sandwich with gravy and mashed, and apple pie. "Sorry," announced Jenny Peters. "I got the roast beef yet, and the spuds. No pie or cake. Been open all night, what a zoo!" Jenny looked to be out on her feet.

"Come on, Jen. You love it," offered another man. "First night you spent with a man for years. And you had a dozen or more." The Crystal Cafe exploded in laughter.

"What a crock," sneered the tired woman. "A dozen, hell! Ain't one good man in the lot, you ask me." She winked at Marta. "Good for one thing. They all eat like horses. Cleaned up the beer, too. I ain't got a can left."

Marta laughed. She took her food and sat beside George Rogers. The man looked defeated. He hadn't joined in the horseplay. Marta said, "Looks like you were one of the people shipwrecked here last night."

"Yep," he said. "After you left I could see she was going to be a tiger. We're not milking, you know, so I said t'hell with it. Got a call in to Helen before the lines went out. You O.K.?"

"Sure." She didn't tell him about the dead animal. The man was beat. "I came by your place on the scooter. Didn't stop but everything looked calm. Want a lift home?"

He was grateful. "That would be a lifesaver, Marty, if it's not any great bother." He sighed. "What a night. I feel for Jenny. The old gal tried to doze off a couple times, but the guys wouldn't let up."

"What the hell, she'll catch up tonight."

"I guess. Jesus, what a storm. Shook the building. I thought one of them front windows was coming in."

Marta asked him, "Any news?" A farmer's question. By that she meant bad news.

"Nothing local. Couple of barn fires in Jaros County. Took 'em right out." Nothing terrified in a storm like fire. No fire fighting equipment could move and the high winds spread the flames, often wiping out a complete farmstead. George Rogers leaned close. "No meeting this week, that's for sure. I think we'll try for next Thursday."

"Sounds fine." Marta was disturbed by George's appearance. Granted, he'd spent the night in the cafe, sweating out the storm. He was a top farmer, purebred Angus, corn yield champion, had served on many state ag boards. The man had connections. George Rogers was fifty-five years old, had been a white-haired handsome charmer. Marta wondered, does Harvest give all of us, eventually, that beaten, hunted look? Is Harvest, in the last analysis, the politics of desperation? Or is the reverse the truth? Has Harvest materialized because only the desperate have survived thus far? All the others, the well-fixed who got out early on a bull market in land, sold at the top of the curve, or those who just plain quit cold and moved on to other things, they've left this impossible scene behind. In another life George, with his eloquence and savvy, might have been an attorney or a corporation V.P. Now, like all of us, he works his land and sells his grain and animals at prices below the cost of production. No way to go on. No way to get out.

"By Thursday we should get a turnout," she said. "I'll help with the phone net. Service will be normal, everywhere, in a day or two."

"We have to keep moving, Marty, bad weather or not. There are three stock and machinery sales within six miles of Shawndo, this month. Growers Bank, on one. The other two are Farmers Home Administration." The eyes, Marta saw, were red rimmed. "We've got to get the folks out. Crowds've been picking up at the foreclosures but we got to double them, triple them," he said, bitterly. "Something I've always believed in. But it takes the numbers to get attention. We have to show the numbers, the solid front."

"I know. People have got to make the commitment," Marta agreed. "People have to drive the miles, make a show of force. It's coming, George, it's coming, even if it's damn slow." She'd finished her meal. "I've got to pick up a couple of things and make a phone call. Lines are open to Prairie I expect?"

"Yeah. That line never went out."

Marta made two purchases at the drug store and used the pay phone. She talked to the rendering plant in Prairie City. She explained that if the dead animal was outside there'd be no hurry. But, in the barn... The man understood. They were backed up with deaths from the blizzard but they'd watch for road clearances and be out as soon as possible, perhaps the day after tomorrow. The man from the rendering knew Marta well. He said the usual things about Mike. Marta thanked him.

In the street, more snowmobiles had gathered. The low slung machines were standing at the curb, like bright toys. Many had sacks of feed and grocery bags strapped to them. Many of the drivers were little more than children, the schools being closed by the storm. Most other vehicles were the four wheel drives — Jeeps and Broncos, the tough tires pocked with deep treads. Brilliant afternoon sunshine bounced off the diamond brightness of plowed banks and the rooftops displayed their own whorls and drifts. The business area of the main street was little more than one block... one side only. The east side of the street opened up to railroad tracks, grain storage bins and other corrugated buildings, and the Farmers Co-op Elevator where, storm or fair weather, the huge corn dryer boomed its muffled blast around the clock. Only dry corn and soy beans were safe to store. Marta walked back to the Crystal. She felt a need to confide in Oscar Thornstad.

The old man was seated at the counter, alone. He stirred his coffee and squinted against the smoke, his cigarette down to a nub between his thumb and forefinger. He smiled. Marta sat down beside him.

"So, sweetheart, you rode the wind last night O.K., huh? Well, damn it, I worried about you, considering all that's been happening lately."

"You did like hell, you old faker." Marta glared. "You going to buy one or be one?"

"I got forty cents left. Might as well be busted." He motioned to Jenny for a cup for Marta.

"Thanks, sport." Marta clasped the old man's hand, her face serious. "I did have some bad luck, Oscar. Lost my best cow last night. Number seventeen."

"Calving?"

"Yeah. Trying. I wasn't much help."

Oscar looked thoughtful. "I recollect the animal. Beautiful, gentle creature. Hell of a thing, time like that, no help in sight. Aw hell..." He wiped his mouth with the back of his hand and mashed the charred butt in his saucer. "Always something."

"Mike could've handled it."

"Maybe. Maybe not. Don't be hard on yourself, we've all lost animals. You put her out of her misery?"

41

"Of course. The thirty-ought-six."

"Good." Oscar Thornstad sat hunched, like a granite boulder, on the stool and wondered about his friend... all his friends. The problems, always one step ahead, two back. Now Marta, alone. He didn't know her financial picture, he didn't need the exact figures. All he knew was that this woman had killed a cow, worth twelve hundred dollars, with a deer rifle.

Marta said, "See you next week, buddy, if not before. At Harvest, I mean."

"Yah, sure. I'll be there, if I ain't dead. I don't really know why I'll be there but ..."

"Don't say that, Oscar."

"I know. It's this war. The war that has no end, only casualties." His voice was thick with an old man's bitterness. "Vietnam was America's great defeat. A terrible, brutal business. But it had an ending. Not the right one, but we're out of it."

"Oscar ..."

"It's alright, Marty. I'm an old guy, I can say what I like." He grinned. "Just like you do. But this war, out here on the prairie, is a second Vietnam. It don't have the stink or the butchery or the terror of 'Nam. But it's a war all the same. We're losing it, and the casualties keep rolling in."

"We'll turn it around Oscar. We will, if we all stick together. There's a chance."

"All?" He shook his big head. He lighted a cigarette and sat, eyes slitted against the smoke. "We'll never get all of us, the bickering's eternal. It's like herding cats. Even if we did get most of the farmers, it wouldn't be enough. A million or two out of two hundred and forty million, something like that. Who gives a god damn?" Oscar was brooding now, deep in reverie. "We ain't got the numbers, Marty. We ain't got the money or the political muscle. We're just out there on the delta, like them sojers. And we ain't got no backup."

Marta laughed. She had heard all this before. But she loved Oscar, she knew the old man was well informed. He was a prodigious reader.

She planted a wet kiss on the boulder face.

"I don't know if we can make it, either. But for sure, not without you." She stood. "Got to go, I've got a passenger to deliver. George."

"Yah, that's good. Helen was left alone last night, too." Another facet of discontent surfaced. "Nobody's got any help these days. Can't get good farm help, can't pay 'em if you do find a man that ain't spaced out half the time. Hell of a damn note."

"George and Helen are solid. They'll do fine."

She said good-bye and turned to Rogers at the big table and

nodded. They went out and mounted the Polaris, Marta driving. At the Rogers farm she steered the machine up the driveway but didn't go to the house. Marta knew that Helen would understand. Visiting with friends was when you could grab it. The milking and the chores were forever.

Marta knew of good herds that had missed a milking or two. From unforeseen events, an automobile accident, a fire, some strange twist of natural forces that left the cows unattended. The cows weren't ruined completely, but many of the distended udders had never been the same again. The Crawford farm had in place, for more than fifteen years, a backup generator, tractor powered. All dairy farms knew the danger of power failure. Thirty, fifty, sometimes one hundred cows, impossible to milk by hand.

So the widow Crawford drove her sleek snowmobile back home and housed it again, in the garage. In a day or two, she could use the pickup. Inside the house she picked up the phone and heard the welcome hum of power. The radio sent cheerful bulletins of a wasteland slowly returning to life.

In the barn, Marta climbed to the hayloft to push down the bales. Sparrows twittered about the cold space above the hay and, in the cupolas, pigeons cooed their ancient melodies of plump contentment. Marta startled as a rat scurried from the feed bin in one corner of the loft. The pesky bastards, she thought. You can keep cats and lay out poison by the pound. But there are always some rats and mice on a farm. They come in from the fields, they gravitate to the feed. It's just a fact of life, just one more hurdle. The alfalfa bales were heavy and bulky, rimmed with a line of frost.

She clambered down the ladder to the cow barn and closed the loft door behind her. Then she continued with all the familiar tasks. Mike's presence did not surface. Not this night or in any of the busy weeks to follow. Marta ran the dairy operation as effortlessly as she turned out apple pies in the kitchen for the church bazaars.

She welcomed the rendering truck that removed the remains of number seventeen and the unborn issue, a bull calf or a welcome heifer? She'd never know. She drove to Shawndo and Prairie City, when the roads were clear, and bobbed along on the Polaris at other times. One day, a week after the blizzard, Sheriff Bill Adams and a deputy came to the farm.

Marta welcomed them into the kitchen and they spent a pleasant hour over coffee and slices of devil's food cake. The paper work on the death had been completed, at least from the standpoint of law enforcement. The report was several pages in length and included Marta's statement at the Sheriff's office in Prairie City. The findings were clear and impartial. Marta signed the report and was grateful to

Adams for the pains he had taken to visit her and explain the law, rather then summoning her to a courthouse appearance at the county seat.

She worried about Adams and wondered, am I seeing this strange malady in the face of everyone I know? This look of quiet struggle and... what? Not despair, but a kind of resignation, acknowledgment of forces, tides beyond the scope of ordinary life. The farmers all had variations of that look , or so it seemed to Marta. Bill Adams and his deputies, sworn officers, enforced the law to the best of their ability. At least two officers attended every farm sale. When there was no machinery or livestock involved, the farms were often bid in from the courthouse steps, the auctioneer flanked by deputies, Bill Adams standing with them. I feel for the man, thought Marta. But I detest what he's forced to do... to help officiate, like some hooded hangman, at the imposition of death. Not death like Mike's perhaps. But death all the same. The banks and the insurance companies win the land, the former owners drift away or come back to work the land like serfs. Bill Adams makes sure that all this occurs. I like the man and lunch with him because he's not to blame. All of us are victims, all at the mercy of an evolution we don't understand. Marta shook hands with the two men and wished them well as they drove away.

Her life, now as before, revolved around Harvest... that movement that had been born out of the anguish of people like her, all across the farm areas of the country. There were chapters forming each week, a third of the nation's states now represented. The sinew of the organization lay in the midwest, fabled "bread basket" of the world. Minnesota, the Dakotas, Wisconsin, Illinois, Indiana, Nebraska, Kansas, Missouri... these were the states where Harvest was beginning to flourish, the farmers despairing of the old, the honored farm groups. The time-worn organizations had proved helpless in the face of forces they didn't understand. The farmers were driven from the land but the land remained, to be mined and plundered by those people ignorant or uncaring about the future. Corn was worthless, unless you raised two thousand acres and claimed the losses against business gains. Other crops, like soy beans, were treated the same. Cows were a quaint luxury, unless your herd numbered in the hundreds and you juggled the profits and losses to fit your accounting needs. In a world of giants and tax shelters, the sweating, shirt-sleeved small time farmer was as outdated as the plow horse.

Into the breech, a last, best hope, marched Harvest. Poorly organized, unfunded, politically inept, the movement floundered, learning as it went along... falling back, surging ahead. Marta attended all the meetings and closed ranks with members at the forced farm auctions. With few exceptions the weather remained tolerable through late February and into March and the snow banks receded in the Crawford farm yard.

March. The month of false spring, false promises... new hope. In the second week of the month Garth Kyllo came back to Shawndo, driving a '78 Plymouth station wagon, the back section loaded with boxes and suitcases. He parked in front of the Growers State Bank and stepped, lightly, through the door. He winked at Gail Samarro, she seemed happy to see him. Next, he walked into Philip Kenseth's office and gave him a check for forty thousand dollars, to be applied on past due interest on the mortgage account of Marta Crawford and Mike Crawford, deceased.

CHAPTER EIGHT

Marta listened, white lips a thin line, while Garth explained what he had been doing in the past weeks. The deliberate calm of her brother's actions sent waves of fury through her. She barely managed to hear the story out, frequently interrupting. She swore and scolded.

"Who the hell appointed you guardian over me, Garth? You get a divine message or something?"

"Hey, that's it. May be I'm reborn."

"And maybe you're a goddamned idiot."

Garth smiled, white teeth gleaming in the lean face. They sat, as before, at the antique kitchen table, drinking strong, hot coffee. Garth, hungry as a coyote, was finishing a quarter wedge of apple pie and sharp cheddar. He was too beat from the long trip to pay attention to the tongue lashing.

"So. You sold your house."

"You might say. Sold my equity in it. You know how that goes. Was a time, when the plants were humming, I had the old shack about paid for. When we got divorced, Thelma got half the house. Fair enough. But she wanted out, wanted her and the girls to live in an apartment. So, I bought her out. Had to refinance to do that." Garth sighed. After the adrenaline flow of the Growers State Bank visit he was heavy lidded.

"So, what did you get?"

"Sixty-eight. I might have got over seventy if I kept it on the market long enough. After all the commissions and closing bullshit, I come out with thirty-six. Threw in all the furniture and appliances, which was a deal for the young couple that bought the place. That was another three. Then I sold the Camaro, what the hell I need with a jack rabbit car out here. Then I picked up the old wagon."

"Which will be in the shop more than on the road." Marta was grim.

"Naw. I know cars pretty good. That old Plymouth will run 'til the wheels fall off. Anyway, I can carry feed sacks in it, fertilizer, whatever."

"I see. For who?"

"Well, I was figuring the Governor. Or maybe the Senator. That tall guy with the black horn rims."

"I told Oscar Thornstad you were a smart ass. I didn't know the half of it."

Marta was deeply disturbed. She had seen her brother only twice in the past twenty years, up to the time of the funeral. This business had an unreality that bordered on madness, a commitment too

staggering to hold real meaning. A man's life, his pitiable estate...
down a rat hole. There was only one solution.

"You're bushed, Garth. My Lord, you can hardly stay awake. You
get some sleep. Tomorrow we go to the bank. You get your money
back, Kenseth can't keep it if I insist. The debts are mine, not yours."

"No way, Marty. Not even if I got to go to court, and who the hell
wants that kind of action?"

She might not have heard. "You get the money back and if you're
so determined to be permanent in this area... well, fine. Get a job,
buy a little restaurant, buy a truck and get into the garbage racket.
Buy a goddamn bar, hell, people will drink when there ain't a loaf of
bread in the house. Any damn thing... you hear me? But don't waste
money on the farm. This ship is going down, no matter what."

"I don't believe that," said Garth, reasonably. "We'll hash this out
later, Marty. I gotta get some sleep or I'll fall on my face. I drove
straight through from P.A. I felt like sacking in when I got west of
Chicago. But, what the hell, I popped a couple of beanies and just
cruised along."

"Wonder you didn't kill yourself. Or somebody else."

"Well, I didn't. Look, Marty. I had to just sort of close my eyes
and do what I did. If I thought about it too much I couldn't have
handled it. Now you and me, we'll figure out the details. But the
money stays where I put it. No arguments, no threats... that's number
one. Number two, I'm gonna help you run the farm." Garth stood up,
his eyes burned in the tan face. "Those two things are basic. Beyond
that I'll listen to anything."

"Big of you," Marta growled. But she was softening. The sheer
audacity of the gesture moved her. Garth had, like the Spanish
explorer... what the hell was his name?... burned his bridges behind
him, or was it ships?

"O.K., we'll talk. Just hit the sack for now. Take the spare bedroom, you know the way. I'll call you for supper."

"Hey, not that late. I want to help with the milking and the
chores."

She was firm. "I said supper time. The chores will be there, again,
in the morning. Them cows ain't going nowhere."

At the supper table the argument continued, all the earlier points
repeated. Marta had slogged through the chores in a fog of
indecision. She had missed Garth so much in the past weeks, she had
been overjoyed when the station wagon pulled up in front of the
garage and the wide smile flashed at her. What a guy? What an idiot?
And how can one apportion a slice of equity in an enterprise destined
to go out of existence? She mumbled, almost to herself, "Part of
nothing is nothing."

"What did you say?" Garth had finished eating, he flipped the tab on a Bud. "Or was that the disposal?"

"No," Marta snapped. "But garbage, all the same." She slumped, the fire was going out of her. "Garth, honey, there may be nothing to save, no way to recoup. Before today I was no better off than the Wilkersons. They were closed out, months ago. Now they're both in Kansas somewhere. Living with some kin of hers, brother, I think, until Jerry finds something." She signed. "My Lord, Kansas. To me, like Siberia, but I guess the natives like it fine."

Her face was dark, brooding with the agony of others. "Maybe the Wilkersons were smart. Some stay around here... eat their hearts out. I know several guys, not all in this county, working for wages on the farms they used to own. Think of it, a landed aristocracy of bankers and insurance companies... farmers turned into serfs. History in reverse."

Garth conceded, "Then you've had, what? The benefit of the widow syndrome, since Mike died?"

"I guess. Ain't that a hell of a thing?"

Garth did not reply to that. He merely smiled, his eyes were bright, almost feverish. "Well, like it or not, the back interest is handled. This year's another problem. But we're gonna pull this baby out. I don't know how but we will." He moved to the stair door. "I got a lot of unpacking to do. Hell, I might want to go to town one of these nights. Good night, Sis."

"Good night, jerk. And don't call me Sis. I didn't like it as a kid and I don't like it now."

In the days that followed, the arguments continued. Not bitter, they were much too close for that. But the hard truth that Marta had voiced, that the debts far exceeded the present valuations, made the mathematics of ownership, the sharing of the pie, moot. Kenseth, and the mountain of revenue owed to Growers State dominated all their conjectures. The milk checks were regular and, slightly, over production costs. A small portion could be spared for the bank but most of the money was needed for seed and fertilizer... all credit from the dealers had long been exhausted. Marta had given up on a replacement for number seventeen.

Finally, a deal was struck, sealed with a handshake and a long telephone conversation with Karen, in Duluth. The news from the tip of Lake Superior was not encouraging. Steve was laid off again, the fourth time in five years. Pellet production in the iron plants was down. Karen was working at a McDonalds while Steve sweat out unemployment checks and stayed at home with the kids. Jessica was five, Timmy, three. My grandkids, Marta sighed. I only see them once or twice a year. They'll grow up without knowing me. Sad.

Unreality creeps into our separate lives. The root of all evil... money. The money you owe to other people, the money that is not there, at the pay window.

But Karen, tough times or not, was the only heir. The farm had been her only prayer, however bleak, for a future solvency. Karen had known for a long time, before her father's death, the extent of the crisis, her parents had taken no pains to deceive her. Still, some hope flickered, promises of tomorrow had helped through long days of uncertainty in the north. Steve was a "Nordeaterner" born and bred... he would not leave the Range country. Her father's suicide... all insurance policies long since cashed in... had been, to the sunny Karen, a final devastation. She had traveled back to her home, on the northern edge of Duluth, filled with a sorrow so deep she became, dully, alarmed at her inability to cope. She had snapped back, of course, she was fine, now. Karen was wild with enthusiasm, Marta could almost feel the glow, about Uncle Garth's return and the forty thousand commitment.

"It's like a story book, Ma," she bubbled. "That is just unreal. How could the man just walk in and do a thing like that?"

"I don't know, baby. You'll have to ask him, sometime when you're down here. I'm still in shock."

"Will the money... make enough difference to... you know?"

"You can say the words, Karen. To save the farm? I've got to level with you. I believe we are still down the drain. But there's a chance... before Garth there was no chance, the mortgages are far beyond the worth." The lines were silent. Marta continued. "We need you down here, Karen. You're the whole litter, kid. Garth has made the ultimate gesture. If we, by some miracle, are able to salvage anything, he's in the picture. Understand?"

"Of course. No other way. But Mom, we're in such a bind here, for money and time."

"I know."

"Listen." Now the sensible Karen took over. "I'm here, you're there... you and Garth. Figure out what's appropriate. You've got my solemn word that any arrangement that's right for you and Garth is O.K. with me. If I can get down there, later in the summer, I'll sign my name, or whatever. Just do it... then write me."

"You're sure?"

"Positive, Ma. I feel wonderful. Like I stepped back from the edge of a cliff."

"A short step, baby."

"I know... I know."

So, over the telephone, the pledge had been given. The sole heir to a lost empire had relinquished all power of attorney to her mother.

For five days, while Garth worked into the routine of the farm work, Marta turned the possibilities over in her mind. She was aware that she should contact a lawyer. But one more large bill was the last thing she needed. Garth was unconcerned with thoughts of legalities. He worked long hours and was content, for the first time in years. The man was a natural with the herd, he handled the welding machine like a pro, repairing and servicing the tractors and field implements for the spring work. He whistled his way through each day. He had coffee, twice, with Gail Samarro and took her to dinner at the best restaurant in Prairie City.

At last, Marta arrived at a decision. Garth could leave his money at the bank, for the purpose intended. Philip Kenseth had not cashed the cashiers check, awaiting Marta's decision. Formal ownership, such as it was, would remain in Marta's name. In that way there could be no judgments against the silent partners. Hot damn, said Garth, the Plymouth is untouchable... what would David Rockefeller say to that? If the future brought any salvage from the wreckage around them, the arithmetic would be simple. Three people, three shares, Marta, Karen and Garth. To all this, Garth was amenable. He seemed almost indifferent. A simple contract was drawn up. George Rogers witnessed the agreement. The original was filed in Marta's bank box, a copy was given to Garth and another sent to Karen.

"This," said Marta, "has got to be the most shirt tail legal document ever concocted. Like two savages, scratching marks on a scrap of tree bark."

"Aw, come on, ain't nothing wrong with it," said Garth. He added the clincher, the finality that rose above laws and regulations. "It's just family."

So the shaky enterprise was set on course. "All I need is gas money and a six-pack now and then." Garth laid down easy terms. He would draw one hundred and fifty a week. The groceries, property taxes, insurance, livestock feed, all the unavoidable costs for the planting season including fuel, fertilizer and seed... all ongoing expenses would be paid out of the working fund in the farm checking account.

Through all the arrangements, Garth thrived. "What the hell," he said, carelessly. "Maybe it is unorthodox... so what? In tough times, folks do what they have to. No big deal."

CHAPTER NINE

The later winter auction was not unusual for the times. In the old days nearly all auctions were held in the lazy autumn months. Farmers found a lull, before corn picking, to bid on standing corn in the field, grain in the bin, field implements for the next season. The weather, then, was comfortable, the farmer holding the sale, jovial and ruddy faced, bantering with his friends and neighbors. They kidded him about moving to town, getting fat and slow and other terrifying prospects of retirement. All of this was a long time ago. Marta remembered a few such sales from her childhood. A young bank employee "clerked" the sale, which amounted to arranging financing for those buyers not paying by cash or check. The Methodist Ladies served the lunch... Marta recalled fried chicken, ham sandwiches and lemonade. Now, auctions were anywhere, any time. Now, a sallow faced young man did not clerk the transactions. The auctions were conducted by a bank, the P.C.A. (Production Credit Association) or FmHA (Farmers Home Administration).

Marta, her parka hood in place, mittens on her hands, shivered in the March wind of the farm yard. She surveyed the herd of Holsteins and the lines of used machinery standing, as though at attention, in long rows. She spoke to Oscar Thornstad.

"How many people do we have?"

Oscar took careful aim at an inert pebble and sent a missile of snoose to the exact spot. He wiped his mouth with his hand. Remnants of the juice clung to the corners of his mouth and the stubble was brown. Marta paid no attention, she had observed this fact of life too long for it to register. Oscar, his mouth relieved of excess moisture, muttered, "Ain't got an exact count, Marty. But at least eighty-five. Maybe more, but less'n a hundred."

"Uh huh. Must be a couple of hundred people here. So we're close to half."

"Yah. What I figure."

A slight shudder passed over her, she hunched into her parka. "Hell of a day, old buddy. Let's go talk to Les before this farce gets underway."

They found the owner, Les Cranston, near the granary, speaking, quietly, with his friends. Cranston was of a younger breed, early thirties, with a black beard, neatly trimmed around a sharp, inquiring face. He and his wife, Nancy, had "owned" the farm for ten years. They had three children, aged three to seven. Les Cranston had endured two hail storms, one a near wipe out. On a busy spring day, the past year, he had lost two fingers of his right hand in the power

51

take-off of his biggest tractor. The mangled hand had healed well. Les didn't consider himself a crippled man. Just busted.

"Hang loose, Les." Marta said the mechanical words in a low voice. "We got a good turn out, the people are in place, just like we drew it up."

"Sure, Marty, I know." Marta could hardly recognize the familiar voice. It was a high pitched whisper, wrenched from the throat. The man was strained, that was plain to see, eyes sunken and red rimmed. The operation looked great, on paper. But this was a cold and blustery reality. Big buyers with cash, the bargain hunters, had come considerable distances to bid on the merchandise... their trucks and semi's were parked along the road and driveway. Marta glanced at her watch. Twelve forty-five, the auction was scheduled for one, sharp. Vehicles were still arriving, some of them Harvest.

"I ain't got much hope, Marty." The whispering tremble held defeat. "Last month at Skalsky's remember? The bidders paid no attention. Hell, Skals didn't come out of there with anything but a couple old cows and a bale elevator that nobody wanted."

"That was then, Les, not now. We only had about forty people out for that debacle. We're in better shape today."

"Muscle?"

Marta was troubled by the question. But she had to level, the man deserved honesty.

"You know better than that, Les. Persuasion... no muscle. The drill will do."

Oscar placed a huge hand on Cranston's shoulder. The craggy face was impassive. "We don't panic, Les, no matter what. But we'll get you your stuff... some of it anyway." He glanced toward the trailer bed that served as a stage for the auctioneer and his helpers. Then he launched a brown stream in the general direction. "Screw 'em," he muttered.

Marta grinned. "I might've said it different, Oscar. But I reckon that'll do, nicely."

George Rogers had joined the group, along with other members. He introduced a sensible note.

"Remember now. We need balance. We've talked ourselves blue in the face on that. This isn't nineteen thirty-three... the sharks are a lot more savvy now. The days of the twenty cent hay loaders and two dollar tractors are gone. We try that, the auction is called off in a minute. Sure, we chase it to another time, another location even, but that's tough." He added, casually, "This isn't old George preaching. Just a last minute reminder."

"Thanks, Uncle George," offered one of the farmers. They laughed and joked until the first cow was cut out from the herd and paraded inside the human ring.

This was a medium Holstein, below blooded standards but a respectable five year old. The auctioneer gave the butterfat record and the sale began.

Les Cranston offered the opening bid. Two hundred. The auctioneer, "Colonel" Hap McCarthy, was appalled. He was nearly speechless from the audacity of the offer. He sputtered. The crowd observed him, mildly, accustomed to the routines of the hawkers. McCarthy, like most of his kind, was a shameless extrovert and a back slapper. But he knew the trade.

The second bid followed in a moment. Two fifty, from a well dressed older man near the outer edge of the crowd. Immediately the man was surrounded by unsmiling men who pressed near the bidder. The men wore green Harvest buttons. They said nothing. Two seventy-five, offered Les Cranston. Three hundred, shouted another man. A different squad of farmers pressed in upon the new voice. No words were spoken, a mere shifting of feet accomplished the fact. The sale had barely begun... the cruel March wind gusted across the barn yard.

Three-twenty, said Les. His voice was reedy in the cold air. It was his final bid.

The auctioneer was dumbfounded. McCarthy knew what was in the air, but the act must continue, the disbelief recorded. He knew that he held, in spite of Harvest, a certain sympathy from the gathering. All sales crews work on commission, there are no guarantees.

"Three-twenty," he raged. "A beautiful animal here, good producer, two heifer calves delivered, no vet bills... strong and healthy. Worth eight hundred if she's worth a nickel." McCarthy turned on the charm... "Come on folks, let's get this party in gear."

McCarthy sang his song of persuasion and encouragement, of profits parading before the eyes of dairymen who needed herd replacements. The next bid was four hundred. Les Cranston, head down, was silent.

The final bid was six seventy-five. A steal, said McCarthy, biggest heist since the Brinks job. Marta was content. Two bidders had backed off. Harvest did not want the sale canceled on the first item. The troops were in place, the long afternoon held promise.

The sale droned on, the circle itself providing great relief from the harsh weather. One by one the cattle were sold. Then, in what amounted to a respite, odds and ends of tools, small engines, dairy equipment were offered. The crowd milled about. Sandwiches and coffee were sold by a vendor, the man did a land office business. Then the major items came under the hammer, the big implements, the tractors, combine, corn picker, baler and wagons.

All afternoon the green buttons moved, in squads of six to ten, through the crowd. Many of the bidders trudged back to their trucks and drove away empty... they hadn't felt up to forcing the issue. But others, desperate for animals or machinery, stood the gaff, survived the ice of silence and made good buys. Several conferences on the trailer bed were held, Marta knew they were on thin ice. Sheriff Bill Adams and two deputies stood near the auctioneer's platform cold eyed, watchful, deadly serious. But the sale was not called off. None of the Harvest people made a bid.

At four-thirty they were finished. For Harvest, a mixed bag. Les Cranston had recovered twelve cows, worth seven thousand dollars on any market, for twenty-eight hundred. He had gutted out the derision of McCarthy to repossess an International Harvester tractor for thirty-nine hundred. Marta knew that the four-plow beauty, twelve years old, was a cinch to go for seven to nine thousand.

Les had other implements, tools and some feed. He could pay for these purchases, this small minimum... he had the bare essentials to start again. Or, as George Rogers whispered, get the merchandise to a different market and pocket the difference. The farm was gone, Cranston's life was devastated. But he was far less destitute than he'd been at noon. Many of the farmers crowded around him. His eyes watered in the wind. He shook hands all around and hugged Marta... she felt his mutilated hand upon her back.

Another day, one more small step. Marta crawled into her old pickup, She was chilled to the bone but the door on the driver's side had been fixed. The hinges had been straightened by a body man who recommended a new door. Marta had declined. The door now closed, she'd live with the dents. Her eyes swept over the Cranston farm yard. Not even that, she thought, it's the former Cranston farm. Only a few dozen people remained, huddled in small groups against the wind. Trucks and semi-trailers were loading livestock. Some of the larger implements were tagged with the buyer's name, for later pick up. Lights glowed in the house and Marta could see small faces peeping from a window. But the whole farmstead wore the look of tired futility. All the buildings needed paint, wooden fences showed gaping spaces between the posts and the wire fences were matted into the weeds. A lovely farm, once, she remembered. When hope leaves, so does beauty. She rolled down the window as Sheriff Adams approached. "Hi, Sheriff," she said.

He leaned one uniformed arm on the dented door. Marta couldn't read his expression and she was too numb to try. But this approach she had to hear. Adams' voice was cold.

"Nice going, Marty. Your guys pulled it off."

Her tired brain responded. I'll play the game, she thought. Aloud, "My guys? Pulled what off? What the hell you talking about?"

"You know. The movement of the troops. The closing in. Everyone knew what was coming down."

"What's all that to me? I'm just another farmer, trying to pick up a bargain. Before the jackals get everything."

"Com'on, you're talking to Bill Adams."

"Talking? Or interrogation?"

"I like the word 'conversation'. But the people in Harvest look up to you, Marty. That's common knowledge."

"Not to me it isn't. I'm not even an officer. I don't have the time, I got too many cows to milk."

Adams grinned, the smile chilly as the March air.

"Not even an officer? Imagine that! Figured you were secretary, at least. Who keeps the minutes?"

Marta laughed without mirth. "You trying to bait me, Bill? You've got to go a little deeper than that sexual shit. The times have left you behind."

"Maybe. But is was close today, you people were on shaky ground. Intimidation's against the law."

In the deepening gloom of the long afternoon, Marta had heard enough. She spoke in controlled fury, her mittened hand clenched in the pickup window. "Don't give me that crap, Mr. Sheriff. What intimidation? I swear, this whole sorry mess was an auction that should never've been held. I did not see one gesture, never heard a voice raised. Not a threat... nothing!" The anger nearly blinded her. "Listen, you fascist punk. How long are you gonna shill for the bankers? You getting a good slice under the table to supplement that fat salary?" Marta's face was a flame, her eyes burned into him. "Just what the hell are you doing, Bill?"

Adams took all this calmly. Marta noted, for the first time, how drawn he looked.

"You know what I'm doing, Marty. I'm doing my job, what I took an oath to do. The law has got to be enforced, you know that."

"So, your job is to front for Kenseth? And for the P.C.A. and the Farmers Home Administration? Your job is to put the people who elected you out on the roadway?" Her voice slashed him. "Mike is dead. I know of at least a half a dozen other farm suicides. Three bankers are dead, Bill, and so are the men who shot them. Some sniper nicked a sheriff in Nebraska, I recall. This part of the Country is going to hell in a hand basket. Today was Cranston... it could just as easy have been me." She felt unutterably weary. "Shit. Tell me about law enforcement."

"I know, Marty, I know. I worry about all this. My wife's getting to be a nervous wreck, since that Nebraska case. Can't sleep."

"That's tough. But Betty ain't got a farm to lose. Nobody's cut off her credit. If that sounds hard on your wife, I'm sorry. But you... doing your job? Maybe. But we've got a job, too. We've got farms to save and lives to save. Harvest works within the law, not outside. If we didn't this farm yard might have seen something very dangerous today. Just keep that in mind."

Adams backed off a bit. His voice was softer. "Yeah, sure, I will. I just hope nothing happens where we clash, Marty. I don't want war with you, or Harvest."

"Neither do we." Marta flipped the ignition key. The old engine roared to life.

"So long, Bill. I always liked you, so do a lot of the members. Wouldn't be surprised most of them voted for you. But we are at war, we know the enemy... we can see his eyes. Don't join the enemy, Bill."

Marta drove toward home, a twelve mile trip that took her through Shawndo. The Crystal Cafe looked warm and inviting and, though she was late, she pulled up and went inside. Jenny served her coffee, the taste was like nectar after her time in the wind.

"Go O.K.?"

"Pretty good, Jen. Not perfect by any means, but you know what we're up against." She sipped the strong brew. "God, I felt for that guy. Les tried his best to tough it out. I could have bawled like a kid. All these deals are so rotten but that bad hand sure got to me."

"Les stopped in this morning. He says Nancy is going to try to get re-certified for teaching."

Marta was laconic. "Great. For what jobs?"

"Well, not around here. But, it's a shot. They might need teachers some day, somewhere." Jenny eyed the world, sourly. "Say, Marty, how's your new hired man doing?"

"Garth isn't a hired hand."

"Hey, I know. I'm kidding."

"Sorry, Jen. I'm uptight. Tension always makes me a bitch. But he's taking to it like a duck to water."

Marta continued on to home. She drove the pickup into the garage and walked straight to the barn.

She felt, for the first time in this rugged day, a sense of belonging near to contentment. The cows were fed, the milking well under way. Garth whistled a merry, off key tune as he went about his work, he might have been doing farm chores for a lifetime. Some things change for the better she thought, as she slipped off her parka and joined him. I didn't tell Jenny no lie. This wild tiger of mine is becoming tame as a house cat.

Between them the work had developed into a silent routine, smooth as an assembly line, effortless as breathing. They spoke very little, moving in that quiet rhythmic way that workers, long accustomed to each other, gain over years of closeness. All this in less than two weeks, to Marta a miracle of progress, time compressed into one small segment. She and Mike had moved as a team through the identical mundane tasks. Now, Garth... was it his resiliency to life itself, an adaptability to different jobs he had mastered in the mills?... was the same. With their new "contract", a fragile paper promise, in place, perhaps the man would prove as indispensable in the fields as in the barn and machine shed.

They wrapped up the work and headed for the house. At seven-thirty, a few days before official spring, the night was full upon them, the wind had died. The darkness was broken only by the yard light, that stab of luminescence that breaks the blackness in farm yards everywhere. Marta had seen, in night flights, returning from some trip with Mike, the pattern of tiny lights across the vast expanse of the prairie. Like the mirror image of stars, the friendly glows were reminders of homes and life and children. As Marta walked with Garth she remembered gigantic drifts that had nearly conquered her, little more than a month before. The mountains of snow were nearly gone, now, most of the yard was bare, only stubborn packs, hard as ice, still lingered in areas sheltered by trees or the shadowed sides of buildings.

Garth was ravenous. Marta had encountered healthy appetites throughout her life, but seldom like this. Her lean brother not only put away the groceries with amazing zest but was uncomplaining. She ladled beef stew into a bowl and added fried potatoes, string beans and brown bread to the fare. They ate together, in tired relaxation. One helping was enough for Marta, she'd lunched at the Crystal, but Garth added a second and a third. He didn't wolf his food, he merely seemed intent on stoking some inner fire. Must be the fresh air, Marta figured. Makes a man that's been cooped up in mill work appreciate plain food.

They lingered, lazily, over coffee. Marta, the trauma of the long day behind, was pensive. In retrospect, the partial victory for the dispossessed Cranston seemed so small.

"So," said Garth. "The auction crowd laid off... just enough to give the man some breathing room, but not enough to alarm the establishment?"

"About it, Garth. Except for the term. I don't really know what "establishment" means."

"You ever been on a picket line... I mean a real hard-ass labor war, then you'd know."

"At one time we were the agriculture establishment, I suppose."

"Yeah?" He was the skeptic. "Well, times change. Now, you... we... are the peons. We'll become the new migrants."

"I know. And that's what Harvest is all about. To prevent that. To put a stop."

"Good for you." Garth went to the fridge for a Bud. A sign of concealed uneasiness? Marta wondered. More likely a sign he liked beer.

Garth drank from the can. "So," he said. "Les Cranston has some cows, a little machinery. The bank owns the farm. Where's Les gonna operate?"

"Who knows? Maybe right where he is. No way he can buy a place. But he might find acreage to rent."

Even as Marta spoke the words, she knew they'd reached the heart of the discussion. Garth lit a cigarette and stared at her, eyes slitted, thinking deep, and Marta's own words rang hollow inside her head.

"I see," he drawled. "Rent from another farmer? Most of 'em are looking for additional acreage themselves, to keep their machinery busy. Same as you and Mike did."

"That's true."

"So, if Les rents, he'll rent from a bank. Or an insurance company... some institution that's become, in the past few years, a mammoth land owner." Garth scowled.

"So?"

"So?" He mocked her. The lean figure tensed, his dark eyes glittered now and the tan cheeks flushed. What goes on here, wondered Marta. She had not seen her brother so agitated before. And, on one beer?

"Therefore," said Garth. "The movement is rendered obsolete. Harvest becomes an anachronism in its infancy. Worse than that... stillborn!" Marta was startled by the sudden passion.

"Your friends become the scab element of the farm crisis, Marty. Like a non-union worker crossing the line. The only way... the only way... to render foreclosure unprofitable is to render the repossessed land sterile. Let the land lie fallow, consumed by weeds and by taxes, because no real farmer will touch the soil."

"Garth, it's too much. That kind of program... a farm belt boycott really... couldn't be pulled off."

He agreed immediately. "I know that. Economic pressure always overcomes dialectics. A fact of life, there's no chance to turn all this around. Not by Harvest. Not by anyone. The financial giants will take the land. The old farming class'll have to serve 'em."

Marta, through the evening and for several days after, pondered the wisdom of Garth's thoughts. Her brother's beliefs had been forged in molten metal and the barren emptiness of unemployment. A quarter century in that environment had produced a man who spoke his mind, who recognized defeat because defeat was always present in some form, a step beyond in others.

Why did the farmers, who detested the money lenders, fight to be the first in line to turn the repossessions of their neighbors into profitable write-offs for the enemy? To raise crops and cattle on the land of their neighbor's defeat? I'll talk to Oscar, she thought. The old man has, distilled in his blood and bones, most of the savage wisdom of the twentieth century.

CHAPTER TEN

The final stubborn remnants of the long winter disappeared. Migrant birds dotted flyways on the return from the south. As March melted into April, the icy holdouts around the buildings melted into slush. A decent spring, the melting had been gradual, most of the water worked back to the black earth... the run-off was minimal. Marta recalled years when the level fields had been lakes, nearly into May. Delayed planting means early, lower yielding strains of hybrid corn and, often, frost damage in the autumn. Farmers, like psychiatrists, are leery of the word 'normal.' Marta smiled, remembering a family doctor who had pointed this out. Still, the caveat acknowledged, it seemed that a normal spring was possible, that field work would not be long delayed. The underground fuel tanks were full, seed and fertilizer and herbicide were stocked in the empty bins of the old granary.

She hardly recognized her own machinery. Garth had repaired and cleaned and sanded the implements to a factory shine. He had overhauled the engines on both tractors, chipped rust, and applied paint where it was needed. Two tractor tires, beyond repair, had been replaced. We'll have breakdowns in the field, machines will bog down, all the inevitable, Marta knew. But Garth's persistence and skill had narrowed the odds. Marta began to miss some meetings. She found if difficult to leave the farm when her brother was working so hard, often until midnight.

At supper, one night, early in April, Marta laid down the law. "Get out of here," she said. "I don't care much where you go." She relinquished the big sister role. "I ain't too far from straight temperance myself. But, even if you get drunk, you've got to have a break for a few hours. You can't keep up this pace... you'll be burned out before we hit the fields."

Garth burst into laughter. His good humor seemed impervious to anything. He had chosen this life, taken the ultimate gamble... with his money and his future. And, taking that step, he hadn't looked back. Garth had closed a door upon all the ghosts of the past, hard years that had seared him. It had taken a miracle, clothed in tragedy... one of life's endless ironies... to bring him back to foundations long forgotten. He said to Marta, "I thought you understood."

"What? Why you're killing yourself with work?"

"Aw hell, Marty. It ain't that. I love the work, therefore, it ain't really work, it's something better. It goes deeper... what I owe to you and Mike."

"Mike?"

"Of course. He... left... because the farm was lost, and it might well be. But because of all that happened, here I am. Mike, a good guy, lost. A worthless ass like me got a second chance. If I give anything less than all out, well, hell then the place is gone, for sure, and I might as well have stayed out in the jungle." Garth was into his vision now, Marta must be made to see his purpose. "I took a pledge, Marty. Not a real oath, just a promise to myself, the day I signed that check over to Kenseth. I told myself that they'd have to kill me before I quit... before I made sure that Mike didn't die for nothing."

"Who's 'they'?"

"I dunno. The whole world, I guess. Whatever you folks in Harvest are fighting."

Marta was moved by her brother's intensity. The man had no eloquence, he had no need for mannered phrases. And she was glad he had spoken out, emerged, for a moment, from his protective bravado. Still, she knew that, at forty-four, he was breakable. She insisted, firmly, that he slow down, at least for a spell.

The following afternoon Garth found himself in the Crystal Cafe. He sat in a booth, across from Gail Samarro. The full bodied figure was sheathed in rust color with no accessories beyond a dull clasp – pewter?, Garth wondered – that pinned her blouse decorously high. The simplicity of her working outfit appealed to him. He mentioned the thought.

"You look like a million, kid. Either that or I've been too long on the farm."

"I figured they buried you out there. On the lone prairie, like the song says," she mocked him.

"I'm too ornery for that."

"That, I believe," she said. "What do farmers do, this time of year... besides get drunk?"

"You're talking about dumb farmers, not me. I work sixteen, seventeen hours, on two cans of beer."

"That long? Being cowboy to a dairy herd?"

"Hell," he growled. He forced a scowl. "For a farm town gal, you don't know much about farming."

"I know plenty. Enough to know that most of the farmers lay around the Municipal in Prairie, pouring it down and baying at the moon about tough times." Garth knew there was some truth in the statement. She continued, not smiling. "Number two, if we're counting, I happen to be a woman, not a gal. You been on leave from the human race for a few years?

"You might say." Garth was contrite. "I'm sorry. I'm a good guy, Gail, but I ain't above stupidity."

"Actually, neither am I." The sequined glasses twinkled at him.

He felt drawn to this spunky person and the night was before them.

"The Municipal in Prairie is a den of iniquity. Let's visit there tonight... as missionaries."

"Are you joking? I don't hear from you in two weeks. Then... wham, let's go boozing. You got a telephone on that ranch?" Gail made no effort to hide her annoyance. Garth was subdued.

But they were smitten. The moment passed and, together, they schemed the hours ahead. All depended on getting a sitter for her children. "But I'll try," she promised. "If I can't, it's Scrabble or gin rummy." She looked at her watch. "Oh shit. Excuse the language, but I'm out of a job if I don't get back with the money changers. You know where I live. Pick me up at eight."

His dark eyes swept her body as she rose, dwelled on the curves. "How much do you weigh?"

"One... none of your business."

"You said I should pick you up."

Gail's laughter pealed in the old cafe. "You're a smart son of a bitch, aren't you?"

"Naw. I just take things literally."

"Uh huh? Well, take this, literally." She thumbed her nose, daintily, the fingers flicking beneath the frames of her glasses. She buttoned her jacket. Jenny had given them separate checks.

"Here, big man," she said. She laid her slip by Garth's. "Fifty-seven cents. Can you handle it?"

"If I can't, I'll stop over. Hit Kenseth for a loan. What the hell is fifty-seven cents against four hundred big ones?"

"Don't even talk to me about loans. Bank employees see nothing, hear nothing. Like the Mafia, a code of silence."

"O.K. Just keep clearing my checks."

Garth had time, hours to kill before meeting Gail. Marta would bitch at him if he showed up on the farm for chores. He eased onto a counter stool beside Oscar Thornstad. The huge face was stony.

"You got that filly broke to ride yet?"

"Hell no, not me. I don't want to break anyone, I like them wild." Garth ordered coffee refills for both. "My interest's in farming, not women."

"Yah, sure."

"Marty told me you were at the Cranston sale. You and George and some of the other locals."

"Yah," sourly. "We were there."

"Marty seemed to think it went O.K."

"Well, Marty. Your sister's a hell of a woman, Garth. Jesus!... I hope you two can hold on. But everything's against Harvest. History plays no favorites... it's just the recorded word."

Garth regarded him, fondly. "Yeah, history. But you're a smart old bastard, Oscar. What's to blame... for all this shit?"

The old man shrank from the question. He had seen too much, lived too long. Now the folly of the decades rolled over him, and all his friends, like a great wave. He knew the truth, but so what? The truth was, often, the most fragile of all weapons, so weak against the forces of distortion and political favor. I'd trade the truth for a lie that'd save this way of life.

"Ah, the blame, Garth, the blame. There's a thousand places this calamity came from. But mostly, it's the government. The politicians, in bunches and alone, turned the desperation of the nineteen thirties to survival. That was an achievement... but they overlooked one thing. They didn't see, or didn't want to, that government aid had to have limits, ceilings... a lid for each farm unit. For the next fifty years that wasn't done. What happened? Well, exactly what was inevitable happened. The lawyers, the doctors, insurance companies, bankers, anyone who owned farm land received the same set-aside and soil bank payments, per acre, as the family farmer. These non-farmers, some with their own little baronies that matched, in size, the medieval enclaves of Europe, received much more, per unit, than the real farmers."

"How could that be?"

"First of all, the landlords had the money to weather rough times... drought or poor markets, for example. If a man owned a thousand acres, he merely smiled, set aside his marginal land... sloughs, knobby hillocks, stretches of sand... and collected his government checks."

"With which he could buy more land."

"Of course. If he wanted to go that way. Anyway, the goal of market stability was defeated. The owner merely poured more fertilizer and chemicals into the land not enrolled in set-aside, soil banks, PIC programs, whatever the catch phrase of the year, and produced more grain than he'd ever grown before. A joke, of course. But fair for one, fair for all, huh?"

"I was coming around to that."

"Not so. The dairy farm, with five kids on a tight little one-sixty or two-forty, needed every square foot of soil to sweat out a living. That farmer couldn't spare the ground to put in set-aside. Or, if he could, maybe fifteen acres. So, the data fed into the great computers in Washington, D.C. and the checks spewed out. Five hundred dollars, two thousand or five hundred thousand, the giant computer didn't know or care. There were no limits... to poverty or to affluence."

"So, the big became bigger, the little gradually got swallowed up... all courtesy of that menagerie in Washington, known as Congress," offered Garth.

Oscar grunted. "You catch on real fast." He sat, a broken, brooding giant. He thinks too much, thought Garth. A fatal occupation.

"Where have all the flowers gone?" Oscar might have been talking to himself. "Remember the Vietnam song? Where have all the farmers gone... long time ago? The average farm, when I was old enough to handle a man's job in the threshing ring... I was maybe twelve or thirteen... was one-sixty, two hundred acres. Now the spreads average eight hundred, a lot of them are three sections or more. And the old farmers are dead, their kids in the cities, some doing well, some just adding to the problems there. Less than two million farms... once there were eight million."

"Sounds like a rat's maze to me. Ain't you simplifying the whole issue?"

Oscar snorted. He eyed Garth with a look near disgust.

"'Course I am. You want a whole textbook? But it still all comes down to this. From day one, there should've been a cap... like fifteen grand... on any subsidy or loan payment. And checks payable to farmers, on the farm. On the farm... only! Would've changed the whole course of history, for goddamn sure for the better."

"Why didn't Congress set it up that way?" Garth asked. Oscar's vehemence made sense.

"Politics, what else? Where d'you think political power lies in the farm belt? On the one-sixties, the guy with twenty cows and sixty pigs? You get big campaign contributions from that crowd? Shit!"

Oscar stood up. "Old song, Garth. I'll sing it right into my grave. And for what? Good night, buddy." The huge figure, denims dirt-caked, a trace of shirt tail flopping, lumbered out of the cafe.

In Prairie City the muni was crowded for a mid-week night. Garth and Gail grabbed a booth as a young couple eased out. The juke box offered a mournful Kenny Rogers. "Nothing but C. and W. in the machine," laughed Gail. "You want metal, even soft rock, move on down the street."

"That solid?"

"Believe it. I've seen size thirteen boots go right through the front glass of the machine when the yammering came on. They know their clientele now."

"Well, a night like this, might as well be the beat. Can't hardly hear old Kenny, over the racket."

They relaxed in the maroon plastic of the booth. Gail had Seagrams and Seven, then another. Garth worked through two cans of Bud Light and started a third. All this was more than enough courage to snuggle against her and chance a casual feel. The operation was a small success.

Between the booths, the partitions were only shoulder high. In the turmoil of sound, voices made a blanket of sound that Garth found enjoyable. He knew Marta was right, he had needed a break. But the sound narrowed down to the men in the next booth. Gail and Garth had no wish to rubber, but the nearby debate was impossible to ignore. The two men were so near, just across the partition, another man facing them in the booth.

"Since noon for that bunch," whispered Gail. "I sort of know one of those foghorns. He's a real jewel. I've been by his farm, the litter would make you sick." Garth took a fast look, turning casually as though searching for a waitress. The three were, sure enough, far down the road.

"That damned Adams,"... the voice cut through the sound of a wailing Tammy Wynette. "They got that sucker in their pocket, like he was a pet frog."

"And when they say jump, there goes the frog." A thundering basso agreed.

Garth turned away. He listened but didn't care who the voices belonged to. He'd met Bill Adams at the funeral.

"To think I voted for that bastard." The disgust was thick enough to cut. "I'd vote for a goddamn rattle snake before I'd ever vote for Bill Adams again." Garth and Gail exchanged small smiles. They were both well aware of the feelings in the area.

"Bill Adams stands around like he was J. Edgar come back to life. Making goddamn sure the blood suckers get the blood. Him and his deputies."

"Never bats an eye. A smile would break his face. One hand right by the old holster, the other one on his hip, like he seen too many television shows. Dodge City – what was that big bastard's name?"

"I forget. But that Dodge cop... Marshall, whatever, always made it. Might not happen to Adams. Somebody, sure as hell, gonna go off his porch rocker. Put a slug into that son of a bitch."

The wild talk went on, exploding into bursts of laughter and orders for drinks. Gail and Garth were jolted by the scene. Saloon bullshit, that they knew. But, in Shawndo, neither had heard such crazy talk. They might have been alone with the wild bunch. No one else in the lounge appeared to have paid any attention.

Three beers were as nothing, complete sobriety engulfed Garth... a harsh stillness gripped him, the noise and confusion around him erased. Is all this comedy, he wondered, the babble of inhibitions vaporized in boozy fumes? I listened in labor halls for twenty years, to this kind of crap. Is violence the only thing the country knows?

But Gail seemed unaffected.

"Hey, let's have one more for the road and get out of here. My sitter's only booked until eleven."

"Yeh, sure. But I'm a little shook."

Garth knew, inwardly, that he'd been too judgmental of the Muni. Most of the crowd was no more or no less smashed than any in a thousand bars he'd known. Many of the folks, singly and in couples or groups were just relaxing, searching for a small escape from worry. One thing we were right about, though. The men here outnumber the women, at least by two to one.

"Come on." said Gail. "It's just bullshit. Guys like that put out that everlasting drivel. They don't have the nerve to face up to their old ladies, let alone Adams. They make my ass tired."

"Well," he grinned feebly. "At least they didn't mention bankers on the hit list."

"Oh, they'll get around to that. Some of 'em smell blood. They read the papers." Gail shared his sobriety now. "God, I love farmers. I've lived all my life in this area. They're such great people. Solid, heroic even. Most of 'em. But you always have a fringe, like the lunatics in the next booth. Free Country... no getting away from it."

At the Samarro house the elderly baby sitter had forgotten her deadline. She had settled down to a late move and, with Pepsi and cookies, had no intention of leaving until the ancient classic was over. Way it bounces, thought Garth. But what the hell, like the ballplayers say, we got the rest of the season to raise the old batting average. He said good night in the front hallway, safely shielded from the television.

Her lips were warm and parted and she pressed against him, arms laced behind his neck. Reborn, thought Garth. There is life beyond Pittsburgh.

He reasoned, "There'll always be a sitter, baby. Or else those sweet kids of yours. One of these times, we got to get away. Like Minneapolis. St. Paul, even, if we're desperate."

She mocked him, but did not pull away. "Jenny told me about your big appetite when you're at the Crystal. Now, I believe her."

"Well, think about it."

"Oh sure. Thinking never hurt anyone."

CHAPTER ELEVEN

In the second week of May, with most of the planting completed, three days of rain put a temporary stop to operations in the fields. We're well ahead of the game, mused Marta. Let 'er rain. Like my Dad always said, it's gonna rain whether you agree or not.

Rain in the spring is always a mixed blessing. Holds up the corn and soy bean planting but it's great for the hay, settles the gathering dust, soaks the subsoil. On a Friday morning Garth and Gail left for the Twin Cities. She'd called in sick for the day and Mrs. Nelson, the venerable sitter, had arbitrated a modest contract for two days and nights with the children. Bart was seven, Sarah four, and both kids well adjusted. Spoiled, of course, said their mother, but aren't they all?

"We'll take my car," Gail announced. "I wouldn't trust that old bucket of yours past the next county." Gail had an aunt and uncle in Minneapolis that she hadn't visited for more than two years. In her '82 Dodge, only a three hour drive. She was dressed in a handsome grey suit... creams and pastels did nothing for her silhouette, or, rather, did too much. Garth dredged up a decent combination of slacks and jacket from what remained in his closet, echoes of the past. He picked the best, but the choice was limited.

I'll stick to the farm, Marta figured. When the cat's away... Garth had been such a bear for work that she owed him one by keeping her nose to the grindstone while he was gone. Good intentions. The rain continued. In the afternoon she drove to Prairie City. There was to be a farm foreclosure sale, a three-twenty with good buildings, at two o'clock at the courthouse front door.

A cruel joke... one more in an endless procession... thought Marta. There'll be only one bid. That will be by a rep from the insurance company that holds the mortgage. The bid will be for the exact amount due. She had witnessed this unreal drama acted out so often that all suspense had vanished. Five minutes, then it was over, the guillotine had never operated more efficiently. The tactical precision of this legal formality, so unlike the farm auction, had continued to baffle Harvest.

Fewer than one hundred people gathered, on the sidewalks and grass in front of the stone steps, half of them Harvest. The weather, as though in honor of the land transfer, had cleared for the hour, a short lived respite. At two P.M. the sun darkened again, black clouds gathered that bulged with new reservoirs of rain. All the forces of orderly procedure were in evidence. Sheriff Bill Adams stood, as the drunks at the Muni had described, and was flanked, on either side, by two deputies. "That damn tin horn," growled Oscar. "Brings an army. Five of them, to stand guard over a flock of sheep." Oscar's melancholy, deep as the Dane's, had grown in the past weeks. The old man was true blue to the movement but his spirits had lowered with each new casualty among the family farms. Marta knew of Oscar's disaffection. Old radicals never die, their voices are drowned in waves of pale indifference.

The legal description of the farm in question was read to the assembled people, word for word as the notice that had been posted. Weak taunts were sounded from voices in the rear, but that was all. The bidding opened, one middle aged man in a spanking summer weight suit bid four hundred and twenty-one thousand, two hundred and four dollars, on behalf of Western Plains Insurance Company. "A fortune," muttered George Rogers. "Still, eight years ago, that farm might have fetched the best part of a million." Marta nodded. "It was Monopoly money, then," George continued. "And we all had lots of it, access to it, anyway. Now... it's hard money and nobody's got any." The lone offer hung in the humid air.

Five minutes passed, the auctioneer continued to cry the sale and the Sheriff and deputies stood, parade rest, their eyes scanning the crowd. Then the bidding closed. Another financial giant owned one more parcel of prairie. Justice was truly done, the loan had been in massive default.

Marta was dispirited. I have to get a fresh outlook, she thought, or else stay away from these funerals. I wonder who'll work the land for Western Plains? Perhaps Garth has the solution. Let dead dirt reward plunderers who use the law to grab what they'd be afraid to steal. She mentioned it to George Rogers. The white-haired farmer pondered the notion, crinkled his eyes, squinting, although the sun, brief visitor this week, had disappeared once more. George Rogers didn't speak without thinking it over.

"The tactic might be ok, Marty. A wave of pressure to keep foreclosed land idle could be a new direction." He laughed. "Appeals to the historian in me. Shades of scorched earth... black embers instead of living green. Now... what? A different form, minus the arson?"

"The idea scares me," admitted Marta. "At the same time, I'm intrigued by the idea of persuading farmers to make a new stand, draw a line in the dust. We'll work no land that's not our own." She frowned. "Hell, that sounds like a TV commercial. But you know what I mean."

"Sure. And speak to Garth. We can use him. The guy's got a direct kind of honesty that's refreshing."

"Aw hell. Garth just likes to drive that tractor. That, and one other hobby that he ought to be outgrowing."

"Oh... that. yeah." Rogers was amused. "It's the season, Marty. Stirs up the blood."

They laughed at the spectacle of lovers, no longer quite so young. George moved on. Helen, he said, would be waiting at the elevator. "She can't stand the legal charades, this or the auctions. Says each one's like the blade of a knife in her heart."

They parted. I'm famished, thought Marta. I pack away more food these days than a lumberjack. She walked to the Saunders Cafe, deciding that she couldn't hold out for the drive to Shawndo and the Crystal.

A slim woman, peering through large blue-lidded eyes, approached her booth. In a quiet voice she asked, "May I speak with you, Mrs. Crawford?"

Marta, dreaming of old times, cafe meals with Mike, looked up. She was startled by the inquiry.

"Why Betty? Betty Adams." She had only met the woman on a few occasions. "Yes, of course. Please sit down."

The Sheriff's wife slipped into the booth across from Marta. Something about the woman's manner bothered her. I don't know her that well, thought Marta. Lord, I haven't seen Betty in more than a year.

"Very nice of you." Mrs. Adams was hesitant, seemed to search for an opening. "Certainly is a patch of rain, isn't it?" Something about the odd phrase, the eye focus... Marta was still puzzled.

"Oh well. The beauty of the spring rains. A mixed blessing, but yes, enough is enough." The hostess in her surfaced. "Coffee, Betty?"

"Yes, please. But you mustn't. I'll get my own." A place mat materialized and steaming coffee in a white cup. Such an extremely attractive woman. So slim. I feel thick as a wrestler, but lots of women do that to me. Ah, the slender ideal... this one, perhaps, to the extreme. Marta said, "Nonsense, you're a nice surprise. I needed someone to talk with. I was just sitting here, kind of remembering stuff. You know how that goes."

"Yes, of course. And your... great loss last winter. January, wasn't it?"

"Yes." Marta did not correct her. For now she realized what had been troubling her. Betty was drunk, she had, at least, the delicate beginnings of a snootful.

Betty Adams said, "I have no one to talk to." The words were like drops of rain... clear and cool, without guile.

"I don't understand."

"What is there to not understand? I could be melodramatic... 'The wagons are circled'... like that." Betty sipped, unsteadily, from the white cup. "I am all alone, outside my family. I've been cut off from the society of women. Except, of course, the deputies' wives. We're fellow travelers, or should be."

Marta said nothing. This isn't real, she thought, like listening to the unbalanced.

"But even that... the deputy connection... has been spoiled. Not entirely, but Bill doesn't believe in, quote, `excessive fraternization.' Leads to problems, like how can he be even-handed with the troops if there's wifely influence?" Betty's laugh was mocking and Marta could feel, like a dank wind, the bitterness. "You ever hear such absolute crap?"

"Well... I can't really judge." I am being drawn into something here that I should avoid? Marta's first thought was escape, what's all this to me? Aloud, "I spend nearly every hour on the farm, Betty. I don't come to town too much."

This didn't seem to register. "I know many farm wives, Marta. Friends for years,... I thought. Now... on the street, in the shops, at church even, they cut me dead. The shop girls, in the stores, are polite... so damn polite! Part of their job, of course. But they hate my guts."

"Is some of this imagination?"

"Oh... who knows? You get ignored, the feelings multiply. Sure, there's some paranoia. And if I can admit that, maybe I'm still all right. Sane, I mean... isn't that the test?"

Mike always called me mush head, the bleeding heart of Black Loam County. God, how he used to rib me. But it was Mike, not me, who built the tree house for the Chicano kids. I don't need this... this added load. I've carried too many. Marta thought, let's boil this down to the bare bones, then get to hell out of here. This woman is in pain, but she hasn't picked the right confessor.

She said, "I'm getting the picture. And I understand your feelings, your resentment. It's not really fair, but what is, these days? I'm an authority on the unfairness of life, remember?"

The Sheriff's wife lit a filter tip, with careful hands that moved very slowly. She whispered, "I know... I know."

Marta, watching the long fingers that tried, so hard, to remain steady, thought of long nights, the labored motions of distorted dreams, attempts to find a way, a flight from danger. The sweep of the net widens, now even this woman, a city transplant many years ago, is caught. This fragile woman who might not know a sheep from a goat, becomes a victim of our problem all the same. How many remain, in this area, who aren't touched? She said, "Seems to me, you're in a vulnerable position. You can't escape what's happening. Therefore, two choices. You cope or you give up."

"I haven't the slightest notion of how to cope. I guess nothing in my life has prepared me for... any of this."

"Oh, you're coping." Marta was short. "By running away. With booze, for sure and, I'd guess, with pills. Right?"

The blue eyes opposite were too bright. But the woman had come to Marta, little more than a stranger, for help. She nodded.

"First thing you can do is try to see the whole picture, not just your part. The farmers are getting closed out. Bill's position gives muscle and validity to the process. You're crying about social amenities. Come with me to a Harvest meeting, I'll show you misery worse than you ever imagined."

"I know the situation. But that is all law... and economics. It has nothing to do with me."

This is sniveling, now, thought Marta. Her voice became a blunt instrument. "Then make it something to do with you. Your husband becomes more hated every day. You could offset some of that."

"How?" The thin voice was barely audible.

"How?" Marta was incredulous. "My Lord, woman, nearly every county, including this one has a counselor now, for farmers. Get in there and help, that office is crying for leg work. Hit the politicians, and when they turn you away, hit them again. Get up to the state capitol and lobby. Get into fund-raising for the families short on food. Christ... do something! People will respond, you'll see. You can turn things around, for yourself at least."

The small homily was wasted. Marta realized that, at once. In the quiet time of the mid-afternoon the pale, handsome woman stared straight ahead and the cigarette formed a long ash above the paper placemat.

"I can't," she said, simply, and, to Marta's discomfort, tears welled in the shadowed blue eyes.

"No? Why?"

"I'm not like you, Mrs. Crawford... Marta. You're strong. I've always thought that, everyone says it."

"Now. please... "

"It's alright. I won't embarrass you. Still, it's true. But I'm a very private person, I couldn't possibly do any of the things you've suggested. I know... " she was struggling. "I know that you've pointed out the way to go. But I'm simply incapable of such involvement. I'm the world's worst politician's wife. And never forget, a sheriff is a politician. Bill's made it this far in spite of me, certainly not because of me."

"Come on. Bill thinks of you all the time. Worries about you. He told me so, himself, at the Cranston sale."

Betty Adams laughed, without mirth, and the tears now coursed her cheeks.

"I'm really sorry I can't be of more help, Betty. But we're on opposite sides." The broken lives of friends paraded before her eyes and the efforts of Harvest seemed so small. She knew that Oscar's increasing bitterness had entered her. "It's not just your husband, Betty. It's all of them. They have to join us, or remain the enemy."

"But we are talking about neighbors, not enemies. Bill and I have long time friends here."

"I know that. You're educated, Betty, you know history better than I do. But name me a revolution that hasn't turned friend against friend, even within the same family?" Marta sighed. "I'm so damn weary, Betty. But I'm fighting a battle, you aren't. You're whining 'cause your social life has gone to hell."

The conversation drifted to a desultory end. There was little more to be said and for Marta, with Garth away, the milking was always there.

Betty said good bye and walked off, a slight, slender woman, swaying slightly on heels Marta would never have attempted, gone – had Betty ever been here? really here? Marta looked vacantly at Betty's spikes She liked farm boots... Red Wing leather, tough comfortable, waterproofed. She'd worn the pair she had on for three years. Hell, she thought, these are just getting broken in. She slogged, in the old boots, to the pickup.

At ten that evening, just as Marta was ready to climb the stairs, the telephone rang. She strained to hear the soft voice.

"This is Betty Adams. Mrs. Crawford. I apologize for imposing on your time this afternoon. I had no right to do that, it was unforgivable. I had been drinking... I was not myself. Please forgive me." One more strange twist to this long day. Marta rallied, though she was extremely tired. "It's alright, Betty... really. Sometimes we just have to find a listener... I've done the same thing myself. It's... " Her voice trailed off, she was talking to a dead line.

A rueful thought... there goes a peaceful night's sleep. The problems multiply, the lines of conflict form strange patterns in this long struggle. Today, a hand reached out, across the line. Tonight, the hand draws back. And why not? the gesture was fueled only by booze. Craig Simmons watched today, his face hardened with sorrow, as his three-twenty was lost to him, almost certainly, forever. Craig is older, by three or four years, than I am... how could he possibly come back? Certainly he has to shoulder some of the blame. Craig made blunders along the way, borrowed too much against land values that plummeted, yields that never came. The cycle will revolve again, it always does. But Craig Simmons, one of Mike's truest friends, will be on the outside, looking in. So, the farms are lost, the tally for our state alone is in the thousands. All the rallies have failed, the politicians are helpless at best, sly adversaries at worst, pandering to urban constituencies... the voters dwell in greater numbers there. All this while making honeyed speeches and other media sound effects.

So many factors... and the Adams family. There was, once, a TV program by that name. Bill Adams, clear eyed protector of law and order... would he have guarded slave owner's rights as rigorously, a century and more ago?... and his frail wife, buffeted by gales beyond her strength. Marta considered these things in the four poster and sleep did not come easily. And later that night, Garth and Gail, far from the encroaching poverty of Shawndo, celebrated a sensuous freedom in the luxury of Radisson Central, room eight-eleven. None of this would have astounded Marta or bothered her in the least. Garth was so solid, he had proved a wonder, beyond all expectations, on the farm. But he was his own man and Gail was an unknown quantity... girl Friday to the man who held her future... and Garth's and Karen's... in his hands. At least, to some extent. This is a situation that requires more delicacy than I can muster. But, what the hell, this old four poster is so empty more power to 'em. For Garth, let the sea seek its own level.

In the waterbed depths of the Radisson, Garth, the dark days behind him, found sweet diversion in a well endowed body, rounded fullness, a handful of pounds above the culture's statistical perfection. The added ounces transmitted energy to match. Below, the noise of the city streets, the kind of harsh sounds Garth had left behind, were muted by the sealed windows. Occasionally a siren wail broke through, the lonesome scream of swift pursuit through the hours of darkness.

On Sunday afternoon they returned, Garth at the wheel, Gail resting, sleepily, beside him. Garth gloried in the beauty of the day, the earth, washed and new from the days of rain. This is perfect, I could only wish this buggy was a convertible... let the air sweep over us. Garth felt like a boy, refreshed as the land around him. "Hell of a deal," he murmured. "A what... mini-vacation? Best time I've had in years."

Gail smiled. "It was nice. I had almost forgotten what jewels Dave and Sue are. They certainly showed us the town."

"Yeah. Great people. What I was thinking, though, was the other. The Radisson bit, you know. Fabulous, huh?"

Gail closed her eyes and squirmed, for comfort, her head turned, cheek against the seat back.

"Oh, that. It was okay I guess."

CHAPTER TWELVE

The Monday morning meeting of department heads, usually Mr. Philip Kenseth, President, Gerald Ryan, Vice President, and Paul Standish, cashier, included, for the first time, Mrs. Gail Samarro, assistant cashier. All the men remarked, with a concern that veiled no hidden amusement, on the excellent recovery that Gail had made from her illness of the previous Friday. Apparently no one had been given reason to phone her house; the excursion remained undetected.

Still, there had been developments elsewhere. Gail had heard of the event on the Sunday night news, although it was then two days old. In the President's office of the Growers State Bank of Shawndo, the death of the bank president in Clayton, just across the border in South Dakota, dominated the meeting. The shooting was not the first, merely the most recent. Now the tally, in the midwest alone, stood at seven, six bank officials and one insurance executive. This, in a period of twenty-four months.

Philip Kenseth read from a printed release: "All of the deaths have been the result of firearms. All killings have been committed by white males, all of them farmers or former farm operators. One perpetrator is in prison, life sentence, one in custody awaiting trial. The other five, including the alleged perpetrator last Friday, are dead of self inflicted wounds, following the incidents."

He turned a page, reciting the names, addresses, ages and surviving family members. Two of the deaths were in Minnesota, one Wisconsin, two each in South Dakota and Iowa. The wide plains and empty spaces of North Dakota were, for the time, unrepresented. Gail felt numb. This was the first inner meeting she had been assigned to attend. She had followed, without undue fascination, the occasional killings. One by one, with intervals of several months, they had seemed to her merely exceptions, blips in the screen of normal behavior. Now, captured in capsule form, a frightening trend.

Kenseth read on: "The entire area of bank officer protection has come under intense scrutiny by the F.B.I., the State Bureau of Crime Apprehension, and all local law enforcement units. The general Consensus is that, in spite of the rash of wanton homicides, many others have been prevented by the continuing vigilance of the above mentioned forces." He paused. Gail, searching for hidden sarcasm in the dry voice, had found none.

No such subtlety hampered Paul Standish, cashier. At twenty-six he was the youngest. He was a State College grad, red faced and vigorous. The cashier had married the previous summer, his wife was expecting their first.

"What a pitiful, self-serving bunch of hogwash," he growled. "The crazy farmers run wild with double barreled shotguns and the Keystone Cops are turned in their tracks. Protection has failed and the law responds with back slapping. A lot of self congratulations."

Kenseth considered this. Then, "Gerald?"

Gerald Ryan at forty-five was the senior member. He had been with the bank for eighteen years, passed over for the presidency eight years earlier when the Board had been impressed by the qualifications and manner of a young Philip Kenseth from a northern town. Ryan's smoldering resentment had long since turned to relief. His strength was in audit and bookkeeping, he had not the slightest notion of how he might have dealt with the human elements of economic turbulence. He spoke carefully, a measured voice... he had no other.

"Statistically, we are extremely safe. We are speaking of a wide geographical area. Actually, in an automobile, driving down the road, you can... "

Standish broke in. "I don't believe this bullshit. What is it with you, Gerry? These people aren't getting blown away by statistics... Christ, they're getting their heads blasted by maniacs." Gail glanced at the bookish V.P. He had not moved a muscle during Standish's tirade.

Ryan continued, calmly. "The danger of sudden death on the highway is much greater than in these offices, or others that are similar. But all of us will continue to drive, continue to ignore the highway fatality figures." Standish groaned.

Kenseth said, "You both have valid viewpoints. The disagreement doesn't bother me. In fact, it's about par for these sessions. We've been arguing in this office for years. Why break tradition now?"

"I know, Phil. But cars... what the hell is Gerry getting at? We all have to drive... and we have to be here, on the job. That's double jeopardy, not a comparison." The athletic young man considered his words. "Besides... a man can drive defensively. How the hell, in this cockeyed farm situation, are you going to bank defensively?"

Ryan was placid. "Easy. Don't loan any money."

Kenneth was amused. He knew that Ryan, the man of computer mentality, was capable of sly humor. Standish, usually adept at gamesmanship, missed it.

"Don't loan?" The cashier was incredulous. "This is a farm bank, in a farm town. And beside the point. The loans are in place, most of them for years.

"Yes, Paul. We know." Kenseth was patient. "The Vice President regales us with a little of his gallows humor. Cuts the tension, don't you think?"

Standish nodded, sheepishly, acknowledging the point.

Kenseth resumed reading: "The clear and present danger to officers and employees of the lending institutions has intensified with this latest killing. While there are suspected affiliations involved, no one group has been identified as supportive of the crimes. The events in Clayton, S.D., or the others, appear to be the results of individual decisions... unbalanced acts by unbalanced minds." He paused. "Sounds a bit antiseptic to me."

"Who writes up that crap?" asked Standish. "What the hell are 'suspected affiliations'? Why don't they call them rabble-rousers, then we'd know what was meant?"

"O.K., why not? You want to tell us who the rabble rousers are?"

"Well... " The cashier struggled to be fair. "We didn't have these troubles years ago, when we had just the traditional farm groups."

"That's true. But in those years we didn't have the financial problems we have now. Where does it all fit in... the chicken and the egg?" The modest office was still. Kenseth chewed on a pencil end. "I'm not about to go on record, even here, in our own family so to speak, as being opposed to a movement that includes at least forty percent of our farm customers."

"Plus the fact," Ryan's voice was precise, "The movement's hands are spanking clean. They preach non-violence."

"As near as we know," said Standish, glumly.

Again the room was quiet. Is this the kind of nonsense that goes on in the bi-weekly meetings of Department Heads, wondered Gail. And why am I here today... even though I've always hoped to be included. We sit here, hashing over the same things the farmers do at the Crystal Cafe. The questions multiply, the answers diminish. Her glance flickered around the Spartan office. Kenseth did not believe in rich decor, the elegant drapes bit. An affluence of decoration and fixtures would not sit well with the rural trade. Kenseth said, "Now, Mrs. Samarro. What are your thoughts?"

"About the killings, about law enforcement?"

Kenseth was patient. "About anything at all. We've meant, for some time, to include you in these discussions. Customer Relations is increasingly important and we consider you vital in that role." There were solemn nods from the other men that she had to believe were sincere.

"Well," she was cautious. "I haven't felt the danger, not personally. I hope that reflects optimism, not that I am unaware of what's coming down. I do know. But we can't run away. And we can't make this place into a fortress that scares away people. Still... I suppose there are sensible measures."

"Such as?"

"I don't know. Electronics maybe. A new buzzer system with a kind of Code Red for the people in front if we see something wrong. A new door for your office. Heavy, bullet proof. Stuff like that, if it isn't too expensive. And something, I wouldn't know exactly what, done to the windows."

Kenseth was making notes. He was impersonal.

Gail went on. "I guess I'm saying the obvious things. But increased surveillance by the Sheriff's department. Of the bank, and your homes."

He looked up. "Your homes? Don't you include your own?"

"I hope not. I'm a small fish here."

"Don't kid yourself. And even were that true, would every loose cannon know that?"

The question was low key. But Gail felt chilled. She shivered in the controlled temperature of the air conditioned office. Kenseth was right, she'd discounted her own visibility, she hadn't considered her children.

She rallied. "You're probably correct, Mr. Kenseth. And there's one more point. We depend on law enforcement. But they may have their own problems... they may be in some danger." She told them of the loud trio in the Municipal in Prairie City. She did not mention who she'd been with.

Standish, to no one's surprise, snorted his disgust. The cashier was a teetotaler, a real health person. He was a runner, he pushed iron every night in his basement. The results were apparent in the linebacker's neck, the sloping shoulders.

"Those fucking yahoos... " he began, then blushed. "Pardon my language," to Gail. She regarded him coolly, and thought, why is this clown apologizing to me, not the others? Have I been invited, finally, to the inner circle to expect special treatment? She said, "I understand the word... Yahoo." The somber Ryan smiled.

Standish tried again but the steam was gone. "Those muni cowboys are always spouting off. Cheap liquor, cheap talk. They're a joke." He added, quickly. "So I've heard. I don't go there."

"Why not? They sell Coke and Seven-Up. Right out of the can... untainted." Gail laughed, she couldn't resist the dig to Mr. Clean.

Kenseth thanked them all for the input and the meeting switched to other topics, specifics of the most urgent and troublesome of the current loans. He listened to Ryan's monotone, ticking off the familiar figures and his mind drifted beyond the confines of the office he had occupied so long. He wondered. Many drifted into banking from other fields. This kind of work is the only thing I ever considered. I was convinced that I had the temperament. A fly fisherman, that's the key... I've heard it so often, the perfect banker attitude, toward life and the wily trout. A man calm and relaxed, in a profession as staid and solid as that of an art collector or historian. The doctor, the lawyer, the banker... three staples, solid as rock, standing out like church steeples in the folklore of the American small town. Shawndo has no lawyer, the doctor visits twice weekly from Prairie City. And the banker is a man who loaned money on six hundred thousand dollar farms and bids them in at little more than half that when the loans are old, drowned in seas of red ink, piled high with the dead weight of interest. The bank itself will surely go under... we totter on the brink... if the loans are not enforced or the collateral assumed. There's no win, I struggle constantly for accommodation and long to forget it all, the rush of water against my waders in a mountain stream. My marriage is a hollow shell. Some colleagues are dead, shot at their desks, and there's no end in sight.

He fought back to the present, to the droning sounds of the Vice President's voice, the numbing march of routine. He straightened slumped shoulders, forced a smile, favored Gail Samarro with an approving glance. He was lucky in his co-workers, if nothing else. He glanced out the window to a street washed in sunlight.

At ten o'clock the meeting ended. They adjourned to the Crystal Cafe. Jenny Peters viewed them, sourly. "The big spenders from the Federal Reserve," she announced to anyone who cared to listen. The four took the bantering in good spirits and enjoyed coffee and Danish at one of the tables. Kenseth picked up the tab. It was Ryan's turn for the tip. He laid down a quarter, reconsidered, the wheels whirring inside him, then added another fifteen cents.

CHAPTER THIRTEEN

Early in June, on a Tuesday night, Garth joined Harvest. The name was inappropriate for him, he hadn't worked a harvest for twenty-five years. Garth knew that commitment was the key, not farming experience. Implement dealers belonged to Harvest, as well as hardware men, grocers, livestock truckers, elevator employees. Jenny Peters of the Crystal Cafe was a loyal member, many of the farm wives and a smattering of retired farmers in Shawndo, Prairie City and across the state displayed the green buttons. Garth was given the who's who of the organization and its aims, short term and past the turn of the decade.

At the initiation Garth listened politely. He could have taught his instructors. Marta had prepared him, drumming into his brain hopes for the future, the movement too young to have a significant past.

"The things is," Marta had said, "Harvest appears, to outsiders, like a loose group. No discipline, no leadership, just a redneck bunch of plow jockeys. Not true."

"How much are the dues?" Garth was a little short. A weekend trip to Minneapolis... alone, Gail had declined... had decimated his cash.

"Harvest doesn't have dues. Members pay what they can afford. Harvest is about the farm crisis, not dues. Forget it." The short, hearty laugh rang out. Marta felt better than she had in months. The new crops were growing like weeds, the weeds obeying, for once, the herbicides. And the hay was lush, first crop already in the barn. "By the time we can afford dues, well, hell... then we won't need the group."

"In one sense, we're like any organization I ever heard of," she said. "Numbers don't means as much as having doers. We got dedicated people, the core group. Then there are the lukewarm folks. They attend the rallies and the auctions, but only if it happens to fit their schedule, or their feelings, on a given day. Then we got those that are virtually worthless. They like to say they belong to Harvest... an 'in' thing. But they don't do a god damn thing, outside of criticize once in awhile."

Garth was laconic. "Sounds like you tapped right in on human nature."

"What else? But all organizations have the problem. Trouble is, all groups ain't life or death to the extent Harvest is. Still... what the hell can you do? You can't say to a prospect, 'we don't want you, we figure you'll be worthless.' Naw, can't be done."

"I know a little bit about the human animal, myself," said Garth.

"You can't eliminate people because you always get surprises. I'd bet my life on that. Some little whimpy guy might turn out to be a real burner."

"Right. You're so smart, Garth. Smarter than you look, anyway," she jabbed. "You chase after that Samarro gal, she might hand you your head on a plate. She's got eyes for her boss, what I hear."

Garth was startled. This wasn't like Marta. His sister didn't pry into his private life, she had been a jewel in that respect. Was there a warning here, a kind of protectiveness? Was this a hint that he should spread out, expand his options in the world of women? Still, Marta was a great kidder.

He was bluff. "I don't worry about that angle. No way, Marty."

"Well, she's in the Crystal twice a day with him. Corner booth. Hell, they don't need all that privacy, they're in the bank all day."

Garth was edgy. "Well, Gail works for the man, she can't ignore him. Anyway, Kenseth is married."

Marta looked him straight in the eye, the kidding was gone. "So were you married, once upon a time. Who cares, these days? Anyway, read the newspapers, the divorce columns are longer than the marriage licenses, every week."

Garth admitted this. "Yeah, true. But what the hell, it's just one woman."

"Now you're talking."

Over the kitchen table they went back to the subject of Harvest. Marta hadn't pushed her brother. The man put in sixteen hour days during the planting and haying season, saving the expense of hiring help. So there'd been no recruitment, only explanations of hopes and goals. She made no attempt to disguise the problems, but called it a fresh new wind, sweeping across the farm belt. She knew that, all in good time, Garth would feel that breath. Now, the time had arrived. Now, there was some respite from the field work.

"You're meeting, with the other new members, at George Rogers' place, tonight?"

"I guess. George said eight-thirty."

"What did he say to you about guns?"

"Not much. Just asked me what I owned. I told him, my twelve gauge shotgun, deer rifle and the thirty-two revolver."

"And he said, forget the other two, just bring the hand gun."

"Well, yeah. How did you know?"

"Because I know. Just do as George says."

"Hell. George gonna give me lessons or something? I can out-shoot him any day. I ain't Clint Eastwood but I ain't bad."

They gathered in the Rogers living room that evening. Seven potential new members, including Garth, plus four Harvest regulars.

The men relaxed in the friendly atmosphere of the farm home. Helen Rogers served lunch. After a big supper at home Garth merely played with the white cake and coffee. Rogers visited with them... Garth could hardly call it a lecture... about a group of people, dedicated, with their lives, to saving American agriculture. He spoke, easily, of the unbearable burdens that a shifting economy, plummeting land prices, high interest, punitive taxes and poor markets had laid on the family farmer... members of a vanishing breed.

Garth listened to the calm voice, doling out the dispassionate views and the researched statistics. Rogers never raised his voice. He might have been a cassette. Clearly, the man, the movement itself, wanted members drawn from a base of conviction, not the enchantment of eloquence. He spoke, knowingly, of foreign trade, crop quotas, of Congress and the actions of the Secretary of Agriculture. Garth and the others, all farmers, drank coffee and took all this in.

In one corner of the room, Oscar Thornstad listened quietly, a statue carved from a rock strewn hill. Rogers paused and called for a refill; the man drank coffee as a desert wanderer drank water. Too much, thought Garth, bad for the guts.

"We come now," said Rogers, "to the issue of violence. We asked each one of you, if you own a hand gun to bring it along tonight. Have you?"

Garth raised his hand. Another man, a swarthy, heavyset figure of middle age, also acknowledged. There were no others.

"Would you bring them here, please." Garth placed his thirty-two on the table. The other man, James Moenke, did the same. The piece was an old forty-five, the barrel and cylinder rubbed to a dull shine, the muzzle of the barrel, gaping, huge.

"Thank you, gentlemen," said Rogers. "Now this is our procedure." He took the thirty-two in one hand. With the other he pulled open a table drawer and brought out a handful of wooden pegs of various sizes. As he did this, Helen fetched other materials, on a tray, to the table. Garth watched with interest.

Rogers selected one of the wooden pegs and sized it against the muzzle. Too large to fit inside. He chose another and pushed it into the barrel until the wood was flush with the metal. Next, he took a green foil tape from the tray. On the tape, in a continuous series, was embossed, deeply, the word Harvest. Garth watched, with growing wonder, as George Rogers continued. The white haired farmer snipped a six inch length of the tape and passed it over the end of the barrel, then pressing it down firmly on both sides. He smoothed the tape edges, then, like a Victorian barrister, he dropped melted wax around the barrel, near the tape's two ends.

"Sealed but not signed," he smiled. Then he handed the hand gun back to Garth. "You see," he went on, "this little operation, a kind of secret ritual actually, is one of the real cornerstones of our movement." He picked up the forty-five. Rogers snipped another length from the embossed tape. In an instant the weapon was snatched from his hand. James Moenke glared at the leader.

"Not so god damn fast, friend," Moenke scowled, and one huge hand shoved the revolver inside his belt. The powerful man looked around the roof in disbelief, the others sat in stunned silence. Rogers was unperturbed. He smiled, gently.

Moenke seemed incredulous. He growled. "What kind of a circus is this?" He leered at Garth. "You let this asshole play kid games with your piece? What the hell kind of a joker are you?" His voice rose on the last question, the man was near to screaming. "I need this baby for protection. Nobody... I mean nobody, touches it."

Garth merely smiled.

"Aw hell, relax, Moenke," he said. "I don't know what's going on any more'n you do. But my gun ain't damaged, why should I worry?" He put a friendly hand on Moenke's shoulder. "George will explain all this. Why don't you sit down and listen, then make up your mind."

George Rogers nodded, approvingly. He was pleased with Garth's response, the leaders of Harvest placed great store on first reaction. Moenke resumed his seat. He did not return the gun.

Rogers poured more coffee. A sign of strain, for sure, reasoned Garth. But the man's hand was steady as a rock.

"Here's the thing, fellows. It's all a drill in non-violence, the central theme of the movement. If we're not peaceful... we're nothing. We don't have a chance. The things is... " He paused, then spoke very slowly, letting each word sink in. "It's so damn easy to talk being nonviolent. It's tough to live up to that, in the face of provocation. So, from day one, we decided on this little litmus test. Just on hand guns. A man needs his rifle for deer hunting, his shotgun for pheasants, grouse, things like that. So we have to take a chance on those firearms... trust our folks not to mess with them. But pistols... any kind of hand gun... they only have one purpose in the world and that's to shoot people. We can't control every blessed thing a Harvest member does. What the hell, this is a free country. But we can make this one powerful gesture. If a man won't go along with it, that's fine. But, we can't use that man."

Rogers paused again and drank from his coffee cup. The room was silent. In his corner, Oscar sat, eyes closed. He'd heard the speech too often.

Rogers continued, speaking directly at Moenke. His voice was kind. "Now you might ask, isn't this an empty ceremony? Also, what's the profit? Well, violence can wipe out all gains, and they're few enough. All it takes is one ugly incident. Sure, it could happen anyway, and even with a handgun, the seal is only symbolic. Or, violence may come from a rifle or shotgun, hell, a crowbar for that matter. But if we attempt to rule out hand guns... seal 'em for the duration... we improve our chances. And, if there is an incident, maybe we won't get blamed... we aren't the only ones that follow the auctions. We'll have socked ourselves into the public consciousness as intolerant of any violence, from our members. Believe me, Mr. Moenke... Jim... the word gets out. We know we're infiltrated. A man would have to be a damned fool to expect less from the F.B.I., and even the BCA. They know our operation and if we seal the pistols it's just a small step. But it's something."

Rogers paused. Garth glanced at Oscar Thornstad. The old man was not asleep, he nodded at Garth and winked. Garth grinned.

"I've been talking too much," said Rogers. "Can't be helped. It's my job to impress on new members that we're peaceful. Peace and friendship... that's the whole ball of wax. We help each other, we stick together, no other rules. No constitution, no dues. We have expenses, of course. If you help out with five or ten when you can manage it... fine. If not, we understand. Nobody's going to dun you. Christ, we're all loaded down now with bills we can't pay."

Garth Kyllo watched as Jim Moenke fought his own private war. The moon face wore a dark mask of concentration. He sat, chin in hand, and did not speak. He might have been alone in a distant field.

The meeting was over. The farmers were now faced with more largess, cheese sandwiches and beer. The tension passed, old friends jawed and gossiped in the usual way. The beautiful weather had mellowed even the most hard-bitten among them, there was laughter, free and easy. Helen visited with Garth and they talked of Marta, the way she'd faced her troubles during the past winter.

"Your sister is a remarkable woman, Garth. A real powerhouse."

Garth laughed. He was fond of this lovely woman and at ease with her. Marta had informed him of the Rogers tragedy. Two children, a boy and a girl... the girl lost at twelve, to a hit-run driver while biking to Shawndo, the boy who never returned from Vietnam. And now, thought Garth, the woman who's lost her kids speaks of strength. Keep it light.

"Well, Helen, don't let Marty hear you talking like that. She can't stand that stuff. Makes her mad."

Helen agreed. "Don't I know that. We'll have to keep it our little secret."

Jim Moenke stood up. Sweat glistened on the swarthy face. He pulled the gun from his belt. Then he handed it, butt first, to George Rogers.

"Take the piece, neighbor. Seal her up. Then put her away. That way I'll never get a chance to go back on my word. Problem is... " The heavy face lit up. "I got a bitch of a temper. I'll pick up the piece in a year or two."

He watched as Rogers took up the tape. Then he nodded, gravely, to Helen, a silent thanks for the hospitality, and went out the door. In a minute the others heard his Buick pull out of the yard.

"I'll be damned," said George, mildly. He permitted himself a small smile. "We got ourselves a new member, fellows. I think."

"What happened here wasn't no great surprise to me," offered one of the new members. "Jim Moenke has a short fuse. I seen him lay two guys on their ass, two booths away, at the muni over in Prairie. My God, I thought he killed them both, two big strappers, at that."

"Cops move in?" asked another.

"Naw. They should have, but it kind of got hushed up. You know how that goes, at the muni. The guys came around. An hour later Moenke was buying 'em drinks, an arm around one, friendly as a brown puppy. The man is an army. But he don't hold a grudge."

Garth noted, "I was going to clip him, right here, if he didn't simmer down. I decided against it."

Oscar Thornstad spoke for the first time, his faced creased in wrinkles of humor. "You keep making good decisions like that, Garth, you're bound to live for a time."

Together, the two men walked out to their cars, Garth's Plymouth wagon and a huge '68 Cadillac that Oscar had driven since the day it left the showroom. The old man was hell on wheels, roaring around the country roads at seventy miles an hour. Rust had eaten out the fenders and the tail pipe was anchored with wire.

"Roger handles this sort of meeting pretty good, don't you think?" offered Garth.

"Yah. George is a fine, solid man. But he leaves out as much as he tells. A recruiter has to. Of course he never mentioned one of the biggest problems of 'em all in the whole sorry farm picture."

"Such as?"

Oscar scowled. He pulled a round tin of Copenhagen snuff from the front pocket of his bib overalls. He tapped the lid, reflectively, opened the box and, with his thumb and forefinger, pushed a big wad behind his lower lip. Talk about ceremonies, thought Garth. The snoose... like a rite.

Oscar said, "You're a bright guy, Garth. I like your style. You tell me what George left out... the biggest problem."

Garth smiled. "Don't grease me up, you old bandit. And how can you put that shit in your mouth?"

"Aw, you been eating shit all your life, it comes easy."

"Anyway, for your answer... simple. The farmers won't stick together. They feel the heat but the old divisions, Farm Bureau, N.F.O., Farmers Union, Lutheran, Catholic, they're all here."

Oscar said, "You got it." He spat, a brown liquid stream, to the cropped grass. "You been learning from Marta."

CHAPTER FOURTEEN

The months of springtime, in the flat country of Black Loam County, had been ideal. Even ancient Oscar Thornstad could not remember a season more ideal. The one prolonged session of rain had not hindered the field work, the temperatures had been balmy. But in mid-June there was a new direction, a twist of the knife for the beleaguered farmers. In their jargon, the rain maker died. In the third week of the month there was one modest shower. From that point on the skies blazed each day with azure stillness, the thermometer soared, continuously, past ninety. And the nights failed to bring relief. A hot, dry spell, said Marta. I've seen my share... the rain will come in good time. But the rain did not come, the second crop of hay was meager, not worth the cutting. Oats and wheat were stunted, ripening too fast.

The Crawford farmstead, situated on a crushed rock road, like most farms not fortunate enough to have a blacktopped county road at the door step, was choked, several times a day, with dust from the passing vehicles. The powdery residue of crushed limestone coated the grass... now turning brown... caked the farm buildings, filtered through windows and doorways into the house. Still, not a dust bowl, no black clouds mounted the horizons, the air was too still for that catastrophe. Marta damned the white dust and scanned the cloudless sky. Garth whistled and went about his work. They lived the dry land life, there was no irrigation equipment, on the farm or anywhere in the area. Frustration and worry were useless. The rain would come, the rain would not come. the cows had to be milked twice daily, the young stock tended, fences mended.

Together with Marta, Garth attended his first forced auction. Pete Johnson, third generation operator of Spring Grove Farm, had debts that exceeded seven hundred thousand, nearly all to Growers State. Land had been scarce on the original homestead. A creek, still functioning, though a bare trickle these days, wound through a rocky gulch. There was some woodland, thinned through decades of clearing and pasturing. The rocky gulch area seemed to spread its tentacles into the surrounding fields and the farm was not as productive, the soil not as deep as other areas nearby. Johnson, in a desperate move, had established a Planned Unit Development resident park, a lure to retired farmers who wished to avoid living in town. The project had failed. The original model house, and one other, stood, forlornly, on the rocky soil while, about them, eighteen half acre lots, platted and planned for cess pools and utilities, grew wild grass and Canadian thistles. Winds had unhinged one shutter of the model house.

With the Development gone bust, Johnson contracted for more land. He paid down, modestly, on two hundred and thirty acres at twenty six hundred per acre. The mortgages, at Growers State, added to the balance owed on the Development Site. The land market collapsed, grain prices stood at depression levels... the house of cards followed the laws of gravity and tumbled. Now a sale was set of all cattle, implements and machinery, the paper against them far above the market value. The land itself was already property of the lending institution. The Johnson family had thirty days to vacate.

"One of our toughest tests yet," said Marta. "We can't let a family like the Johnsons get tossed off the land, like squatters that had stayed too long. The man has made some mistakes, used poor judgment. Now he's supposed to let everything go, end up with nothing. We have planned an action to delay all this." Garth wasn't so sure. "But, what the hell," he thought to himself, "I'll go along for the ride." Like the correspondents who monitored wars and volcanoes, an observer. With the temperature at ninety-four, observing sounded strenuous enough.

"What's Johnson plan to do when all this is over?" he asked.

"God knows. George Rogers has offered his old hired man's house to use for awhile. They're old friends, you know." Garth hadn't known. "But George is in tough shape, himself. He's just cash cropped the past few years. He doesn't really need a hand, couldn't afford one at any rate."

Garth grunted. "So then, Johnson will be like all the others. Either move to the city and look for work or rent a farm... most likely from a bank or insurance company. Goes around... "

"Well, for sure, he's flat busted – or near enough. Pete will, most likely, never own a piece of ground again, unless it's a forty by one twenty feet to plunk a mobile home on."

"Scary."

"Tell me about it." How many more can I endure, she wondered, these scenarios of grief, these bits and pieces of a puzzle too complicated for me to solve? She knew that Harvest was considering her for the next county chairmanship. Christ... a dummy like me! I'm so damned unqualified. But again, aren't we all? Garth brings a healthy skepticism, almost disdain, to all this, even though he's joined. I've got to think more like him, to keep my hopes small. I'm so tired of failure.

They drove past George Rogers' farm, two miles to where the land dropped slightly in the beginnings of the rocky Johnson gulch and pasture land. All around them the corn was green and healthy, the soy beans fanning out, thickening in the rows. "Lovely crops, everywhere," said Marta. Her salty reservation surfaced. "So far. Getting dry, though. We sure could use some rain."

"It'll rain. Always has. A fact of nature."

"Yeah, it always rains. Not always on time."

"Like the buses, back in P.A."

The Johnson farmstead was set well back from the road. A long driveway led up to the building site, through a hay meadow. The cars and livestock trucks were parked along the driveway and on both sides of the township road. Garth parked the pickup and the two walked down the drive. He was puzzled. All the people, in the hundreds, milled about on the driveway and into the hay meadow. He could see only a handful of figures in the yard and near the buildings. Machinery was lined in a long row. Cattle were corralled in the barn yard, plastic numbers pasted on their rumps.

"What's the deal, Marty?" Garth looked around. "How come the folks are laying back, out here? According to the flyers, it's sale time."

"You'll see."

They pushed their way through the quiet, subdued crowd. As they neared the entrance to the farm yard Garth saw the fresh black soil, piled high across the drive. Tons of soil, with the damp, fresh look of recent excavation... the soil of an open grave, without the cosmetic green cover. "Sweet Jesus," murmured Garth. This time the words held reverence.

The dirt was not from a grave, unless symbolically. A ditch, fully ten feet wide and six feet deep, had been gouged out of the earth, across the driveway, up flush to the barbed wire fence rows on either side. The ditch, a gash of defiance on the flat land, lay like a message in front of the old farmstead. The sight took Garth's breath. Marta observed the scene with calm satisfaction. A modest furrow, she thought. But there isn't a truck or even a four by four that could cross it. With only a few others, she'd known of the plan.

The plan, the operation... The "sabotage" it would be named... had been conducted with the stealth and swiftness of a Ranger strike. In the darkness, obviously, a machine had completed the job, then disappeared. There was no machine in sight with the equipment to carry out such a dig. The audacity of the plan struck Garth as no less than magnificent. Lethargy toward the movement left him. There's hope for this tired crowd of shit kickers, he thought.

He scanned the faces around him. They were quiet or spoke in low voices. A cathedral hush seemed upon them. They waited, with that patient curiosity Garth had come to know, for the next move.

He whispered to Marta. "What happens now?"

Marta reached for a handful of the soil. "Nice to see some damp dirt," she murmured. "Even if you got to go six feet down for it." She ran the soil through her fingers, thoughtfully. "Damned if I know," she admitted. "I don't know enough law to even guess. Most likely, none of the farmers do. But this is Johnson's farm, at least while he's still here."

"What becomes of the heist?"

"The auction? Good question. Of course, Harvest hopes it will be called off. We exist on hope, you know that."

The laconic answer seemed, to Garth, inadequate.

"Well, you've thrown 'em a challenge, for sure. But won't the auction simply be rescheduled, after they sort all this out?"

"I suppose." She smiled. It was hard for Marta to stay down for long. "It's just a tactic, Garth. A thousand knives, attrition. Keep the banks off balance. Maybe the whole business will go to court. Then, if Johnson loses, which he will, appeal to a higher court. The enemy's own playing field. We'll use it if we can."

"How come you didn't tell me?"

"What for? You know now." The logic was indisputable. But the operation was full of holes. Garth turned as the law approached. The official car of the sheriff, with Adams and two deputies aboard, nosed down the drive. Behind, another car, full of uniformed men and, behind that, the county attorney, Roger Carlson. Marta remembered how decent the man had been, the day after Mike's death.

Adams shouldered his way through the crowd. No one stood in his way. He viewed the gash in the earth, passively. He said nothing until Carlson had also inspected the damage. They conferred together, quietly. Garth watched them, in fascination. This was drama with an ending he couldn't imagine. The shouting, profane violence of the picket lines at the mills had never been like this.

The sheriff and the attorney clambered down into the ditch and climbed the opposite bank. Gobs of dirt clung to their shoes. Their trousers showed specks of mud and their hands were soiled. Polite applause sounded as they reached the other side. The conference continued. This is the Marx Brothers, thought Garth, Animal Crackers on the farm.

Adams, from across the ditch, addressed the crowd. His voice was flat but the handsome face showed strain. The man is in a bind, thought Garth. But what the hell, I never did like cops. No particular reason, they never did anything to me, outside of a couple of speeding tickets.

Adams' voice carried clear in the hot, still air.

"This is a bunch of foolishness, folks. We will... " his voice was drowned in a sudden wall of sound. Laughter and cat calls from the farmers swept across the scene.

The sheriff was in no hurry. He waited. Then he said, "We're sending to Prairie City for equipment. We will fill this ditch and proceed with the sale." Loud dissent from the farmers resumed. But the opposition seemed, to Garth, not complete. He sensed that not a few in the crowd wanted the sale to begin. Marta had told him, often, as had Oscar Thornstad, of the divisiveness among the farmers... greed and sympathy mixed.

Mostly, he figured, the crowd was waiting for the central figure in the drama to appear. Pete Johnson, slim and clean shaven, a stooped man in his late fifties, clambered across the ditch and approached the officials.

"There was an auction booked for this farm today." Johnson spoke with the easy manner of a man who has no more to lose. "But some damn fool cut the road." A wave of laughter came from the crowd. Garth grinned in appreciation at the innocent remark. He admired the man's poise in a tough position.

"Therefore," said Johnson, "the sale I guess should be postponed." He added, gamely, "Or canceled." The farmers beat their hands together, applause mingled with the laughter.

Johnson said, "I suggest, Sheriff Adams, you get in gear and try to apprehend the misguided person who wrecked my driveway. Arrest him... or her, as the case may be." Marta chuckled, softly, at this. Johnson continued. "And no other earth-moving equipment will be permitted on this property. Not while I'm here and I still have some time. This damage must have been done during the night, while my family and I were asleep." He looked, contemptuously at the sheriff's holster. "I see you're well armed, Sheriff, out here among your peaceful neighbors. Well, I have a gun, too. Up at the house. I will use it on any machine operator that invades my property. I believe the law permits a man to defend his property." The laconic farmer turned to the county attorney. "Wouldn't you say that's true?"

The crowd had quieted. They were intent, hanging on every word, appreciating the ballsy performance. The man showed courage. In a depleted arsenal, courage was about all that remained.

Roger Carlson didn't answer. He and the sheriff walked a few steps from the ditch to confer again. Friendly advice was showered upon them.

"Hey, Carlson. You need a secretary to keep the minutes?" Laughter. "Hell, Carlson wouldn't know what to do with her." And, "Better get Kenseth in on your confab." Another agreed. "For sure. Kenseth is your boss, better pay attention, he doesn't want to pay you boys for nothing." The role of the mortgagor was, clearly , on the farmer's minds. In the brilliant sunshine they stood and sweated. In his hard nose days in Pennsylvania, Garth had never encountered such a gathering. Still, that naked sense of power, dangerous, potentially explosive, came off the orderly crowd like an aroma. One more skirmish, Garth felt, in a war of attrition. Lives and futures hung in the blistering air. Yet there was humor and bantering... defiance cloaked in derision, not violence. Not yet.

There followed more advice, more questions. "Hey, Carlson, what did they teach you at that William Mitchell college about bulldozers?" "Next time you run for Sheriff, Adams, better bring in the Mafia to count the votes." A diversion: "The county's full of dope peddlers, Carlson. Don't waste your time on them, you got farmers to put out on the street." Another agreed. "Yeah, Carlson, you got your priorities in order." The two officials walked, slowly, back to the ditch, still murmuring in low voices. They seemed not to hear the jibes.

Adams started to speak, the words seemed clogged with phlegm. The crowd waited while he cleared his throat. He said, "The auction is called off for today." Cheers from the massed crowd. Those disappointed by the announcement remained silent.

"The auction will be rescheduled. Notices will be published. Thank you." Adams stepped back, indicating that the county attorney had something to add. Marta was struck by the tremor of Adams' voice, the lines of strain on his face. The man has clearly aged, she thought. Join the crowd.

Carlson was forceful in his statement. It was apparent, to Marta, that the attorney had made a conscious decision to show no weakness.

"There has been an unlawful act committed here," he announced. A crescendo of noise greeted the words. The boos and cat calls were thunderous. The colorless county attorney... no one had opposed him for election in sixteen years... had been castigated recently by the local press for his constant plea bargaining on behalf of the drug dealers. The man was, for the first time, politically vulnerable. He'd sent a few dealers to jail, most were freed on suspended sentences. Now, he spoke of the law.

Carlson waited for the storm to quiet. "The auction sale, planned for today, was a legal procedure, prescribed by statute, to partially... I repeat, partially... satisfy a judgment." He raised a hand as the vocal opposition resume. "We could, very legally, in spite of what you have heard, repair the driveway and continue, today. In the interest of the community we will not do this. We wish to safeguard life and property in these matters... " Again the noise was deafening, a wall of sound rolled, in waves, through the air. The attorney did not flinch.

"Mr. Johnson will be dealt with in a separate action. You have all heard his threats of violence." Another wave of protest greeted this.

"Hey Carlson," the voice was deep and penetrating. Garth, turning, recognized Jim Moenke, the reluctant gun toter from the Harvest initiation. "I'll bring my tractor into town, run it over your yard. I wanna see if you'll take it lying down." Garth smiled, the man was a handful.

But, for the day, the officials were clearly beaten. They crossed the ditch, the crowd parting, politely, before them. They joined the waiting deputies and drove away. No one made as much as a gesture against them. Before leaving, the sheriff spoke to Marta, touching his hand to his hat brim in a courtly manner. She acknowledged the greeting, saying, simply, "Hello, Bill."

Garth did not know whether to laugh or to join the celebration that broke out at the official's departure. He felt unreal, as though he had watched a film, projected off-focus to a tilted screen. He knew he had stood witness to a gutty confrontation, one more in a long line that might hold historic implications. But aside from Johnson's statement, which was merely a determination to defend his driveway, he had heard no threats. There had been none of the physical contact he had known in the east. No bloodshed, no clubs. He could not understand the mental process. Garth walked slowly back to the pickup, with Marta.

He asked her, "Did the whole operation come off about as planned?"

She considered. "More or less. There are always the unexpected turns. Pete Johnson's statement was a bonus. The man was great."

"Was he right?"

"Right... wrong?" Now the weariness returned to her voice. The heat was getting her. "Who knows? The whole thing was a gimmick, of course, a delaying tactic. And Pete's remarks sent the legal boys back to their books. Maybe they'll need an opinion from the state attorney general. Then, whatever the opinion, it might be challenged. Court hearings, divisiveness... it all takes time." Marta slammed her fist against the pickup door, still carrying the dent marks of the blizzard wind. "It's a war of attrition, Garth. We've become guerrilla fighters."

"Very well mannered ones, I'd say."

"God, we hope so. As long as possible."

"Sounds like you're hedging."

"I suppose. George preached to you about all this. We won't be able to stop the violence forever. Harvest isn't strong enough to control all the hot heads. All we can do is try. That, in itself, is another delaying tactic. But don't fool yourself. The volcano is there, ready to explode."

"Yeah. Gail brought me up to date. About the killing of the bankers. I hadn't realized the extent."

She shuddered. "We can't possibly plug in every potential action. When a person goes over the edge, there's not a lot that can be done. The best we can do is counsel against the ultimate."

Marta brooded. She was reduced to a black mood by Garth's reminder. "Lord... the brutality. And all it gets the rest of the farmers is terrible press. We all get tarred with the same brush as the nut." She softened. "That isn't true, completely. I'm just tired. Folks know there are extremists in any movement, not just the farm struggle."

They drove back to the farm and went to work, preparing for the evening chores. Number seventeen still hadn't been replaced. On the following day there was no rain and the heat was, again, intense. The drought continued, day after day, the fourth of July hit a record high for the date, one hundred and one. The skies were blinding, not a cloud in sight, and the waves of heat shimmered above the flat prairie, dancing in the still air.

Two weeks after the events at the Johnson farm, and following legal maneuvering and the issuance of a court order, a county highway department road grader entered the Johnson driveway and filled in the ditch. Harvest explored possibilities to halt the action... they couldn't find an attorney willing to take the case without a large retainer up front. The auction sale of machinery and cattle was held three days later. Harvest, quiet and unobtrusive, was present in force. The auction was less than successful, the big buyers, from distant areas, did not return. Likely, they suspected still another ruse. Pete Johnson recovered a considerable amount of property. Somewhere, no one knew the source, he had come up with some money. Rumor held, he had floated a loan from relatives in Chicago.

Pete Johnson and his wife moved into the hired man's bungalow on George Rogers farm. The group responsible for the excavation of the driveway was not determined. The investigation was dropped.

CHAPTER FIFTEEN

Garth Kyllo wiped his brow, the sweat ran in rivulets and salt stung his eyes. The work was brutal... mending fences, replacing some of the scarred and rotted wooden posts with rusted steel posts he had salvaged from a bankrupt lumber yard. Tough, grimy work, the dry earth was as solid as concrete and the post driver slipped and turned in his hands. In past years Mike had maintained a fierce pride in proper line fences, the barbed strands taut, straight as an arrow. Then, the crunch, no materials, no help. Now, there was so much to be done. Good fences, good neighbors... the old bromides held. Within the confines of any farm the temporary electric fences were sufficient but the line fences had to be adequate to protect the livestock from wandering. Garth, perspiring in streams, felt a sudden stillness in the air. In the thirty-first consecutive day without rain, a low bank of clouds gathered in the west. There was still time enough to finish the job. The wires must be tightened, a half dozen more posts driven down.

At three in the afternoon the temperature hovered just below the one hundred mark and the air was breathless, dry as whitened bones in a borax desert. A world of harsh quiet, heat waves shimmering. The farms in the flat country north of Shawndo lay beaten, dust laden upon the cracked earth. The grass, in meadow land and pastures, turned, each day, another perceptible shade, more blanched and lifeless than the previous day. And the corn, that resilient super forage, hybrid descendant of the fabled sustenance of bison and camel... could we dream, even Mammoths?... turns its leaves inward in piteous spirals, the ancient memories of protectiveness. The corn, shriveled into itself, a dormancy of survival that would weather temperature and thirst and bring forth something resembling grain... if the drought did not last too long. But the planet is marked, scarred, with vast areas, sub-continents, where the creeping evolution of wind patterns, cloud formations, diminished streams and depleted aquifers had turned rich pampas into the loneliness of drifting sand. Such assaults on the earth and its peoples had occurred, for the most part, in Africa and Asia, even the lifeless outback of Australia. In the fertile headlands of America such cataclysmic marches could never form. On this July afternoon, Garth was not so certain. In half a brief lifetime he could see, a slice frozen in time, a landscape that reached out, periodically, in supplication for the water that had always been so plentiful, just beneath the surface. Wells that once reached down fifty feet now searched four hundred and more for potable water.

Water was one thing; the dark, roiling clouds, swiftly gathering on the breathless day, were another. With two posts to go, Garth knew he had miscalculated. He knew, memory from one childhood moment of terror, the power that could hide in the low slung sky. After long drought the still, burning air, he remembered now, could throw down wind and water... mixed blessing to the parched earth.

Garth started the tractor, then unhitched the wagon, moving with swift, sure motions. He threw the tractor into high gear and headed for home, more than half a mile away and the eerie cloud bank, awesome shades of purple and yellow, closed in upon him. The tractor bumped along the rough field road, shards of dirt spinning out from the heavy treads. Daylight had turned to a strange, still haze and Garth shivered as the temperature plunged.

The garage doors were open, an announcement that Marta was not at home. The doors of the huge machine shed were closed. Garth's mind flashed as he brought the tractor to a halt. I haven't the time to open those big shed doors. The tractor will not fit in the garage, the cab is much too high. Leave it... head for cover. What cover? Only the basement of the house offers some protection. Garth knew he had delayed too long at the fencing. He had, stubborn as ever, put the job at hand above everything, perhaps survival. He looked behind him, the direction from which he had come, a funnel cloud, black serpent of destruction, had darted from the clouds... it was almost on him, the roar of a freight train was rising in his ears.

The farmstead numbered few buildings; it was one of the lesser spreads. The huge red barn, two silos attached, the machine shed with lean-to, the house, the garage, an ancient chicken house long unused and, near where Garth had halted the tractor, the empty granary, waiting for the harvest. In seconds the picture cracked, distortion came from the heavens in a twisting spiral of power. Catching only one corner of the building site with its full force, the darting snake obliterated the granary in a panorama of explosion like the thunder of cases of dynamite. The roof mushroomed in blasted sections, siding shot through the air, odd shaped spears hurled by a colossus. The noise was a wall of sound. The air, thick with dust and debris, was a dark void that stilled all light. Garth, for one blinding moment, could not move, a paralysis on his limbs. Then he half turned, twisting into a falling crouch, a shell-like instinct of preservation, arms raised in shield. A great weight struck his back and shoulders.

He fell, face down, upon the ground and was covered. Waves of pain encased his back, air exploded from his mouth. And he knew no more. The twister moved on, uprooting trees, snapping power poles, a dervish that lifted, then disappeared into the clouds as swiftly as it had first emerged. All this in seconds, a time span that the crumpled figure beneath the granary roof section could never measure.

In days to come Garth could never distinguish the fragments that coursed his brain in the minutes that followed his fall. Shafts of memory, suffocated and diffused by gasping pain, a struggle for breath, numbness in the arms and legs... the lean farmer hovered in a forgotten land between oblivion and a kind of wakefulness. He knew the power of the steel mills, smelled the acrid furnaces... the heat was that of molten metal and his own imprisonment beneath the broken roof. He saw Thelma, plain as life, and the girls. They were young, swinging home from grade school but the heat was the scorching midday of summer where the green of life was coated with dust. Slowly his mind cleared, the violence of the present coalesced. He knew intolerable pain and the terror that comes from being pinioned, crushed beneath the pressure of weight.

Part of the blackness washed away. Garth could see, ahead, a small slice of light. He could not judge the distance. He tried to move. He could not budge, even a fraction of an inch, and his efforts met another wall of pain in his back and shoulders that, for a moment, swept him again below consciousness. Galaxies swirled. He was lost. Then he fought once more to the surface. He lay quiet, his only choice, and wondered why he was still alive and if his back was broken. Survival gripped him. He would not sink without a struggle, he would chance his future as a crippled man. At the moment of truth, the instant he might have let go, his sardonic sense of humor saved him. Crushed in the dirt, immobile, he thought, somehow I am still alive. I will fight to live. Sex and Budweiser... I thought they rated high. They are nothing, survival is all. Garth forced a smile, the grimace of the undefeated, and tried to think.

He hardly knew how to begin, focus eluded him. Crushing weight, grinding pain, immobility, the struggle for breath. He had nothing but the tiny shaft of murky light ahead of him. To fight the terror, the paralysis of despair, he concentrated with all his power... the supreme effort of his life... to look for a way out, to retain consciousness. Garth was struck with the conviction that if he slept again he would never waken.

Why was he pinned to the ground but not dead? The smothering weight was not only above him, pulsing his back with waves of pain, but on both sides. He was crowded, pinched, as though in a box too small. One arm had been caught, in the crucial instant, at his side. The other, the right arm, was stretched ahead of him. Gradually he realized he could not be paralyzed. There was a sense of feeling in his legs and in the hand and arm reaching ahead. And the stabbing pain in his back and shoulders went on. Garth's eyes filled with tears from the agony and he cursed... the first words that escaped his lips.

Then he knew, suddenly, what had happened, why he still lived. The roof section had collapsed upon him, with the rafters lengthwise to his body. He was pined, immobile as a mummy wrapped and bound, between two of the rafters and the roof nails, sticking through, unclinced by the carpenters of a lifetime before, were gouged into his back and shoulders. That section of his body had taken the brunt because it was the thickest part. And ahead of him, he now guessed ten feet, the rafters rested on the ground and provided his small window to the world. The window, a tiny rectangle, grey and filmy as unwashed glass, was in direct line to the garage and house. The garage still stood, the doors open, no pickup in sight. In spite of mind control, panic gripped him. God... must I die here, a stone's throw from the house. Someone... please help.

Again he tried to shift. And again the metal, driven into his body, sent a shaft of pain that seared his eyeballs, balancing him, once more, on the brink of consciousness. Garth moaned and sweat and wept. He waited for rescue, or death. He had solved the paradox of his survival, he could do nothing to alter his fate. He sought to clear his mind, to focus on the rescue that might, even now, be near at hand. But analogies flashed... the woodsman caught beneath a jackknifed tree trunk, mountaineers buried beneath huge avalanches, survivor in a life boat stranded in stagnant calm. Waves of claustrophobia engulfed him. He could not move. Marty might be off the road or injured, the neighbors, caught in the jungles of their own destruction, would not arrive. Garth lay still, in depleted pain and tears.

And then... the greatest horror of all. He felt a probing sensation on one of his extended fingers.

Something had stirred in the passageway between the rafters, he thought. A weed, a blade of grass, some chaff from the bins trapped here?... now a draft of air from my window moves it. He felt the pressure again, a flickering touch. Garth peered into the gloom ahead, toward the grey rectangle. Then he screamed, a piercing sound of agony escaped him and he sought, with a madman's strength, to pull the trapped arm back. He could not move a muscle, he screamed again, a primal shriek of death and his mind moved through a red mist to the thin brink of sanity... that razor edge where the wall of the mind weakens, the breech where the chasm yawns.

The new pain was beyond bearing, worse than the nails in his back. Nerve ends were in agony as the teeth of the lost and terrified animal ripped into the tip of his middle finger. Then he felt no more, not even the shredded flesh on his back, as the granary roof was lifted from him and thrown aside. Two grim faced men lifted the unconscious Garth and carried him to a cleared area. Another man

Northfield Public Library
210 Washington St.
Northfield, MN 55057

grabbed a broken board and flailed at the bewildered rat. The rodent was killed, then kicked aside. The rain was falling gently on the parched ground and the air was calm and cool. Marta wept, her tears mingled with the rain. She ran ahead to hold open the kitchen door.

The men carried the body, face down, they could see, at a glance, the damage to the back and shoulders. George Rogers and Phil Johnson each grasped an arm and shoulder beneath the arm pit. The blood on the back was a mottled mass, bits of shirt and skin crusting together. The men laid Garth down on the kitchen table, cushioned the body with blankets. Marta took one long look, then decided. There was no time for lengthy discussion.

She said, "Before an ambulance could reach here from Prairie we could be there ourselves. It's our only chance, get him to the hospital as quickly as we can."

Oscar Thornstad, who had just arrived, came over to Marta. Oscar had brought a family of eight, and many grandchildren, through every possible crisis on the farm. He checked Garth's pulse... the beat was there, he felt mild reassurance.

"Yah," he said. "The man is hurt bad. There's a lot of blood loss here, may be bone damage, too. But shock is the big danger. Wrap him warm, all the blankets you can find."

"We'll take him in my car, it's the biggest," said George Rogers. They moved swiftly, working the blankets around the still form.

"No way," growled Oscar. "The man can't sit up, we might ruin his back. We don't have a hatchback or a station wagon, Garth's buggy caught a tree branch. We'll have to use Marty's pickup." The old man took charge, he saw the problem clearly. "Get straw into the pickup, we got to cushion him and he's got to be on his belly. Get a tarp to keep off the rain."

George Rogers considered this. Then, "You're right, Oscar. Only way we can handle it. Marty?"

The woman had buried a husband that she couldn't save. Now... a brother. Her mind sought answers, Oscar's seemed the only one. "Right," she said. "Bring him out." She ran to the barn. There was a broken bale of straw in front of the calf pen. Perhaps enough. She wrapped her arms, partially, around the half bale and hurried back to the pickup. She spread the straw in a three foot band on the pickup bed. The men laid Garth, face down on the straw and snapped the back gate. Pete Johnson had raced to the shed for a tarp. They unwrapped enough of the canvas to cover Garth. "Sweet Jesus," Marta sobbed. "Is this my life? I'm always covering someone up." No one heard her voice. Pete and George Rogers crouched in the rain, one on either side of Garth, holding the stiff tarp, shielding their friend. "Hit it, Marty," growled Oscar. He slid into the seat beside her. The Chevy jumped ahead, wheels spinning on the wet grass, down the driveway and out on the crushed rock road. Fifteen miles to Prairie City... she held the pickup at a steady pace. Part way there, Garth revived. He opened his eyes. George Rogers' muddy boots were directly in front of him, he heard the steady beat on the tarp above his head.

He groaned. George bent down to hear him. Garth muttered, "What the hell we doing, out here in the rain?" Rogers grinned and winked at Pete Johnson, old friend, old neighbor. "Well," he said. "Thought we'd all drive over to Prairie. Have a round of beer at the muni, if you feel up to it. First though, we really oughta stop at the hospital. You got a little scratch there on your south side."

CHAPTER SIXTEEN

The doctor said, "The rat was clean."

Oscar Thornstad nodded. The rat had been his biggest worry. Now, in the afternoon following the plunge of the dark spout from the sky, he felt relief. As soon as the pickup had arrived at the hospital, Oscar had known, even before the matter was mentioned, that they had all screwed up. He borrowed a car from Doc Hawkins, an old crony, drove back through the steady rain to the Crawford farm to make amends. There was still some murky daylight. Oscar augmented that with a flashlight. He poked around the granary debris in the area where they had uncovered Garth. He found the smashed and sodden body of the rat. He put it in a burlap bag and returned to Prairie City. What a bunch of assholes we were, the old man berated himself. If I didn't find the carcass, Garth, sure as hell, would be in for rabies shots. If the nail holes and the bad finger didn't kill him, the shots would. Well, hell, his thoughts rambled on, I did find the damn thing. Now, the only hope is it's clean.

It was. The lab found no traces of the dread malady. The rodent had bitten because of fright, not the madness of rabies. A wonder, said the doctor, the countryside is full of the disease. Skunks, squirrels, gophers, cows even. Plus the rats. But Garth is safe, on that score. On infection, Hawkins had his fingers crossed. The gouges from the rusty nails, ten separate wounds, were deep and ugly. They pumped tetanus shots into Garth and hoped for the best.

Garth rested on his stomach and tried to sleep, the throbbing pain in his back and finger softened by the pain killers. Now, to change positions and protect the bandaged areas, he sat on the edge of the bed and talked with Oscar and Marta. He was flaunting orders but could endure the belly position no longer without a break.

Marta, the rock, was still recovering. She had discovered a new weakness within herself in the wake of the near-disaster. The woman felt the dark void, knew that a second death would have devastated her beyond help. All night she had brooded on the capriciousness of the Universe, the odds against a darting whiplash from the clouds. The small tornado had touched one building, one man, then was sucked back into the clouds from which it came. The granary was gone, some shingles from other buildings, power poles, and a few trees in the windbreak. That was all, just Garth. I'm truly shaken, she admitted. But no one must know. Now, for a time at least, my burden on the farm is heavier.

She said, fondly, "You are one battered cowboy, baby. But you're alive. I'll take it...no complaints."

100

Garth grinned at her. "Aw hell, I'm O.K. Give me a day or two..."
He winced and gripped the bedside table.

"Ah! ...now." he muttered. "Little stab there. Got to expect some
of that. Who..ee!..." He wiped his face with a tissue. The stubble on
his face shredded the kleenex. The hospital bed table had its mirror
out, and, glancing into it saw traces of grey in the stubble. He liked
to keep clean shaven.

"Garth, you better lie down. It's too soon."

"Yeah, yeah. In a minute." He smiled again, bothered by the
sudden weakness. "I'm fine. How's the farm, and the herd?"

"No trouble, Garth. George helped me, last night and this
morning. We had to use the backup generator. The REA is repairing
the line damage. We'll be alright for tonight. George can get back
home, where he belongs."

Oscar broke in. "Rest easy, partner. Everything's under control.
Your wagon is rammed pretty good, totaled most likely. What the
hell, take the insurance money and get another one. Have you back
chasin' puss in no time."

Marta howled. She squeezed Oscar's hand in gratitude. The old
boy knew how to break the tension, restore perspective. She was
used to his salty talk.

"Yeah?" Garth was quizzical. "Right now I couldn't catch a one-
legged woman in a telephone booth." He ran a hand through his
mussed hair. "What kind of wheels you think I should get?"

"I dunno," said Oscar. "Them Mercedes ain't bad. Less'n you don't
like foreign jobs. I guess you got to keep them old buddies of yours
in the P.A. mills, busy."

"I know. It's an obligation. Guess I'll have to pass up a Porsche,
too. Not to mention a Ferrari." Garth was swinging back to normal.
Marta could hardly keep from weeping with joy.

Garth leaned forward, gingerly. He was tired. Marta and Oscar
helped him back to his prone position in the white bed. He thanked
them.

"You know, all bullshit aside, I'm one lucky S.O.B. A gift from
the gods, something I didn't deserve." The half smile was peaceful on
the unshaven face. "Way I look at it, when your times comes, that's it.
Fair enough. Hell, my time came and I missed the boat. I got a free
ride for a few years that wasn't in the books."

"Yah. Maybe." Oscar was not so sure. "It's the breaks. A kid can
get run over, an old bastard like me can hang around for eighty-some
years, just getting in folk's way. I don't try to figure it out any more."

"Well, from here on, every day is sweet. You know, I wasn't too
bad under that roof. I could handle it." A spasm wracked his slim
body. Marta didn't want to hear this. "It's alright, Garth," she said,

softly. "It's O.K. Let it go."

He did not appear to hear.

"I was fine... really. " 'till that rat got me. God, I couldn't handle it. Man ought to be able to handle anything. But I couldn't."

Oscar placed a big hand on Garth's arm. He leaned close.

"We all get things we can't handle, partner. All of us. You're a solid guy, Garth. I ain't never seen a better man. Don't fight it. Gradually the whole business will fade away." Oscar smiled. "You got to trust me on this one, Garth. In a couple of weeks you'll be laughing. You'll want a big brown rat for a pet."

In the white bed, Garth relaxed. Oscar winked at Marta, perhaps the treatment worked. Marta kissed the old man when they left the room. Garth dozed. The nurses flitted in and out, the bandages were changed. Then it was time for supper.

Garth finished his meal, leaving nothing. His appetite was strong. He lay on his belly and remembered the things he had said to Marta and Oscar. Bravado perhaps. He'd flaunted nonchalance to respond to Oscar, to buoy his own spirits. But the rat had diminished him, flashback had brought him to the verge of hysteria. God. He shivered beneath the blankets. Thought to himself: "I only hope Oscar is right. I know he was reaching for a way to help me. And he's wise, deep in humility." The knowledge of the mind, its hidden reaches, might well be there. He held out his hand, studying it. When he thought of the finger, the pain came back. A primal thing, Garth reasoned. I shrink from the rodent because my ancestors did. The beady-eyed scavenger, carrier of the plague, disseminator of diseases. My forbears shrank from its touch and so do I. The finger was encased in bandage and splint. The damage isn't serious. It'll heal, with a scar, the nail's intact. With an aluminum shield, the farm work won't have to suffer. Shape up, Garth. He bumped his chin with the heel of his hand, a discipline. Gail Samarro walked in the door. The room brightened, his wide smile returned.

"Well, Hi." Gail was bouncing bright, all curvature enticing in a cool blue dress. The neckline was square and modestly measured, her arms were bare to the shoulder straps. She wore new glasses, the sequins had been replaced with modish steel. "Orphan of the storm, so I've been told." She kissed him, lightly, on the cheek.

Garth eyed her with naked appreciation.

"I'm an orphan, for damn sure. Like to mother me while I recuperate?" He indicated a chair. Gail relaxed in it.

"Shit. I know what kind of mothering you're talking about." Her smile was brilliant. "This is the first time I've felt safe around you."

"I know. Ain't it hell?"

"Well, you're such a case. You'll be pleased to know you're famous. Shawndo famous, at least in the Crystal. The guy that beat the reaper. Keeps the babble going around the tables."

"I imagine."

"Not the first time they've talked about you."

"How's that?"

"I don't know where the leak came. For sure, not me. But the bank has several employees. People know where your forty grand went."

"That god damned Kenseth..."

"Oh, come on. Philip keeps his own counsel. But there's bookkeeping. A thing like that is just too hard to hide. Anyway, it makes you kind of a local hero."

"Jesus!"

"I know. Personally, I think you were out of your mind. I dream of enough dough to feed my kids, buy them clothes. You pour a small fortune down a rat hole."

"Hell of a metaphor," he grumbled.

"Huh? Oh, yeah. Sorry." She broke up in laughter, paused, and then continued. "And that's another part of the Crystal talk. How's the finger?"

"Sore as a bitch. But it'll be alright."

She looked at him, fondly. "Well, you're a tough hombre. And real nice. I just wish you weren't so damn scatter brained. I mean, like, with the money."

"Growers State need the Crawford farm that bad?"

"God damn it," she blazed. "Cut that out, Garth Kyllo. I can't change the world, neither can the bankers. They don't want the farm, any farm. They're just fighting to keep afloat, like everyone else."

Garth was essentially a fair man. He considered this. "I suppose you're right. I just been getting one side of the picture."

"That's O.K." Gail was forgiving. "The whole thing is a mess. Harvest can't deal with it. We can't. God knows how it'll all turn out."

They visited for half an hour, throwing it back and forth, until the night nurse appeared with strict instructions. Gail rose to leave.

"By the way," she said, "a bit of news. Betty Adams was stoned out of her skull at the Muni. Now she's out of town, for what?...a rest cure."

"I'll be damned."

"Undoubtedly. Our grim faced law man has his own problems, just like the common folks."

"Seems like." He turned the full power of his best smile on her. "Good night, Gail. Thanks for coming, I really appreciate it."

"Sure. Get well." She favored his cheek with another fleeting kiss, then breezed out of the room.

The drapes in his room were not drawn. Garth gazed out the

window to the water-soaked hospital lawn. The rain had ended, the priceless water from the roiling clouds had, he hoped, revived the crops. But why had the rain been needed so desperately...why did rich soil crack and bake like red clay?

Garth remembered yesterday, the fence line... had it been just thirty hours? He had wondered then, where has the water gone? A dozen brooks that splashed his boyhood days were dry beds, stone bottomed, thick with weeds. Water, the lifeblood of existence, the element more precious than iron ore, the oil, all the gems. All natural resources are nothing without water. The answers mocked him. He knew the causes, or some of them. The water is gone, the tables have been lowered to the far reaches of the driller's bit. We've squandered our water, our blood, with tile, sunk deep, and huge drainage ditches that criss-cross the land. We took the marshes, nature's sponges, the habitat of wild birds, and wrung them dry. And what did this perversion of nature produce, this tampering with checks and balances that eons had set in place? More arable acres, fields where moisture drained, like the run-off from a city street disappearing down a storm sewer. Grain in abundance, the storage bins overflowing with metric tons, measured in millions, glutting markets, depressing prices. All this while third world children dragged skeletal bodies to barren camps, to die. We should have saved the sloughs, held back, for future generations, the reserves of nature. We didn't do it, now Minnesota topsoil extends the delta. My childhood, my precious water, down the Mississippi and, Huck, I ain't got no raft.

Part Two

The Prophetess

CHAPTER SEVENTEEN

Marta listened to the words and knew she was hearing the truth. But the capacity for unbelief lies deep. Her mind shrank from this latest revelation in much the same way her hand would have drawn back from a flame. In the early days of August, in a year that had piled heartbreak upon tragedy, Marta had reached a watermark. She heard the calm, soft voice, devoid of self pity or anger, revealing to her a fact she could not accept. Limits are reached, the human spirit hits a wall... then new limits are established. Helen Rogers explained to Marta that the Rogers farm, lovely showplace of the area was lost. Not possibly or even probably...irremediably gone, beyond any power, short of a miracle, of saving. The auction sale was just ten days away.

"George and I never got involved in building houses, none of that sort of activity," said Helen. Otherwise, our situation is about the same, a carbon copy really, of what Pete and Alma Johnson went through in June. The debts are at least forty per cent greater than market value. On land and machinery and the beef herd. We don't have dairy cattle, of course." She sighed. "One more mistake in an interminable line. The dairy herd is helping you hang in there. That and Garth."

"Helen, you're talking like a reporter. This is you... and George." Marta stared at the chipped green wall of the Crystal Cafe. She was numb with grief, engulfed in a sea of helplessness. Harvest had won minor skirmishes, small partial victories. Now...

"Remember, Marty, the grief stages that you said you went through, with Mike, when things were rough?" Marta nodded, blindly. Helen, precise and efficient, measured her words. "We've made a conscious effort to do the same, now."

"And...?"

"And...it isn't working. Not for George, at least."

Marta said nothing.

"For me? Well, somewhat, I guess. Women accept."

Marta looked at her friend and knew, again, that this was perhaps the most beautiful person she had ever known. Beauty in every sense of the word. Helen slender, tall, immaculate. The woman had strength but little endurance, the residue of a severe bout with hepatitis many years before. I always feel like a clod when I'm with this woman, thought Marta. I feel thick, stolid... a peasant. Betty Adams had somewhat the same effect on me. But Betty is much too thin. In a swirl of fragmented feelings she savaged herself. Why am I thinking of looks, impressions? My friend and her marvelous husband stand at the crossroads, a life crisis. I just cannot deal with the facts.

"I'm worried about George, of course." Helen was thoughtful, she might have been lecturing in a long ago classroom. "There is a devastation there that is so unreal. He has really seen this coming for a long time, but knowing it and actually facing it seem worlds apart. You know how George is. Urbane, informed, articulate. He's always been a leader of sorts. Now. it's like a return to adolescence, childhood even. Absolute non-acceptance."

"Mike was the same. Without George's polish."

Marta's words had been pure reaction. She knew, at once, the words were wrong, the implication dangerous. She attempted to back off. "What I mean is ..."

Helen reached across the table and touched her friend's arm. They had been close for more than half a lifetime.

"It's alright, Marty. I know what you mean."

Helen Rogers sipped her coffee and the Danish lay untouched on the plate. "We can't generalize, people are much too complex for that. But, somehow, women seem to cling to people... to husbands, children, whatever. Men cling to possessions and no possession is as basic as land."

"I know." Marta's voice was bitter. "Sometimes I hate the land. Not the soil itself, but the power it has over people. Men become blinded. All they can see is the land."

"Yes. And we have no children. Not now. Maybe, that way, it was worse for George."

"What about you?"

"Oh, I'm like you, Marty. Not that I flatter myself that I have your depth of character."

"Watch it!"

Helen smiled. She continued. "I just have your love of life, some of your perspective. I don't want to leave the farm. But if – when – we do, I'll be all right. We'll still be better off than three-fourths of the people in the world. That's a thought I cling to, a life raft."

"That raft is loaded with a lot of good people."

"And, hey, I almost forgot. George has prospects for an agricultural appointment. He's been in touch with old friends in, what do they say, high places? How could the government pass up a man like that?"

"When you put it that way, no chance?"

"Something will turn up. Like Garth says, what the hell!"

The cafe was nearly deserted. Jenny Peters slipped into a chair next to Marta. She looked tired, hair straggling. Typical Jenny, Marta admitted.

"Hi." She had brought the coffee decanter and poured them a free refill. "Heard you mention Garth. How is that wild hunk these days?"

"Oh, Garth." Marta waved a hand. "He's great. Only stayed in the hospital four days, you know. Doc Hawkins was mad enough to shoot him. But Garth just ambled away. Doc wasn't smart enough to hide his clothes."

"He's a tough son of a bitch. Excuse the remark."

Marta laughed. She liked Jenny. She knew something of the tabs Jenny carried, worthless bits of paper, uncollectable.

"That's sweeter language than we usually get from you, Jen. Forget it. And Garth would appreciate the concern. The guy's rugged, for damn sure. He still has a couple of places on his back where I have to change the bandages. And his finger bothers him at work. He hates that splint he still has to wear to protect the end. Where the little friend chewed on it."

"What I mean, tough." Jenny studied her red hands. "I'd like to change his bandages. But I wouldn't know where to stop." She laughed. Marta grinned and winked at Helen.

Marta said, "Control yourself, Jen."

"Aw, hell. Garth's too young for me. Oscar is way too old. And Clint Eastwood never stops in." She sighed. "Clint doesn't know what he's missing."

"Poor guy."

"Age is funny, the way people think. I really believe, far as Garth is concerned, that the Samarro gal thinks she's too young for him."

"Think so?" Marta wanted to hear this opinion. Jen saw a lot of Gail, and Kenseth.

"Yeah. But it's the money, too. Gail has two kids. Real sweethearts, I'll admit. So who needs a busted farmer?" Jenny laughed without mirth. The farmers struggled, she struggled. "Again, excuse the remark, Marty. Garth's your brother, I shouldn't be talking about his finances. But I'm just giving you what I think might be Gail's view."

"Of course. And you may be absolutely right, Jen. The same thought has occurred to me."

Helen said, "I've always been a romantic. Just my nature. And I feel for all the young folks today in the farming business. Even if Garth isn't exactly young. But the rug has been pulled out. What is the future, for any of them?"

"You know the answer, Helen," said Jenny. "They can drive a tractor and pick corn for some corporation. At three-forty an hour." Her voice held bitterness. "Shit, might as well work for me. But I can't even afford the three-forty. They can all go to work for 3-M or Honeywell. Let the land go to hell."

Jenny stood up. "Nice vistin'," she said. She walked back behind the counter where Oscar Thornstad had taken his regular stool. Marta looked at Helen. George Roger's wife sat silent, her eyes wet.

"It comes down to that, doesn't it, Marty? After all the fine talk. It's the truth, in this god forsaken corner of the Universe. Let the land go to hell." She extracted a tissue and wiped her eyes. "We're good farmers, Marty. You know that. And we're beaten, right into the dirt. George and I are just two, out of thousands. Maybe they'll get to you and Garth, too. Then what?"

"Well, we're working on the problem."

The two women sat in silence and behind the counter fresh coffee perked in cheerful bubbles. Helen's voice was flat. "I know George and I've soldiered for Harvest, just like we did for Farm Bureau in the old days. Still, the enemy's won." Helen brushed a kiss on Marta's cheek and left, head held high, her step firm. Marta, watching her leave, felt a new desolation. She straddled a stool next to Oscar.

Marta saw at a glance that he knew. Oscar, seated at the counter, seemed his true age. The old man sat hunched and glowering, bib overalls nearly to his chin, eyes sunk and slitted against the usual cigarette. Black coffee in front of him was cold and scattered ashes were strewn on the counter. "Hey," said Marta. "Kind of sloppy today, looks like to me. You bummed out?"

The deep creases did not soften to the sunny smile, to their old badge of camaraderie. He eyed her, sourly.

"Naw. I'm great. Never felt better."

"You're a lying Swede. Or Norwegian. Hell, I never can remember. Not much to chose between them anyway." She couldn't get a rise out of him.

He crushed the butt in his saucer. "You heard?"

"Just now. From Helen."

"Yah. I figured."

"So, what happens?"

"Mostly, not a god damn thing." Oscar spoke with an intensity so sharp that Marta stared in disbelief. "I've preached nonviolence, same as George and the rest. What's it got us? Nothing!"

Marta eyed him with a level gaze, said nothing, letting the storm run.

"We get knocked down. We get up, bloodied. We get knocked down again. Millionaires turn into billionaires. Fortunes are being made all over the country. Yet the most basic of all industries suffers this humiliation. Christ, isn't there no end to it?"

Marta drank her coffee, never mind it was her fourth cup. How could she answer questions she'd asked, so often, herself?

"I been like Ghandi," the old man muttered. "So have you. We might just as well wear a white sheet. For what? The law persecutes us, the politicians have failed us...the big money people chew up the remains." Oscar fired up a fresh smoke. Marta had never seen his hand shake before. Her mind cringed before the spectacle of a crumbling boulder.

"Aw, hell." He spoke softly now. "I'm just an old fart that the world has left behind. I'm all talk, I wouldn't cause any ruckus. You know that, Marty. It's just..."

"I know. George and Helen."

"Sure."

"Oscar, I feel the same as you. We've always been on the same track. But we can't just give up."

"No. 'Course not."

"Harvest meets Thursday night. Maybe we can come up with something. A special effort."

"Sure, Marty. Sure. I'll be there." Oscar spoke the right words, he couldn't lay any more havoc on his old friend. But his voice was listless. Oscar Thornstad did not mind being old. He was too much the philosopher to rebel at nature, forces that, like planting and harvesting, continued the cycle of life, the greening of new seasons. He had been born when the century was new. He'd be long gone when the century ended, the millennium folded into history. Oscar had plodded, tirelessly, through wars and depressions, the flu epidemic that carried away two brothers, fires and windstorms. One son had endured a shortened life with a withered limb, twenty years too soon for Salk vaccine. Oscar Thornstad had no quarrel with life, he asked no favors. But depressions and hard times should punish people with an even hand, prosperity reward every man and woman that worked hard, kept at least some of the Commandments...stayed out of jail. The scholar in the old man railed against forces he couldn't control, an enemy he could not fight. He didn't know who the enemy was, he couldn't see his eyes.

Back at the farm, Marta broke the news to Garth. The man was impassive, she couldn't read his thoughts. Garth studied the skyline, the ripening corn which had made a valiant comeback from the weeks of dryness. The man is deep, thought Marta, and so hard to really know.

"Hell of a note," was all he said. He was working on the barnyard fence, repairing damage that had been left untended during the rush of the busy season. He picked up his tools and carried them to the shed.

When the milking was nearly completed, Garth spoke to Marta.

"I'm cutting out early, kid. I want to see someone."

"Yeah? What's her name?"

"His name, as it happens. Jim Moenke."

"Thought you didn't like the man?"

Garth stroked his chin and considered this remark carefully. He had relayed the story of the forty-five revolver to Marta. She had questioned the sanity of a man so redneck.

"He's a hard case, Jim is. But I've gotten to like him since that night. The man is a Commando...like a bull."

"I've had bulls that busted down fences and didn't amount to a damn with the cows."

"Maybe the cows weren't all that good looking."

"Well," she said. "Watch it. Now get going, I'll finish up." She couldn't resist, "Then I'll know it's done right."

Garth crawled into his station wagon, a '79 Merc that had replaced the totaled Plymouth, and drove to Prairie City. In the lounge of the muni he met James Moenke. They each had a couple of beers.

They spent the next couple of hours hassling three farm operators, renters who were making crop on land leased from the banks or FmHA. Two were strangers to Garth. Moenke seemed to know everyone.

The talks were forthright and persuasive. No trouble resulted. Garth was eloquent and soft spoken. He talked with short gestures, the bandaged, splinted middle finger of his right hand stabbing out his thoughts. His partner talked less, but the presence alone was powerful. No one had any wish to tangle with the squat Moenke. There was no changing the lease arrangements for the present year. The crop in the fields had to be harvested because the investment was in the ground. Garth and James Moenke talked of next year, letting the fucking ground grow weeds.

The two men emphasized the point again and again. Garth talked of his past. There were scabs in labor disputes. Workers crossed the lines in droves to protect jobs, to feed the families. I know these things, said Garth. I've lived with both sides. But if we work for the money lenders, instead of standing up to them, then there's no hope for any of us, we die with hardly a whimper. The three farm operators were left dazed and uncomfortable. They had received no threats, no promises of recrimination. The battle of pure confrontation and resolve caught them unprepared. They left the muni, nerves shaken, sober as black-robed judges.

"A start," said Garth. "Jesus. These guys make Benedict Arnold look like a winner."

"Screw 'em," said Jim, in a low chuckle, "I thought those guys would wet their pants."

"The word will get around, buddy." Garth was confident. "We won't have to run no classifieds in the paper." The lean man flashed his white smile and regarded his empty schooner. "How about another beer?"

"Hell of a deal!"

CHAPTER EIGHTEEN

The word did, indeed, get around. Much of Black Loam County buzzed with fact and fantasy on the new direction that Harvest, or some portion of that organization, had taken. Garth and Jim Moenke spent much of their precious spare time spreading the message that they looked with disfavor upon the men who chose not to refrain from renting the foreclosed farms. If you want to work those farms, buy them, said Garth. Moenke nodded agreement. If you can't buy the farm or odd eighty or one-twenty, stay away.

"We know you need land," was Garth's clincher. "No question about that. You got to keep your machinery busy, some of you need more hay land to feed the livestock, the kids need new shoes. We know all that, we'd be blind not to know. But they need us, the new owners, that is, more than we need them."

"That's right." Jim Moenke offered his views in a rumbling basso. "Then see what happens. Them sons of bitches like to own farm land so bad, let 'em get some dirt under their fingernails and do some real farming. Wouldn't last half a day. Be like a pimp trying to shingle a roof."

"Most everybody in the county has a grand daddy or great something or other that came to this country to escape the land barons and serfdom in Europe. Our people homesteaded the prairie. Read your history, man. Sod huts, terrible blizzards, grasshopper invasions, drought... you name it, they lived through it." Garth sighed. He wasn't sure of his facts but he had a slight talent for melodrama. "Now, what? History turns on itself, we drift back to the fiefdom and the peasant. We do business with the very banks and the other money-bags that close us out. Like the miners, buyin' at the Company Store."

And so the rhetoric went. Garth doubted that he and Moenke made many converts. But for the first time since joining Harvest he felt a sense of purpose in the organization. Strike and boycott were the words he knew best, his heritage from the labor wars he'd known. The words were in his veins, he had little understanding of compromise or the innovative solutions of better financing and prudent planning. Both Garth and Moenke had an almost instinctive dislike of politicians and, therefore, the whole political process. Neither man was acquainted with the local state representative or the area state senator. This was understandable. Both legislators had, on the record, been virtually worthless to the farmers, the senator from aloofness, the representative from bumbling stupidity. Elections were more than a year away, there was little help in sight. At the state capital the governor wobbled gently in every political breeze.

But one local official was concerned, even though that involvement came from a different perspective. Sheriff Bill Adams eased into a booth in the Crystal Cafe where Garth and Jim Moenke were deep in planning. They looked up, more in amusement than annoyance, at the uninvited visitor. Sweat glistened on the sheriff's face, the temperature was, once more, in the nineties.

"Well," grunted Moenke. "If it ain't Marshall Dillon hisself." He grinned, hugely. "Lookin' for good men for a posse, I reckon." The words were mocking. Adams smiled, thinly. He'd clashed with Moenke before.

"Naw." Adams was affable. "Just a cup of coffee. Maybe a danish. Hey, Jen," he shouted. "Three rolls over here and more acid. These guys are starving."

"Shucks," said Moenke. He played the rube. "Ain't that a nice thing to do?" He poked Garth's arm. "The Marshall here eats off'n the taxpayers all year. Now we gonna eat off him." His eyes were bright, the moon face was crinkled in a mirth. "Who said there ain't no justice, huh?"

Adams took the ribbing in good grace. Garth said nothing. He studied the square face of the sheriff. He had met the man only a few times. He knew, so well, of Marta's ambivalence toward Adams, her enmity with him at the farm auctions, her old respect for his professionalism. That, and some sympathy for his present domestic problems. Garth studied the man in silence, content to let Jim flail away. Garth knew the visit couldn't be pure accident, not in these times. The sheriff looked five years older than he had when Garth first met him at Mike's funeral. Lines in the face were deeply etched, the close cropped hair was peppered with gray. Even the sheriff's uniform had lost its band box sharpness. Adams was in his third four year term after spending a dozen years as a deputy. The man knew no other life. He had no children, no hobbies to speak of and, for now, no wife. His life was hollow and his enemies seemed to multiply.

Adams wasted little time. He asked, "How's the crusade coming along?" A useless gambit, the two men stared at this, their eyes blank, un-answering.

"I see." Adams drank his black coffee and chewed, thoughtfully, on the danish. "Well, only fair to tell you — gentlemen (Adams had nearly said "boys", a familiarity he struggled to avoid) that there have been, well, complaints. On your recent activities."

"Um," muttered Moenke. "That's kind of a strange word, complaints. Could you just sorta explain what the hell you mean. You got me interested."

"You know."

"Hey, Garth." Moenke poked his partner's arm again. "Ain't this somethin'? We're playin' games with Mr. Dillon."

"Yeah. A riot." Garth spoke for the first time.

"People feel intimidated, gentlemen. They don't like it a bit. In a free country they got a point."

Garth was laconic. "Who are They?"

"I'm not really at liberty to say. Not at this particular time." The sheriff's voice was level.

Garth asked, "Any complaints signed?"

"No. Not as yet."

"Then," now Garth's voice was cold as ice. "Like Jim said, we don't know what you're talking about." He paused in reflection. "The intimidation appears to be coming from you, not from us. Like at the auctions. You recall the auctions, I'm sure."

"Oh, cool it." Adams wouldn't rise to the provocation. "Garth, we're just having a friendly conversation. There's nothing formal here, not even quasi-legal. I just happen to believe in stamping out grass fires before they get out of hand. Seems sensible to me."

But Garth had assumed his stance. He knew that the issue must, eventually, be forced. And now as good a time as ever. Garth had never been a man of infinite patience in the steel conciliation meetings. Most of them had struck him as little more than interminable drivel. Paper pushers, attorneys, government officials, squeezing the rights of the Union workers.

His voice was a knife. "A lot of things seem sensible, Mr. Sheriff. Like farmers hanging onto their farms, especially those that have been handed down, father to son, or daughter. American farms should be owned and farmed by farmers, not bankers, not government lenders. But you ain't concerned with sensible things like that."

"You're changing the subject, Garth."

"I called you Mr. Sheriff. My name is Mr. Kyllo."

"Sure. But you're still changing the subject. You're talking financial and social structure, plus a touch of history." It was plain that the sheriff didn't want to get beyond his depth. "I'm not into all that. I'm in law enforcement."

"There's only one subject." Garth stood up. His eyes were bright, the lean face was taut. He felt a surge of the old combativeness. "Only one subject in the last analysis. And only two sides. Harvest and the farmers are on one side, you and the bankers on the other."

"It's my job."

"That's what the oppressors always say." Garth didn't like his own statement, it had the ring of posturing, borrowed words. But, hell, he'd been pushed.

Adams began to simmer. "You really want anarchy?"

"Of course not."

"What then?"

"Just decent markets for our produce. And some debt readjustment. Is that too much to ask?"

"Garth, sit down." Adams was drawn, almost pleading. The long months, the years showed on him. He couldn't absorb the unending dislike of the people he admired. He tried once more.

"You might be surprised by this, gentlemen. But I agree with you one hundred per cent. I was raised on a farm, ten miles from this spot. I know the picture. Things have got to change, we need new financial arrangements, new laws, grandfather clauses on old homesteads, a whole list of changes have got to come from Washington and the state capitol. Jesus, fellows, get after those people. A lawman can only work with what's on the books. And you'd be surprised at how much I overlook." Adams' voice thinned, he wasn't used to talking that long, making speeches. Garth sat down, thoughtfully. Jim Moenke was unimpressed.

"Nice speech, Marshall," he muttered. "But you forget why you came in here. To lean on Garth and me. And, ..." his voice was hard as concrete, "Without official complaints, without warrants – nothin'. Just leanin' on Garth and me, showing the badge."

"Not true, Mr. Moenke. Just a friendly gesture, that's all. You actually think I'd like to see the day I have to arrest guys like you? Shit!" Adams grinned. "For one thing you're too damn big."

Moenke snorted. "Big, little, what's the difference? You pack a gun, mine is in hock." He winked at Garth. Adams did not understand the reference to the taping ceremony at the Rogers house. This was, for the time being, intelligence beyond his files.

Now, Adams stood up.

"Thanks for your time, gentlemen. I've learned a lot. I can't ask you to really understand my position but you might look at things like this. If I'm gone, there is another sheriff. If one isn't elected in a special election or appointed by the commissioners, the governor or the attorney general appoints one. They have this funny attitude in St. Paul that rapists and arsonists and such like ought to have some law on their tails. Even dealers, pushing their little plastic packets to the local snorters. Seems like somebody ought to mind the store against such folks." The voice was casual but now the lawman was all business. "Maybe, from your standpoint, the county would get a lot better man than me. But maybe a lot worse."

He picked up the check. "You're right, gentlemen. This one is on the tax payers." Adams walked to the cash register, paid Jenny, then left. Jim Moenke started after him and scratched his head.

"What a load of sheepshit. A man needs hip boots. I don't know any more now than I did before."

"Me neither."

"Well, screw 'em. I'm glad some of them yellow bellies are crying. Shows they're paying attention."

"Yeah. And you notice George Rogers never came up in the conversation. I wonder how boy scout Adams feels about that deal, about his precious duty."

"Shit!" Moenke's favorite word spoke volumes. "Adams will claim he's bleedin' inside. But he'll be there when McCarth's hammer falls. Kenseth'll see to that. The corporations've gotta be protected, that's priority number one."

The name Kenseth stirred uneasy feelings in Garth Kyllo. He'd become skittish on the subject of the bank president. He said good-bye to Moenke and left the cafe with a wink and a smile for Jenny. He stood for a moment, considering, on the sidewalk, then walked into Growers State Bank.

The cool interior, the soft, grey carpeting, was like an oasis, a center of sanity after the meeting with Adams. Deception is everywhere, thought Garth. Jen's cafe is reality, Growers State, efficient and exuding the rich aroma of money, wears the mask of make believe. All of us are actors in an unfinished drama. Or soap opera? And Garth caught the anomaly of entering a bank, one of the strongholds he preached against to the farmers.

Gail Samarro was not at her desk. One of the young women at the teller windows informed him, with no expression, that Mrs. Samarro was in conference with Mr. Kenseth and the vice president, Mr. Ryan. Garth thanked her and left. He drove the station wagon back to the farm and went to work.

That night he phoned Gail. She told him that one of the children was ill. She couldn't possibly go out with him for at least a few nights. Gail was firm on this point. Then, in a sudden softness, made a date with him for lunch on the following day.

Garth pondered this information. He fingered his billfold where he had the telephone number of one of the waitresses from the Municipal Liquor in Prairie City. Gloria had been coming on strong during Garth's frequent stops in the muni in the company of Jim Moenke. The moon faced man had kidded him, without mercy, at the prime stuff he was passing up. The temptation was great, he owed nothing to Gail Samarro and she was so, well, he couldn't get a fix on the elusive department manger.

"Hell with it," he said. "I'll play out the string a little longer. Gloria'll always be there."

I'm a chauvinist bastard for thinking like that, he mused. He couldn't get Gail out of his system. Sweet Mama, girl Friday to the enemy, the man who would close out, send on their way, the elemental pair, George and Helen. Still, that wasn't Gail, that was the machine, the faceless force that Bill Adams had talked about, the force that turned long time friends to enemies. Even Kenseth, Garth could dismiss, just one more cog in that remorseless machine. But Gail... the woman invades my senses. I see her as I did on our first weekend together when we had the excitement kids get when they steal a half day from school... taste her , feel the warm soft skin against my own, touch her breasts, full and firm as a girl of twenty... exult in her ...

Before heading for bed Garth glanced at the daily newspaper from Prairie City. He looked at the headlines and the sports results, then searched the local items for news of Harvest. There was none. But his eyes caught a special item in the county statistics that sent him to the refrigerator for a fresh Bud. One Black Loam County divorce was listed. On some nights there were as many as half a dozen. This one listed Philip and Corrine Kenseth, after fourteen years of marriage. Custody of one minor child was awarded to the mother.

Bound to happen, thought Garth. None of my affair. But sleep seemed distant. He slouched in the big chair in the living room and the dancing shadows of the Tonight show were meaningless, flickering on the black and white screen.

CHAPTER NINETEEN

Garth did not mention to Marta about the strange meeting at the Crystal Cafe with Bill Adams. The life and times of the sheriff of Black Loam County were unimportant to him, easily dismissed. Garth had, in his new role with Harvest, pegged Adams as a light-weight, a man lost in a job he could never handle, certain to be defeated when his term was up. But Marta found the troubled lawman increasingly on her mind. She had made the surprising discovery of being riddled with premonitions about Betty Adams. She regretted deeply the lack of understanding she'd displayed to a woman faced with attitudes beyond her understanding.

At three in the afternoon Marta sat at the kitchen table and reached for the phone. Her hands shook slightly, she was drenched with perspiration. A sudden weakness had come upon her in the farm yard and driven her to the house at this unusual hour. Hey, this better not be a sign of getting old, she thought. Hell, I can outwork most men in Black Loam County...at least Shawndo Township. But the blaze of ninety-five degrees had gotten to her. Garth, oblivious to any caprice of weather, was continuing his work on the fences, just as though the tornado had never intervened.

So Marta had worked at the tedious, never ending job of cleaning up the debris that was still scattered about, piling odd pieces of wood and metal in neat piles, sweeping the grain that would sprout in odd clumps if not gathered. A contingent of neighbors had swooped down upon the farm while Garth was hospitalized, clearing the bulk of the granary mess, trimming the uprooted trees. Still, much remained to be done. The work was interminable; she'd nearly collapsed before heading for the cool kitchen.

I have to make the call, she told herself. Not easy, considering the hot words at the March auction sale. But I have to live with myself. The river of life flows on whether farms are lost or saved, no matter if crops flourish or fail, if our enemies triumph or are defeated. My life is here, on this flat land, in this black soil. There's no place where I can hide. Mike was old fashioned, stubborn, a terrible manager of money. The man had limited vision, he was impervious to changing times and volatile markets. But he kept his simple humanity, built the tree house for children he scarcely knew. And I wept when the rough boards were all in place and the Chicano kids found a few hours of happiness in a tiny kingdom of their own, twelve feet above the orchard grass. Marta put in the call to the sheriff's office, the sheriff was not available at this time, could she leave a number? On impulse, she phoned his house. He answered, in a voice she could barely recognize.

They talked for half an hour. Bill Adams was wary at first, the memories of conflict too recent. But he warmed to old friendship and, gradually, spilled his grief and bewilderment to Marta.

Betty was not merely sick, he was sure that Marta knew as much. There had been a massive crumpling, a devastation of mind and body that years of drug dependency and alcoholism had made inevitable. She was residing now in the state's finest facility, the prognosis was not good. Betty lived her days and nights in a secured area and vacillated between roller coaster bouts of depression and vague oblivion. The cost was staggering and the care professionals held out only the most guarded hopes, statements hedged with every possible factor. Bill visited his wife as often as possible. The drive, six hours round trip, was a cut his schedule couldn't handle. Each visit left him more uncertain than the one before.

Marta was not surprised by any of this. She was merely fulfilling a natural function by her call, making the appropriate sounds that sympathy demands. She spoke cheerily, like a Hallmark card, she voiced the soothing, hopeful sentiments of comfort.

"You're doing great, Bill. I really admire you so much."

"Cut it out, Marty."

"No, I mean every word. You've hung in there. You have taken some tough shots without flinching. A lot of guys would have gone to pieces."

"I'm not tough. And I am in pieces. I try not to let it show but I feel like I've gone through a corn shredder."

"That's in your mind." Marta kept the right touch, the ultimate friend and den mother. "You've stayed on the job, you're working it out. Takes guts and class, Mr. Sheriff."

That's what Garth called me, he thought. "Oh, God." The first chuckle crept over the wire. "You're such a B.S.'er. I love it, I had to talk with someone like this. You must have known, you are one hell of a gal."

Marta had steeled herself to make the call. Now, it all seemed worthwhile. She had learned, in six months, how desperation breeds, how the shadows multiply. The bantering tone of the sheriff's last remark was all the thanks she needed. One tiny step. Christ, how important that was for the hurt and desolate of the world. She spoke with bluff certainty.

"You'll be fine, Bill. And Betty will be back, sound as a dollar. Much sounder, I hope," she added. "But you know, I've two other worries. George and Helen."

"Marta, what the heck went wrong there? Just when you get accustomed to the shock of failure, another greater blow comes along.

Impossible...yet, there it is."

Marta spoke carefully. There are dark corners in every house.

"George is a complex man, Bill. So damn smart – brilliant, I always thought. But the man had a love affair that did him in."

"Love affair? Come on."

"Oh, I don't mean that. George could never see past Helen. Or the other way around. George was in love with, quote, The Family Farm, the hope and salvation of the earth.

"Yeah. But where did the money go?"

"For more land, for new buildings. For veterinarian bills beyond belief. When trouble struck his Angus herd he should have dumped the lot. Not George. Those dumpy animals were like his children – the ones that died. He's paid for three herds...he has only one, and not worth much at that."

"George is smart, no doubt about that. Guess the tide over-whelmed him, just like other folks."

"Worse. His sunny nature was his worst enemy."

"I hear he blames it all on Kenseth."

Marta was troubled, she had heard much the same. "Well, for sure, when things were going smooth, Kenseth had loads of money to lend. What better A-1 prospect than George Rogers."

"Still, if not Kenseth, then someone else."

"Of course."

Adams said, "Well, I heard from some of the boys at the Crystal, and from Jen herself, that George said he might be free and clear today if it wasn't for the blood sucker financiers – like Kenseth."

Marta laughed. "Shit, that's just farmer talk. We all spout the same line. Lets off steam."

"I know, I know. But George Rogers ..."

One more mystery in a land, an area, where nothing was as it had been. Marta and Bill Adams talked of other matters, the flaming international situation and how events in other lands might affect the farm belt. They spoke of politics, and rains that had brought the crops back from the edge. Then Marta, mission accomplished, said good bye and went back to work on the remains of the granary debris.

Only the foundation of the building was in place. Nearby stood two new steel corrugated bins, purchased as replacements by the insurance settlement. I detest these shiny monsters, thought Marta. They stand, like oil tanks, displaced from an Arabian desert. But the insurance companies do not rebuild the old fashioned granaries, the cost prohibitive.

Her mind was on George Rogers. The white haired farmer she had admired, nearly worshipped, for more than twenty-five years had

121

come, at last, face to face with a destiny he had never visioned. The master farmer, known and admired far beyond the boundaries of Shawndo Township, was soon to be, like thousands before him, shunted into a new way of life, one he could hardly comprehend.

And the master farmer, at the very moment, smiled and joked with Helen and tried his best (I'm a failed actor as well as a bankrupt, he thought) to conceal from the woman, his best friend as well as his wife, the torments that lodged his spirit in a sunken world where the sun did not shine and laughter was extinct. One life isn't enough for a man, he mused, a point of reference to his time on earth. I should, of course, explore the excitement and challenges of new endeavors. Psychobabble. Straight lines from television gurus streamed through his mind like advertising jingles you can't not think about, that you can't shut off. This farm isn't the end of the world, there are other fields where my talents might flourish. I've got old and grumpy with my financial troubles. A new start, a different job, best thing possible for me – and for Helen.

And so on. George Rogers' thoughts ran wild, a crazy pendulum that sought, desperately, the balance and rationalization that might make the days of August pass quickly, the nights bearable. He was a man of great knowledge in agriculture and human organization. Opportunity lay in all directions... the term agri-business was a fact of life. Both business and government cried out for gifts he possessed. Helen had spent thirty years in this one house, a change might be a tonic for her.

George Rogers played the mind games that were, in some obscure science, a last cry for salvation, a final hope for survival. He could not bear to leave the land, the fields and animals were like his children, looked to him for protection. His buildings, well painted, trim and solid, were old friends, he knew each cranny, every solid beam. The farm buildings were showplace fresh. They were not, like so many barns and sheds and granaries, caked thick with dust and residue. George Rogers kept his castle as clean as Helen's kitchen, for someone else to inherit. For Philip Kenseth and the minions of Growers State. The ownership was to be not even local, directors lived in Prairie City and more distant towns. They were the new landlord class, lords of the land. The phrase held shades of classism that stilled his blood, the stratification of society had always turned him cold. People thought of me as a leader. Bittersweet thought. And I have been, always, deep inside, the ultimate everyman, a man of the masses because they're all my neighbors.

Now, Growers State – all the banks and insurance firms and government lending agencies will own, eventually, most of the land. Philip Kenseth, a lounging money pimp with sixty dollar slacks, and others like him, will riff their papers, consult their attorneys, own the rich black soil.

Rogers walked the fields, testing the fences, checking on weeds and insects, scanning the crops as though they still belonged to him. He strolled through the lower pasture, casting a critical gaze on the blocky Black Angus cattle. They browsed, sleepily, and lazed beneath the trees, escaping the hot sun. All was right, all familiar. George Rogers could even forget that the health of the black critters had cost him a fortune, money borrowed at disastrous rates of interest.

So went the days of George Rogers, while the tall corn ripened and the pods on the soy bean plants began to fill. Waves engulfed the man, each bout of common sense, of rationalization, was swept aside, inundated under waves as dark as the ocean's floor. He smiled and laughed and helped with the work of lining up equipment for the auction sale. And Helen watched him, though he was unaware, and knew her own secret sorrow, her own helplessness in the face of total defeat.

Helen's thoughts, these days, were increasingly on the two who had shared their home for such short years. Technology has brought so many blessings, comforts that had lifted the back-breaking drudgery from farming, that controlled the weeds and watered and fed the animals with the touch of a button. Diseases conquered. She thought of Oscar Thornstad and his son, lost to polio because he was born too soon.

The machinery of the earth has changed our lives. She remembered, we still milked cows by hand and trudged from farm to farm in the threshing rings when I was young. And split the kindling wood by hand and gathered eggs from angry hens that nested in strange hidden places. When I was a girl and had never known George Rogers. But machinery of sorts, a kind of technology, reached out and killed our little girl with a pickup truck and crashed our son into the jungle in a helicopter riddled by ground fire.

When I was young, she thought, all things were simple. But of course they were not. Her parents had cried against changes that would be ruinous, of a depression so long and harsh that the nation and its farmers would be lost forever. Her parents were more than twenty years dead. Perhaps their prophesy would be fulfilled, a generation or more delayed. Now, Helen watched her husband and kept, hidden deep, her own secret despair.

CHAPTER TWENTY

"Do we have to have Mrs. Nelson again?" asked Bart. Gail was not worried, she knew the kids liked the old lady. Bart was jut being possessive of his mother's time.

"No, we don't, Bart. We can get Janice Knowles." Janice was seventeen, a senior.

"I hate Janice. She's mean." Bart was positive. Sarah, four, made a face and rolled her eyes, agreeing with her brother.

"Well, there you are." Gail was brisk. "Mrs. Nelson it is. You kids behave for her, I want no bad reports. And go to bed when she says."

"You going out with Garth tonight?"

"For awhile."

"Where are you going?"

"Oh... just out."

"You going to marry Uncle Garth?" The boy was unrelenting in pursuit. Gail laughed.

"What ever gave you that idea?"

"I don't know. I guess 'cause you like him."

"Well," she had to put a firm halt to this line of conjecture. "No one around here is getting married. Remember, I am married. To your father. And Garth is not your uncle."

"I know." The boy was thoughtful. "But I don't even remember my Dad."

"Of course you do."

"Well... sort of. Are you going to divorce Dad?"

"Maybe. Maybe not." The woman was struck with a sudden burst of tenderness. So much, so soon for children to understand. "You two are such good kids. I'm sorry we don't have a regular family. But your Dad just likes to work far away. He's a vagabond. You know what that means?"

"Yes."

"Well... some day we'll all... " All what? Gail Samarro seldom lied to her children. The three, the mother, Bart and Sarah shared a small cocoon, based on trust. And Mrs. Nelson, more like an aunt or a grandmother, was a treasure. She didn't pry into Gail's affairs, she had maintained a vague disinterest in the weekend jaunt to the Twin Cities in the spring. Mrs. Nelson's life centered around her soaps and the nostalgia of the late-night films. A devout church-going lady, she possessed that rarest of virtues, charity. Mrs. Nelson knew the life of the deserted wife was not without complications.

"Now, come on, Bart. You really like Mrs. Nelson, don't you?"

The boy considered this. The old woman was strict, in a gentle way. But, compared to the pouting Janice, an easy choice.

"Yeah, she's nice. But I like you at home better."

"Well, thank you, dear."

"Me too," added Sarah, not to be overlooked.

"That is very noble, both of you. But your mother has to get out of the house now and then. All grown-ups do. OK?"

They consented. At eight-thirty Garth arrived, the Merc wagon running smooth as silk.

So, on a Thursday night, five days before the scheduled auction at George Rogers' farm, Garth Kyllo and Gail Samarro sat in their favorite booth in the lounge of the Prairie City Municipal Liquor. From the noon time lunch date the two had drifted, naturally, with an afternoon of work intervening, to this accustomed spot.

Garth was at peace with the world. His full strength was nearly back, the brash ebullience had never left. Even his finger had ceased to ache and the protective aluminum tip would soon be gone. He was dressed sharply, Marta made sure that her brother did not acquire the rough untidiness of the bachelor farmer, that fabled character that considered worn denims and a frayed flannel shirt the ultimate sacrifice in conformity. The bachelor farmers wore three days of stubble and a Copenhagen breath to town and never knew why waitresses turned away, eyes watering. Garth's clothes were neat, with a knife crease on the grey slacks. And Gail was serene. She had accompanied Garth this night to end, for once and all, her sleeplessness. The tossing and turning, the indecision had worn her nerves. The children had lost their laughing mother. Perhaps, thought Gail, it's not too late to bring her back.

Now she stared at Garth across the narrow width of the booth. And Garth thought, at the moment, he looked into the eyes of truth, level, unswerving. The flirtatious woman, that bouncing possessor of sly graces, hints, promises was gone. For so many months the two of them had balanced, finely tuned, on the thin edge of serious involvement. Gail's look told him plainly, an honesty as sure as salt, the games had all been played.

She said, calmly, "Garth, you are a stupid son of a bitch. I could despise you... perhaps I do." The words did not surprise him, they were an affirmation of the long hot summer that had followed a beautiful spring.

"We had something," she said, her voice a dull knife. "For such a little time. A nice little interlude... a walk in the park."

"Until reality intruded?"

"Of course." Gail sipped her drink, the hard eyes softened. "The real world, the world of groceries and doctor bills and pennies stashed away for a college education that may cost a King's ransom, near the year two thousand. That world."

"I know all about it."

"Do you?" Gail laughed, a bit wildly he thought, but then... three drinks. "Do you, really, Garth? Forty thousand dollars is not a hell of a lot these days. But it was enough for a start... for a chance for us."

He could feel his cheeks burning in the soft light of the lounge. "I figured we'd get to the forty grand."

"You figured right, friend."

"I thought at the time... hell, I still do... I done the right thing. You think otherwise?"

"Oh shit, Garth." She seemed, suddenly, very weary, her voice held sadness. "Right, wrong... who the hell knows? Those words don't mean much when the electric bill's too big... when there's no check in the mail from that wandering asshole I married."

Garth said nothing. The floodgates have gone down, he thought. No stopping now the rush of words that he could do without.

"I think when you gave that money to Marta... and that's what it amounted to... it was the nicest, the most decent thing I ever knew a man to do. Noble, that's the word that comes to mind." Gail finished her drink and pushed the glass to the edge. Garth caught Gloria's eye. He motioned for a refill and another beer. Still twenty minutes short of midnight. Enough to play out the comedy.

"The thing is, hon... and you've got to know this as well as I do... that little gesture sealed your fate. Mine, too, in a sense. You're strapped. Flat-ass busted from here on in. My kids aren't gonna scratch for bread crumbs." Gail stopped. She couldn't bear her own dishonesty.

"Cancel that last remark, Garth. That's a prize copout. I can't lay my feelings on the kids. It's me. I been too long dirt poor. No more. Not for you, not for any man. Not if I can help it, that is."

"You've got a good job, haven't you?"

Gail jeered. "Good? Yah, OK. I like my job. But if you think small town banks pay much more than minimum wage, you're nuts. Sure, I get a little more than the gals at the window. I make about one half the pay of the guy that reads the gas meter. If I take home eight bills it's a good month."

This was an education for Garth. He had never talked personal finances with Gail before. Department head... he had supposed she was making about fifteen grand.

"So... Kenseth and the two V.P.'s make the big money. Nothing for the slaves?"

She shrugged. "Sort of. The veeps don't make all that much. Philip does O.K. but, hell, look at the heat the man takes. Like from you and that James Moenke, for instance."

"Then why don't they ease up on the farmers?"

"Ease up?" Gail blazed. "Christ, Garth, you're even dumber than I thought. This bank is damn near belly up. Just because Kenseth's been too lenient. The parent corporation is on him all the time about the default mortgages. If people only knew. Even sensible fellows like George Rogers, putting out all that crap about Kenseth. I don't get it."

"Yeah? How would you feel in George's place... or Helen's?"

"Lousy. Just like them. But what can Philip do? He's gone the last mile. George and Helen owe eight hundred thousand. The farm and stock and equipment are worth five, maybe six. The arithmetic doesn't add up."

Garth was uneasy... the ratios were uncomfortably close to the Crawford situation. But the down playing of worth bothered him. He said, "I know George's spread. Worth a million, easy."

"That's farmer talk. The old love affair with the home place. Damn it, Garth, a spread is worth what it will bring on the open market. No more, no less." Gail brooded. "Here I am, talking shop about other folks' property. Not supposed to do that. Unethical."

"But all this crap going around... " Garth looked at her, fondly. He detested Kenseth but he admired loyalty.

"I've said too much, Garth." Gail bit her lip, her eyes, bright with drink, glistened. "Let the tail go with the hide. So I'll say this, too. Sure, when money was plentiful Kenseth and the other bankers pushed loan money to the farmers for expansion and improvements. But it was still the customer's decision. George Rogers, intelligent guy that he is, lived in a land of make believe where prices never stopped going up, where all investments doubled. Well, the bottom fell out... now the banker is the bastard that caused it all to happen."

"Um. What's the answer?"

"For me? Get out. There must be something better. For you? I don't know. Your forty thousand is down the drain. Stick it out and hope for better days I guess."

"And for Kenseth?"

In the dim light of the muni, Garth caught a faint blush in the oval cheeks opposite him. But Gail faced the question squarely.

"I think, I'm not sure, that Philip is looking at an offer from the Twin Cities. Some of the big financial people up there like him. He has been through fire without cracking. They like that in a man."

"He leaves, you going with him?"

"Possibly. He could use an assistant."

"I didn't mean that."

"I know what you mean." Gail turned her drink, her fingers white on the glass. "Hell, Garth, I don't know for sure. I'm leveling with you, hon." The endearment was as natural as rain. "I like you better than any man I know. We have fun, my kids like you. But I won't go on forever like we have. It's not fair to you. I won't be a farmer's wife, hell, not even in good times. For sure, not in these times. The women get wasted, most of them are bitter and worn out."

In the long, lonely moments of the night, with the hands of the Miller Lite clock passing midnight, the honest woman had spelled it out for her friend. The unspoken messages of the past months, the innuendoes and excuses were all explained. Garth knew a sudden emptiness, a pain as wrenching as the nails that had nearly finished him. He had bounced back from the trauma of the twister because he was a physical, confident, sardonic creature, flame-hardened by the blast furnaces. This blow might be more difficult. He grinned, wryly.

"First time I ever got turned down by a woman before I even got around to asking," he said.

"Garth, I'm leveling." Gail's voice was a hoarse whisper. "I like you, hon. I suppose I love you, whatever that means."

"Thanks for that."

She might not have heard him. "But we can't make it. Money doesn't wreck families, it's the lack of money, the financial ruin that does them in."

"I could show you dozens of couples that refute that."

"I suppose. But I can't get into that kind of situation. We'd end up hating each other."

"I couldn't hate you, baby."

"That's what you say now." She was struck with a perception, keen as a razor. "You're not far from hating me right now."

"No." Garth was honest in his own right. "Not you, Gail. Never. Philip Kenseth perhaps."

"But why? If we're not going to make it, what's the difference? Kenseth, Joe Palooka, all the same."

"Joe Palooka is a stranger. Kenseth holds my sister's mortgage... among others. Growers State owns George Rogers' farm."

"We're back to that. Full circle." Gail stabbed her cigarette in the plastic ash tray. "God! I hate this garbage talk. From you. You're too much man for that, Garth."

"Naw. Not me, kid. No man really has the balls when things are coming down."

"Look at it this way, I'm giving you an out."

Garth raised his glass of beer in salute. "Hell, you put it that way... " The white teeth flashed in the lean face.

"I'm so god damned fond of you, you goofy hayseed. But... " Now Gail was struggling visibly, she viewed with distaste the fragments of her present existence. "I'm going downhill, Garth. I've got to get on with my life. You don't know what a woman in my situation has to battle, what the odds are. I'm like the farmers, in a war."

"Yeah, sure. And I do understand." Garth glanced at the Miller clock. "Let's go."

"OK." In a sudden impulse, she leaned across the booth and touched her mouth to his, her eyes glistening in the dim light of the muni lounge. On the jukebox Kenny wailed, hoarsely, of gambles lost.

CHAPTER TWENTY-ONE

Two days before the scheduled auction sale, George Rogers drove his pickup to Shawndo. He and Helen had been granted thirty days grace, beyond the sale date for the house, an indefinite period beyond that if they decided to rent the house. This, of course, if a renter for the farm was not found who demanded the building site and house as well. George Rogers knew the farm would not likely be sold to an operating farmer. None were left with the credit needed to save Growers State from taking a huge bath on the mortgage. George and Helen would likely remain, as long as they could manage, in a house whose walls and roof and rooms belonged to others.

Helen Rogers grieved at the deterioration, as she would have mourned a landscape destroyed. A tree had been felled, she knew... the forest could never be the same again. Her quiet presence and encouragement were all she could offer. But the restlessness and sleeplessness – George roamed the house each night until daybreak, then slept in tossed mutterings – she could not manage. Her husband had a tough time to get through. Still, some signs were encouraging. George had contacted old friends at the state capitol for a possible post in the Ag Department. He reported to Helen that the reception was warm. Prospects for a position could firm up within weeks, perhaps a regional post, more likely a move to St. Paul.

At nine A.M. he drove to town. He entered the Crystal Cafe, a reflex. There was no other place to go.

"Hi George."

"Morning, Jenny," said George Rogers. He hobbled to one of the square tables and pulled out the chair.

"Hey, what is this? What's with the leg?"

"Nothing much, Jen. Fell down in the barn this morning. Twisted my right leg. She's froze right up, at the knee. Stiffer'n a board." He turned sideways and slid onto the chair, then swung the right leg out of the way. "Coffee and a cinnamon roll, Jen."

"I'm way ahead of you." Jenny placed the roll and steaming coffee before him. The cafe was nearly deserted. Most of the early morning crowd had left. The coffee break people from the bank and the few stores had not yet appeared. Warm sunshine bathed a section of the bare floor. An occasional fly, disdaining the spiraling rolls of fly paper, buzzed against the front window. Jenny sprayed the entire place each night at closing. But, like the farmers, there were always survivors.

Jenny had a motherly streak. She was fond of George.

"You better get to Prairie and have Doc Hawkins look at that leg.

Maybe you got a busted knee cap."

"No," George laughed. "It's nothing. Just a strain. I've had this happen to me before."

Jenny crouched by the table. "Here, let me have a look at it. I got some rubbing alcohol in the kitchen that might help." She reached for his trouser leg.

"No!"

George's voice was, uncharacteristically, sharp. He pushed her hands away, thrusting the stiff leg beneath the table, boot clattering on the floor.

Jenny rose, red faced.

"Whoa... hey, sorry, George. I wasn't gonna glom onto you." The woman was embarrassed. One of the men, seated at another table, laughed. "Just wanted to help," she said, lamely.

George Rogers sat erect. He had a strange regal posture and the stiff leg stretched, ignominiously, beneath the wooden table. He forced a wintry smile.

"Jen... it's OK. Please." He looked at her, earnestly. "You misunderstand. I fell down in the beef barn, the pants leg got a little smeared. That's all."

She grinned. "Well, I touched that stuff before, too. Never killed me."

The tension was broken. The men at the other table resumed their conversation. George Rogers drank his hot black coffee. He didn't touch the roll. His eyes swept around the old cafe. He might have been seeing it for the first time. The six booths along the wall, the tables and chairs, worn and comfortable and the round stools at the counter. This was the hearthstone of the town. He had spent hundreds of pleasant hours here, visiting, kidding, with friends and neighbors. He had, in fact, spent one whole night here while blizzard gales swept the prairie, in February, the night that Marta had battled the sudden storm to reach her farmstead.

George Rogers sat in reverie. Past times, familiar faces crowded around him. He heard the coarse jokes, the randy laughter, he could smell the odors of good food... warm food that stuck to the ribs, that sent a man back to the barns or fields refreshed. Women's voices, too, the sweet and musical lilts that had blessed his days... all the sounds of the farm women and the working women of the town and the school were blended into the warm walls. He thought of many of the folks he had known, all fine people, and was glad that none of his favorites... Mike and Marta, Oscar Thornstad, Phil Johnson, Garth Kyllo... all these and scores more, none of them were here today. Why have I thought of Mike, he wondered. Mike is long dead, because he thought his farm was lost. I felt such sorrow for the man.

Now, my farm is lost, for certain. I was a young man in this town and then a middle aged, white-haired farmer, well thought of, comfortable... reasonably happy. Now, it seems a mere instant, an old man, worn, defeated, turned out like a beggar by guys who've never planted a crop, never tended a sick animal. George Rogers drank his coffee, refilled by Jenny, and thought of the people he had known, the events leading up to today. The stiff leg rested on the floor beneath the wooden table. And he thought, too, of the lies he'd told to Helen. Had she believed his hearty assertions of jobs crying for his experience at the state level? She had demonstrated belief... bright optimism for a new and exciting dimension in their lives.

"Tough row, George." Jenny poured him a second refill. First refill was free, second one a quarter. But she brushed aside the coin. She added, "Just remember, you've got a lot of friends. We're all behind you." Jenny Peters had some difficulty with her voice. She cleared her throat, noisily.

"Yes," George roused from his reverie. "Thanks, Jen. I'm fine, no sweat. Got some great prospects. Coffee's good today. Got a new supplier?"

"Naw. It's August. Every year, about this time, I clean out the pot." She hooted. George smiled, warmly, Jenny was a true original.

He finished his third cup, then got up, awkwardly, and hobbled out of the Crystal, raising a hand in half salute to Jenny as he left. He walked out, blinking into the brilliant sunshine of mid-morning. He waved at a friend pumping gas at the Co-op station on the corner. Two girls walked by, children of eight or nine, daughters of folks he knew in town. He smiled at them and said hello.

The girls, deep in private secrets, said Hi, Mr. Rogers, how's your TV show? They giggled and went on down the sidewalk. Not much of a sidewalk, George Rogers thought. Heaving sections, broken curb... the towns go sour, along with the farms. Even bigger places, like Prairie, creaking and crumbling. Beyond the railroad tracks the Farmers Elevator was quiet, he could see one pickup loading sacks of feed and salt. Elevators are funny, he mused. Right now, sleepy and peaceful. I've seen the time, October, November, the trucks and wagon loads of beans and corn lined up for half a mile, waiting their turn to unload. Rogers had a few hundred shares of elevator stock, worth, at best, a penny on the dollar. The humor of the farm belt was always the same. You run out of toilet paper, no big deal, you always have your Farmers Elevator stock. George Rogers moved, nursing the stiff leg, along the sidewalk and entered the front door of the Growers State Bank. He walked across the carpeted floor of the lobby. Gail Samarro, busy with a customer, smiled at him.

"Hi, Gail. Had too much coffee at Jen's. Gotta use your facilities."

He managed a grin.

"Yeah, sure." Gail waved a red nailed hand, lazily, to her left. "You know where it is." George nodded and made his way to the men's room. He entered and locked the door behind him.

Next, he unzipped the front of his denim coveralls, reached inside and grasped the twelve gauge shotgun. The double barrel of the gun was inside the denim of his right leg, the muzzle nearly to the ankle. The butt rested in the pit of his right arm. George Rogers extracted the weapon and adjusted his clothing. Then he walked to the sink and washed his face and hands. The image in the mirror was that of a man he had known long ago, white hair groomed and perfect above the lined face. He tapped the dispenser several times for soap – an obsession was upon him for cleanliness – and carefully wiped his hands and face with the white paper towels. He combed and re-combed the white hair. Next, he took two shells from his left coverall pocket and inserted one in each barrel, cocking one side only.

He unlocked the lavatory door and walked, briskly, out to the lobby, crossing to the office he knew so well, the shotgun cradled in his right arm.

Gail Samarro looked up as he pushed Kenseth's door open. She tried to cry out, a word, a scream... the sounds were silent in her throat. She willed her right foot to touch the silent alarm.

George Rogers pushed open the door with the barrel. He fired once at the blue suited figure by the desk. He cocked the second barrel and fired again and the staggered figure crumpled to the carpet, hands clutching a sea of red against the blue vest. George Rogers turned and, glancing at no one, walked, without haste, out of the front door as Gail, recovering sooner than the others, dialed 911 for an ambulance. Then she forced herself to enter, with the others, the silent office.

George Rogers walked to his pickup and climbed in behind the wheel, placing the empty shotgun on the seat beside him. He fastened the seat belt, started the engine and drove out of town, heading north along the same crushed rock road that snow had obliterated from human eyes in February.

He drove carefully, without haste. George Rogers, the calm and thoughtful man, the law-abiding citizen had never been stopped for a traffic violation. He considered hurry a waste on any project. Now, in the warm sunshine of the humid August day the discipline of a lifetime encased him and the speedometer stood at a steady forty-five.

One mile north of Shawndo, he drove for the last time past the intersection that, like the touch of a switch, flicked his mind with pain. The crossroads where Becky, on her bike, blindsided by tall

133

corn, had been struck by the pickup of a drunken kid, whipping past the stop sign, careening on down the road, neither knowing or caring about the broken body lying in the shallow ditch. Years had eased the sorrow somewhat. Now the memory seared him, mingled with the knowledge that he had put off too long his visit, and Helen's, to that black slab of honor where the names of the Vietnam warriors stood in final parade. The radio spoke, in dry figures, of the livestock prices for the day from South St. Paul and the other markets. Cattle lower, hogs steady... sheep slightly higher. The numbers were familiar, he listened attentively to quotations meaningless to his existence.

In minutes he approached the farm. On a slight rise, thirty rods from the building site, George Rogers stopped the pickup. His eyes searched the farmstead for a sight of Helen. He had hoped she might be in the garden, picking sweet corn or digging out early potatoes. But all was still, only a few Black Angus beef cows stood in the shadow of the barn, cattle he no longer owned. They had wandered back to the barn yard from the pasture. The black tails switched languidly. Flies were always a problem in late summer. He glanced at the rear view mirror outside the pickup door and the road behind him lay white and deserted.

George Rogers climbed out of the truck. He reached back inside and brought out the shotgun. Then he crossed the shallow ditch and stepped through the barbed wire fence, spreading the wires with that easy motion of old farmers who never snag a piece of clothing as they slip between the strands. He had placed the gun beneath the bottom wire. Now he picked it up, brushed off shards of grass and reloaded both barrels.

Will the corn make it this year, he wondered? Each year a struggle, first to grow a decent crop, then to get it ripe... fit for storage or feeding. The blistering drought of early summer had set back the crop. Ninety bushels per acre, he figured. He had hoped for at least one-thirty in the green days of spring when the world was young. He turned back the green husks on several ears. He was satisfied with the stage of maturity but the ears were not well filled, the grain would be a bit chaffy. One mile down the rock road, in the direction of Shawndo, a maroon and white car appeared and dancing red lights on the roof sparkled, revolving in the sunshine. They made good time, he thought. I wonder if it was Gail that sent the warning. Gail... lovely, laughing, full of spunk. They were all fine people, all save the dead Kenseth... a man without mercy or humanity, a man who had never plowed a furrow. Now he was gone, one more message delivered, one more testament that those who live on the land will not retreat. He thought of Harvest and, with the mind of a stranger, of George Rogers and his homilies of peace. There is too much forgiveness to seek, now. There's no time. The whirling bubble was a quarter mile away and the wail of the siren, the world's loneliest sound, penetrated the silence of the field of corn. A small flock of black birds, ravishers of the ripening corn, swirled from the field and circled, then settled down in a large elm tree near the pasture lane.

The birds were a minor nuisance on the prairie. Only in the bottom lands, near streams, did they do much harm. George Rogers smiled at the birds in their nighttime residence. He placed his right forefinger on the trigger of the cocked gun and rested the muzzle against his forehead. He could barely stretch his arm the distance. The sheriff's car screeched to a halt on the rock road as he pulled the trigger. The right side of his head was sheared in a red haze as the white haired man fell to the ground. In the elm tree the black birds stirred and a few of them fluttered into flight.

The right eye was smeared with blood but he felt no pain. Only a disgust near to loathing. He muttered aloud. "I screwed up my whole life. Now I can't even kill myself... the ultimate worthlessness." He knew, in the instant, that the screech of the tires on the roadway had startled him. He had flinched at the final moment. Now the deputies were out of the car, crouched, guns drawn, approaching the barbed wire fence. "Too late, guys," he whispered. "I still have the other chamber."

George Rogers pulled a shirt sleeve across his bloodied eye. He pushed himself to a crouching position on his hands and knees while fresh blood blotted his sight and dropped in rivulets upon the grass. The world before him reeled in the sunshine and the air, next to the standing corn, was still.

He cocked the hammer on the second barrel. Then he placed the muzzle to his head once more. This time he moved the metal to the front, near the center of his forehead. He pulled the trigger and the world dissolved. The deputies dropped on their bellies in the ditch, heads down, and the black birds stirred once more in the big elm.

Two more maroon and white cruisers, the back-up force, pulled in behind the first car. The deputies conferred together, briefly. They knew the moment for swift action had forever passed, the farmer had breached all boundaries of pain. One of the deputies found a wire cutter in his vehicle. They snipped the barbed wire strands, a gesture of respect to a body they did not wish to snag between the strands or hoist over the top wire.

They waited for the next phase, the arrival of the investigators and the photographer... the moment, the place, the ballistics must be recorded. The men had no need to ascertain death in a figure blasted beyond all recognition. Sheriff Adams drove down to the house to speak to Helen. She was standing in the front yard. Helen had heard the shots, she had followed the turmoil and the arrival of the back-up vehicles. The silent testimony of the abandoned pickup, door standing open on the drivers side, had told her all she needed to know. Like Marta, she had sensed, deep inside, the truth for a long time. She stood, dry eyed, a plastic bucket over one arm, her hands encased in canvas gloves. Death, on the farm prairie, was no longer a surprise, only a confirmation.

After Adams had left, Helen walked to the garden. She watched the proceedings, the busy workaday world of the lawmen, competent, professional as they removed the limp form. "And they shall bear him up on golden shields"... how did it go?... she could not remember. There were no shields, no flashing armor or coats of mail. The court held only jesters, grim faced men, sweating in the hot sun in the breathless stillness beside the tall green corn. Field corn, the very best in hybrids for Black Angus cows and young stock, blooded stock, prize winners at the Fair. Sweet corn was another matter. Helen picked just two ears, more than enough for the noon meal, alone. Gently, she placed them in the plastic bucket, careful not to bruise them.

By mid afternoon, the gaunt body with the shattered head lay in the Hanson Funeral Home in Prairie City. No autopsy was required. Nor was there more than an official notice of death on the second still form in the same room... Death by Homicide.

The face of Gerald Ryan was as calm and expressionless in death as in life. The vice president, victim of a mindless fate, had entered the empty office of the president to check some papers he had left on Kenseth's desk. Intent as ever on the business at hand, he had never seen the twin barrels of extermination or the white haired man who stood, for one brief moment, in the doorway.

The auction sale was postponed one week. The auctioneer, Colonel Hap McCarthy, was livid. His vacation schedule was knocked, he and four cronies had planned ten days in the Canadian wilds, dragging the big lake trout into the boat. Now, he had to change the fly-in date. Always something to screw up the deal. But business was business, he had agreed to cry the Rogers sale, one of the biggest of the season in Black Loam County.

CHAPTER TWENTY-TWO

The men were buried on the same day, in plots of ground less than a mile apart. While a cruel sun beat down on the flat prairie, the body of George Rogers was interred in a solemn ceremony before midday. And Gerald Ryan, a quiet, introverted man who had tried all his life to help others, was laid to rest in the afternoon. A Methodist minister performed the service for the farmer. A Catholic priest from the tiny country parish of St. Andrew spoke the message of comfort for friends and family of the banker. Many people attended both ceremonies because they had known and liked both men.

The town of Shawndo was stunned to its depths. The hot sun of August beat on the broken sidewalks and the lawns were, once again, brown and sparse. Two thousand people, more than double the assemblage of the February ceremony for Mike Crawford, milled through the streets around the Methodist block. The old church held only a few hundred. A loudspeaker system, tinny and vibrating, carried the words of the minister and other speakers. The crowd was silent, not even a child whimpered as though they knew, felt inwardly, the solemnity of the occasion.

Marta was among the eulogists. She spoke briefly, without anger or passion, of a friend she loved and would miss. Others... it was inevitable... railed a bit at circumstances that had brought to pass this tragic ending. Oscar Thornstad had been asked to speak. He refused. "A solid man, George," he muttered. "I won't insult the man with the kind of empty words I could manage." Marta suspected the old man did not trust himself to speak of peace and forgiveness. The black, bitter harvest of the eighties was becoming too much to bear. Philip Kenseth attended both services. He was alone, his estranged wife with a different group. Kenseth faced the hostility of the crowd with seeming indifference, his face white and chiseled. Marta sensed... she could not be certain... that some protection was being afforded the bank president. There were certain hard eyed young men about, strangers to Marta but they might well have been distant relatives or other banking people.

Around noon, after the Rogers funeral and before the Ryan service, Harvest attempted to provide a lunch at the Legion Hall. The food ran out before half the people were fed. All businesses in town were closed for the day, but Jenny was persuaded to open the Crystal and do what she could to help provide an alternative. Additional help was pressed into service, the old cafe bulged with the pressure of sweating bodies. Many food tabs were uncollected, the press of people and the confusion too great.

With the passing of a friend and a broken romance behind him, Garth decided morosely, that it would be a good time to get drunk. Jim Moenke seemed of the same persuasion and, like a runaway tank, proceeded to accomplish the task. But Garth changed his mind. After three beers the enormity of the occasion, the death of hope and promise, encompassed him in a way he had never known, not even in the hospital with the sharp teeth of the rat a scorching memory. "I'm knocking off," he muttered to Marta. "I couldn't get smashed if I put away a keg." He brooded. "Just doesn't seem right."

Marta squeezed his hand and said nothing. Since her brave words in the church, a Herculean effort, she had been unable to manage her voice. She kept busy, knowing that continuous action was the only hope of getting through the day.

Media attention on the separate funerals was intense. Editorials had commented, some sensibly, others shrilly, on the events leading up to and culminating with the murder-suicide. Who was really guilty in this mad confrontation?... so ran much of the conjecture in print and on the air. Which man was perpetrator, which one victim? Or was there a way, an infallible way, to choose? Marta knew the answer. Both were victims, as were all the others who had gathered, for this one day, in the town of Shawndo. Garth, his attention pointed in new directions, helped post the notices... a meeting of Harvest at eight the following evening, in the school cafeteria.

"Without George we'll flounder, like a beached whale," Marta said. Garth agreed. But they could not let too much time elapse. With the county chairman dead and buried the local chapter was wounded. The will, the commitment could well fade in the cruel heat, the discontent of late summer. Once vanished, could the drive be resurrected? And who could possibly replace George Rogers? "There are a lot of good men." Marta spoke bravely, but she wasn't that sure. The most informed and respected person, by far, in the local organization, now, was Oscar Thornstad. Marta couldn't say the words, they stuck at her like daggers. Too old, by many years too old. And Oscar would be the first to agree. There must be younger blood in the leadership, brains, savvy, a mind unencumbered with the bitterness, the bile of passing years, too many defeats.

That night Marta and Garth milked the cows and tended the chores in a vacuum of silence. Both retired early but sleep was elusive. Marta stared at the ceiling in her room and slept fitfully, her dreams riddled by the ghosts of those she had known and loved. The dreams were violent, fragmented... the days are filled with violence, she thought. We've sought the peaceful solutions to our dilemma. We've marched, in peace, to the capitals of our state and nation. We've picketed in peace and lobbied the politicians in the most respectful manner. Nothing matters, nothing helps. There must be some glitch in our leadership, some elusive ingredient is missing in our approach to a nation that turns in boredom from our problems. Why can't we break through? Is Harvest a bad joke, irrelevant to agriculture and the problems of hunger and malnutrition in the world? We farm, we raise the livestock, produce the milk and eggs. We do all these things better than any group of agrarians in history. Still, we go busted. And now, violence. I always knew it was coming. I just never dreamed the catalyst would be a treasure like George. Beads of sweat were on Marta's forehead, her pulse was a racing beat. I'll be a candidate for a coronary, she groused. Marta, the solid rock, they call me. Sweet Christ, I'm a bundle of nerves, charged up like a Die-Hard Battery.

Garth, in his room, smoked and pulled at a can of beer while an FM station brought him the wailing melodies of Willie Nelson and the other country artists who sang of tough jobs, sweet women and long dusty roads. Garth saw the continuing struggle in elemental terms. Them against us. And, for now, we're taking a real shit kicking. Wars are lost as well as won, an idea hard for Americans to accept. But this one we're sure as hell losing. Jim Moenke and I have tried, in our way, to turn things around. We make as much difference as a fart in a whirlwind. Farmers are like most folks in the world. They see, and feel, their own special plight. The big picture eludes them. But I've cast my line in this stream. With all the problems, the heartaches, I'd never go back to the mills. Garth's thoughts turned to his daughters. Wonderful girls, well, women really. I can't sleep tonight, I'll drop a line to each.

He crossed to the small bedroom desk and got out the tablet. Then he went downstairs, as noiselessly as possible, for a fresh Bud, the last one in the refrigerator. Things go better with Bud, he grinned, I need help to write a decent letter. But I should cut down on the brew. Since I hit the wall with Gail the drinking has crept up. I'm an undisciplined son of a bitch but, for sure, I'll never end up on that dead-end street.

So went the meandering thoughts of Garth Kyllo in the dead hours past midnight as the laconic man sought, in his own way, to stifle the torments of his heart. A good friend buried, a sweetheart lost. Tough times. He knew the loneliness of the crap shooter when snake eyes stare back from every roll of the dice. Garth finished the letters and the room, tucked under the eaves, was suddenly too hot to bear. He grabbed a sheet and pillow and went down the stairs again. He opened the front and back doors and stretched out on the sofa. In the comparative coolness of the living room he managed three hours of troubled sleep before the alarm clock sounded. The brother and sister had set their workday beginning each day for five-fifteen. With twenty-nine cows and lacking the convenience of a milking parlor an early start was essential.

At seven-thirty that evening Garth and Marta drove to the Shawndo school building. Marta was pleased to see a large turnout... it looked to be the best attended meeting in months. There was a certain hiatus of labor on the farm in this season. Most of the haying was finished, the cutting of silage corn still weeks ahead. Oscar Thornstad, hunched and shuffling, greeted them at the door. He greeted Garth with a smile and handshake, then drew Marta aside on the school yard grass.

"You got a choice, Marty. Cut and run, right now, or dance for the fiddler."

Marta grinned. "I got a lot of choices, you old coot. And one of them is not to talk riddles with you."

The jibe failed to bring the expected chuckle.

"Hell, Marty, I ever steer you wrong?"

"Naw. Not on purpose anyway."

"Well, hell, Marty. I ain't above being wrong. But not this time."

The old man was so serious, Marta had to laugh. She asked, "Why don't you tell me what you're talking about, Oscar?" She touched his arm. "I can't play games if I don't know the rules."

Oscar sent a large brown jet into the school yard grass, near the sidewalk. He leaned closer.

"They fixin' to run you, Marty."

Now he laughed, heartily. The old man, for truth, usually knew what he was talking about. But this was crazy.

"What you been smoking, Oscar? That stuff is for the kids, not us old folks."

Oscar wiped his mouth. The red flannel shirt sleeve, stained with long use, dried the brown moisture.

"Suit yourself, Marty. Just being a friend."

Together, they walked into the meeting. Marta was struck by the lack of animated conversation, the buzzing of small groups discussing the latest in farm movements. A strange quiet hung over the cafeteria, the members moved almost silently as they took their seats. The chapter vice-chairman, Don Kliest, called the meeting to order. The secretary, Mrs. Madsen, read the minutes of the last meeting. The treasurer's report, a sad commentary that brought chuckles, followed. The chapter was nearly broke, fund raising efforts must be resumed. The treasurer, a serious farmer, Bob Jasper, offered, with little hope, suggestions. A barbecue picnic, open to the public (would someone donate a hog?). A raffle, garage sales? We need operating capital, he said. Give this some thought, maybe we can reach a decision later in the meeting.

So went the preliminaries. Oscar Thornstad proved, not for the first time, to be right on target. Nominations were opened for a new county chair to replace George Rogers. At this point a minute of silence was evoked for the memory of the deceased man. Marta, who had not cried at the funeral, could not see. Tears welled and ran down her cheeks. She felt the loss more keenly than at any moment until now.

Marta was nominated for county chairperson. A dozen seconds filled the room. A husky farmer... Marta could not make out the face, the tears were still blinding... proposed that nominations be closed. A chorus of approval rocked the room, there were no dissents. In sixty seconds the coup was over. Marta never really knew what happened, her mind and heart were on the fallen leader. Oscar Thornstad grinned. He had left his chew in the yard outside. Now he reached for the round box, tapped the lid, took a sizable wad of the moist tobacco and punched it into his lower jaw.

Garth was flabbergasted. He and Marta had never even discussed such a possibility. He shook his head in wonder.

Jim Moenke punched his arm. "Hey, nice goin', pal." The man wore a smile from ear to ear. "What a choice. Your sister's a great gal." Jim was, blissfully, unaware that Marta considered him a jerk. "Bet you're surprised as hell."

"Knew it all the time," said Garth.

CHAPTER TWENTY-THREE

The searing heat had returned to Black Loam County and all the farm belt. Milk cows sought the shade of trees. Clothes hung in limp compliance on the line and the handful of windmills in the area... spires of remembrance, steel towers from a simpler past... were stilled. With no breeze and a temperature of ninety-four F, the shimmering waves were dancing above the flat fields.

Oscar Thornstad felt nauseous in the driver's seat of the old Cad, his foot heavy on the pedal as he wove his way along the crushed rock road toward the Rogers farm. I'm getting too old for this shit, he thought. A day like this, fry the balls off a Holstein bull. And I ain't eating right, lately. Got to slow down on the fried pork and the gravy biscuits. Jenny better put in a salad bar to shape me up. He jerked the wheel, violently, as an errant woodchuck lumbered out of the ditch. Oscar righted the car, cussing the empty air.

"Christ," he muttered. "Damn near hit the ditch, just to miss that little bugger. Useless little son of a bitch." The hint of a smile was on his lips, rimmed with the damp brown of snoose. "I know all about useless. That's me. I've got something in common with that fat little sucker. The fat and the slow and the unprotected of this world better stick together." The old car, rusted to the door hinges, went over a slight rise. Oscar stopped the car, near the spot where the strands of barbed wire had been cut by the deputies. The wires had been spliced back together. Spread before the old man was the panorama of the approaching auction. Rows of machinery, stacks of tools and small equipment and the black cattle, corralled in the barn yard, rumps showing the paper stickers of their numbers. Cars were lined on each side of the driveway and scattered throughout the yard. Nearly an hour to sale time and the deputies flanked the maroon and white vehicle of the county sheriff. Oscar no longer spoke to Bill Adams. There had been no communication between the two men since the day of the big ditch across the Pete Johnson driveway.

Oscar Thornstad was not a man without compassion. A thousand instances in his life testified to his great humanity. And he felt, deeply, the tragedy of Betty Adams' troubles. He knew... or thought he knew, the conventional wisdom... that Mrs. Adams had gone away for just one reason, to get dried out. But the unbending attitude of the sheriff, the steely-eyed, unsmiling face, the right hand so often in the area of the gun butt... Oscar had become... unknowingly, a victim of mannerisms more than morality. The old man had never asked himself, honestly... as Marta had asked herself... what he would do if he were sheriff in Bill Adams' shoes. In despising the ebb and flow of events which had brought the farmers to the precipice he despised the man with the badge, sworn enemy of riot and anarchy. Oscar left the Cad parked on the high ground. He didn't want to be pinned in by other vehicles if he decided to leave early. He had the walking stick in the seat beside him.

Oscar got out of the car. He took the stick, a stout blackthorn, a gift long ago from a son when Oscar had been laid up by a kicking horse. Now, in later years, he often dragged the black stick out of the closet when he knew there might be some distance to walk. He had thirty rods to walk to the farm yard, so the walking stick was a blessing. Before starting he spat out the remnants of his morning chew and, after the ceremonial tap of the box lid, scooped a generous wad of Copenhagen into his lower jaw. He chewed, reflectively, gazing with watering eyes at the gathering crowd in the farmstead area. The auctioneer had not yet arrived.

A fleck of color caught his eyes, beyond the repaired fence. Deep red, near to black, color on the grass, not yet overgrown, where George Rogers had spilled his life's blood The area had been cleaned up... the one spot of matted grass, tinged with the testimony of a man who had fought his final battle, cried out to Oscar. Here George Rogers, a man who had fought, his mind a spiraling montage of small victories and one last defeat, had gone down. The old man, stick in hand, hobbled across the shallow ditch and leaned against the wires. He could see the blooded spot more clearly now, he noted the half dozen ears of corn with husks peeled back, the measurement of grain maturity against the seasons. Oscar sobbed, his pale eyes were wet. He had not wept in forty years, not since the boy with the twisted leg and thin, wrenched body had slept quietly away. Oscar tested the wire strands with a practiced hand. Someone had mended the fence well, there would be no stray cattle in the corn field that belonged, now, to Growers State. The corn stalks stood straight, free of weeds, the field of a master farmer. There had never been in Black Loam County, to Oscar's knowledge, a better farmer than George Rogers. Now, his machinery oiled, well kept, was about to go on the block and the squat black cattle would provide breeding stock for other cattlemen, for new herds of beef.

Oscar glanced down the rock road. The pickup truck with the auctioneer's platform hooked to the hitch was in sight. He left the fence and worked his way down the road, the blackthorn stick a welcome aid. He thought, George Rogers chose a nice day to make his statement, this ain't too bad a day, either. People tend to cuss hot weather but, in August, we need solid heat to get the corn ripe.

Thornstad gained the center of the driveway. He barely acknowledged the greetings. He turned and faced the approaching pickup of Hap McCarthy's. The pickup ground to a halt, stopping just short of the old man. The horn honked, a bare flip of sound, the driver understanding the confusion of a man over eighty years of age standing in the hot sun. Oscar rapped the hood with the blackthorn. The heavy stick rang out, a metallic clang, cutting through the babble of voices all around. A slight dent showed on the surface of the hood and the air was suddenly still. This is interesting, thought Garth Kyllo. He watched the old man closely. Marta approached and gently took Oscar's arm. He shook her off, glared fiercely at his friend, then swung the blackthorn again. Marta backed off. Bill Adams and a deputy closed in. Two more official cars had arrived on the scene.

"Come on, buddy." The sheriff spoke quietly. "Let's just step out of the way here." The men had been friends since Adams was in high school. Now the old man whirled upon him, they were like strangers.

"Don't lay your hands on me, you stinking Judas." Oscar's gravely voice was thick with rage. "I ain't letting that blood sucker McCarthy into this yard. You can go to hell."

A small problem. Obviously the sun, the heat, the turmoil had gotten to the old man. But, somewhat ominously, the crowd began to back Oscar. They murmured encouragement to his stand. All but Marta. She stood silently, grieving for one more aberration, the crumbling of a Gibraltar, pebble by pebble. She had seen this coming, the rumblings had been low but distinct. Marta moved into the area. She slipped past the others and touched Oscar's arm again.

"You're right, Oscar," she said. "The sale's a travesty. McCarthy needs his vacation money."

"The son of a bitch would cry a sale for his crippled grand-mother," Oscar snorted. He staggered and Marta and the deputy steadied him. Adams had dropped back a step, deferring to Marta's experience.

"He would certainly do that," she said. "And never bat an eye. But we can't keep him out." Marta turned to the sheriff, her eyes imploring him for time. Adams nodded. "Listen Oscar," Marta said, "The members are here in force today. Things might go fairly well."

"Yah. A cakewalk." His voice had a funeral tone. Marta had never heard or witnessed more sorrow... a devastation beyond hope. "Same shit as always," Oscar mumbled. "And all of it too late for George." Unexpectedly, the old man turned away. With Marta on one side, the deputy on the other, they moved off to one side of the pickup.

Adams nodded to the driver. The pickup shifted into gear and eased ahead and the farmers were parted to each side of the drive-way. It was nearing time for the sale to begin, the auction sale of the personal property of George Rogers, deceased, and Helen Rogers. The crowd had thickened now, more than two hundred cars were strung along the driveway and on both sides of the township road. Some farmers, further back along the drive or making solemn judgments on the merchandise to be offered later, paid no attention to the antics of the old man and the people restraining him. All auction sales are a hubbub of noise, action, constant movement, continual appraisal. When money is short a bad buy can become a small disaster. So perhaps fifty people were witness to the subjugation of the ancient protester.

Then it happened. Later, some would say, with great swiftness. Others would hold that the action was so unexpected that all the onlookers, including Adams and the deputy, were frozen in a tableaux of time. They could not respond.

Oscar Thornstad wrenched free from the arms that supported him. He stepped back in front of the moving pickup. The blackthorn walking stick had been dropped, he faced the moving vehicle and both arms... once they had been oak trees... reached out, the big hands slammed into the hood. A road block, one man, one single human being against the tide. The driver shouted and his foot went to the brake pedal.

Too late. Oscar slipped to the crushed rock driveway. The right front wheel rolled over one arm and across his chest. The pickup stopped, then backed away.

The old man lay on his back and bubbles of blood mixed with the brown snoose around his mouth. Marta screamed, her voice a lonesome sound, as she rushed to kneel beside the still form. She cuddled the white head in her lap and, all around, determined action took form, maelstrom of voices, milling figures, above the prostrate form.

Bill Adams spoke quietly into his walkie-talkie. An ambulance was ordered from Prairie City. Harvest members would have no part of such a long wait. The accepted method of transportation sprang into reality once more. Garth plunged in to help. As a pickup bed was readied with hay and blankets he remembered his own rain swept journey, his life in the balance. Time is precious, each minute ticks off the chances. The battered, smashed body was lifted from the roadway, four men on each side moving carefully, and laid, with tenderness, upon the cushioned blankets for the trip to the hospital. Oscar's eyes were open, he made no sound. Marta used her handkerchief to wipe the blood from the mouth and nostrils. All this took hardly more than a minute. The farmers, no strangers to either accident or illness, moved like a team.

The pickup drove away. Marta and Garth were in the rear with Oscar. Ted Michals, a young Harvest member, was at the wheel and two deputy cars, lights flashing, accompanied them, one leading the way, the other following.

The auction, delayed by the driveway altercation, went on as scheduled. Harvest members played no part except to carefully refrain from running up the bids against each other. Many from the organization ranks left for their homes, the fatigue of utter discouragement showing in lined faces, slumped shoulders. Helen Rogers had expressed a desire not to be involved. So there was no victim to protect, no wrongs to right, no determination to restore another farmer to a position of operating base. Helen sat in the house, staring straight ahead, the tumult of auction might have been from another place, a distant time. Other women tried to visit with her. But Helen had reached, at last, a sheltered recess from reality. She had been, since the death of George, a marvel to all who knew her. Now, the drawing back. She spoke to the others, kindly. She did not really know when they entered the house or when they departed.

The pickup reached the Prairie City hospital without incident. Marta stayed on for the admission and to do whatever she could. Garth left for the farm after returning, briefly, to the auction site to pick up his station wagon. He spoke to no one. He wanted to scream to all the people gathered there to trash the sales goods, to burn, to destroy, to send the Black Angus cattle streaming down the road. Instead he drove home; he would have to do the evening chores alone.

The auction sale, desolate, without spirit or force, drew to an end. Cattle and machinery were loaded on the big trucks, the sales clerks tallied the receipts... a huge loss. More red ink, another setback for the absent owners of Growers State. Death and debits haunted the financial institutions of the midwest... the mortgages might as well have remained insolvent. Foreclosed, they were proving to be good money after bad. So thought a weary Sheriff Bill Adams. At eight in the evening he drove to his empty house. A lonely dinner, the night time news on television, one more attempt at ragged slumber.

Oscar, rallying, passed the point of danger. The old man had five broken ribs and a hairline fracture of the sternum. The right arm was bruised and discolored above the elbow, some of the muscles torn. But he managed a grin for Marta and a wink for the nurse. Oscar Thornstad faced a long period of idleness, a painful sentence for a man of action.

At seven-thirty Ted Michals drove Marta home in his Ford pickup. Ted was twenty-three, with one child and (praise God, he muttered) a slightly older school-teacher wife approaching tenure in the elementary school of Prairie City. "We're hanging in there, Mrs. Crawford", he said, politely. "Thin as tissue paper but without Pam's paycheck, no way."

146

Marta knew the truth of this. "Crops O.K., Ted?"

"Oh, sure. Hurt by the dry weather, some. But you know... two dollar corn. The market says different but time it's dried and shelled and graded, more like one-eighty."

Marta sighed. The words were a refrain beating against her brain. Only the voices changed, and this one so young.

Late that night the telephone rang at the Crawford house. Marta switched on the bedroom light and groped her way down the stairs. It was Bill Adams. But Marta couldn't recognize the whispery voice. She asked, sharply, "Who is this?" A long silence. Marta was about to hang up when the voice found itself.

"This is Bill. Bill Adams."

Now she heard him clearly. "Bill, what's up? It's the middle of the night." Bleary eyes sought the kitchen clock. "Past two."

"Is it? Oh, sorry. It's just... " Another long silence. Is the man drunk, she wondered. I've never heard of that happening. But how would I know?

Bill said, "You remember last February? You called me, with bad news... on Mike?"

"You think I could have forgotten?"

"No. Of course not. You had to call me... regulations, remember? And I wasn't much help."

"Bill!" This was ridiculous. "Go to bed. Sleep it off." Marta had short patience with drinkers, disturbers of healing sleep.

The sheriff's laugh sounded strange.

"Reason I called, Marty, is that, well, everything comes around. I'm kind of lost tonight." He paused, then added simply, "Betty is dead."

Oh God, thought Marta. And I as much as accused the man of being drunk. She could not speak.

"I called... because you were Betty's friend. And I was Mike's friend."

"Yes." Marta whispered the words. What little cost to lie. Had Betty been so lonely that a farm widow she hardly knew was counted as a friend? Perhaps. She remembered the thin, nervous woman who longed for acceptance she could never find. Now... I can't ask the cause of death. But the woman's last look will haunt me.

"Betty wasn't strong. She was in this Minneapolis hospital for treatment." He seemed to have forgotten their last conversation. "Anemia, you know. Then... like that, tonight, a heart attack."

In this crazy world of ours the truth is lost. Marta was thankful for the chivalry in Bill's lie. She hoped the cause was not what she had feared. She would never know... she would accept Bill's word.

"Are you leaving tonight?"

"No. I couldn't make it. First light of day. I couldn't stay on a highway tonight."

"That how I felt, Bill."

"I know. And I gave you hell. I've been ashamed ever since. Now, more than ever."

"Forget it. You were nice to me. We've crossed swords since but... but not for lack of friendship."

"Betty was devastated by all this. She couldn't handle it, Marty. God... she was lost and I was so god damn blind." The sheriff was a lost man himself, his were the words of despair, a wisdom that arrived too late. "This place. All the unhappiness got to her. She couldn't handle it."

"I know, Bill. She told me."

"She liked you, Marty." The man was rambling now, the voice was that of a wanderer. "Betty admired you. Said that Marta Crawford was a champion. She did, you know."

"Bill, get some sleep." She dreaded the next question but felt compelled to ask. "You bringing her... Betty... back?"

"Huh? No... no. Her home was there, her folks. Let her rest there... away from this."

"Perhaps for the best." She had to get out. "Goodnight, Bill. I'm sorry about all this. A tough time for you." She thought he was gone but the line was still open. The distraught man was not through. In a minute he spoke again.

"We were strangers, Marty. All my fault. I let what was happening here... this county... overpower me. All my time, all my thoughts. Tough it out, duty first, all that crap. I soldiered this... undeclared war. I left Betty out there... all alone. No wonder she... " Adams did not complete the thought.

"Don't punish yourself, Bill. Goodnight." Quietly she put down the phone. Her hand was shaking.

Sheriff William Adams was gone for several days. Deputy Allan Kendall took over in his absence. There were no forced auctions in this period, the dog days of August were upon Black Loam County.

On the fifth day, Bill Adams returned to Prairie City. The following day, a Tuesday, he attended the weekly session of the county commissioners at the court house. He asked for time and made a brief statement, resigning his position as sheriff of Black Loam County. The decision, he said, was irrevocable, he would not reconsider. He walked out of the meeting and left the building.

The commissioners, after some deliberation, appointed Deputy Kendall to the position of Acting Sheriff, pending the next election.

148

CHAPTER TWENTY-FOUR

A match is tossed, a campfire not extinguished... even the hot exhaust from a field tractor. Of such are prairie fires born. Some sweep the fields and ditches, threaten farmsteads, pushed by the winds, fed by drought, altering the landscape.

From one small deed in one small town, virtually a throwaway item on the national agenda, a new fire swept the farm belt. The fire was in the hearts of the people, the spark had been ignited, finally, by one lone action. Bill Adams took off his badge and tossed it on the commissioner's table. A single act, the force of the murder-suicide, the injury to Oscar had coalesced with his personal problems to seal the end of his tenure as sheriff of Black Loam County, one of the leading counties in the United States in farm foreclosure.

Harvest, old nemesis of the disposed lawman, applauded the action. Old scores were considered settled, old enmities forgotten. Bill Adams, comfortably fixed but far from affluent, had sacrificed income and position for a principle. Not true, exactly, but so viewed by most. Now, went the talk, Adams had been a fair man. Anecdotes were recalled of his generosity, his kindnesses, concerns for the unfortunate that had been overlooked in the past. The slit-eyed enforcer, hand on hip near the gun belt, had vanished. And a new hero demanded a new villain. Allan Kendall, the promoted deputy, was a man of rigidity, unbending in the application of paper justice. All this, of course, unfair to Kendall but fairness was a vanishing element in the sun baked days of late August.

Marta recovered swiftly from the shock of the Harvest meeting. In all modesty she could see the motivation behind her election. She had been active. She was capable of original ideas, fresh perspectives. George, with all his exceptional qualities, had been a figure of conservatism, a man not given to the innovation, much less the radicalism, that changing times might demand. Well, mused Marta, I'm not Ma Kettle much less the earth mother of the tribe. But they've trusted me with a portion of their future. I'll have to give it a fair shot. And the opportunity for a master stroke was at hand.

Prairie City, Minnesota became, within a week, the hot news center of the midwest. The stories multiplied, they built upon each other in a careening explosion of attention. A few members of the local media grabbed the story. Then the large metropolitan newspapers, the television and radio stations and even the networks could not resist the continuing drama. Bill Adams was besieged. Nothing in his stolid past had prepared him for a blizzard of attention he neither wanted or, he honestly felt, deserved. He had resigned out of depression, not for principle. The media would have none of that. A hero was necessary, as vital as the breath of life, in the exodus of the farm family. A sheriff, point man of law enforcement had informed county officials that he had endured enough. Best of all the man fit the mold, he might have been summoned from actor's equity, handed the uniform and gun.

In desperation Bill turned to Marta for advice. The farm widow was equal to the task. Twin tragedies had drawn their lives together and the bitter residue of past exchanges at the farm auctions faded. There was a common bond but much more was involved than the drawing together of victims. Marta sensed – she could not have expressed the thought exactly – that new options had appeared in the long struggle of the farm families. My God, she thought, I can't be callous, opportunistic at a time like this. I hope I'm not. But there may never be another such break-through – not until it's too late.

She drove to Bill Adams' house in Prairie. He had an interview with CBS., scheduled for broadcast on the evening news.

They talked over the kitchen table in Bill's white-shaked rambler. Even in town old ways die hard. The kitchen was, to Marta, the room for coffee and talk. The ex-sheriff was drawn and thin, the man has lost fifteen pounds since winter, thought Marta. Bill was racked with indecision.

"This is a whirlpool, Marty. I'm getting sucked in."

"Shit," she laughed. "Screw 'em. Just be yourself, Bill. You always were a charmer."

"Oh sure."

"I mean it. Don't let them lead you with trick questions. Just stick to the facts. That way you're sure of yourself. If they want to read more out of this situation than you give them, well, let them."

"Yeah. Easy to say. But I tend to freeze up when the little red light goes on."

"I wouldn't touch that remark with a pitchfork handle." A strange wisecrack to a bereaved man, she thought. But Marta knew, instinctively, she had to keep the man relaxed. He obliged with a small, tepid chuckle.

"It's just, I don't want to claim more character than I've got. I wish to hell I was a man of principle, that I'd resigned in protest to all this trouble."

"Perhaps you did... subconsciously."

"Maybe." Marta was troubled, watching the inner struggle. He doesn't give himself a chance, she thought.

"Oscar making it O.K.?"

"Oh hell," Marta laughed. "Is Mount Rushmore still standing? I saw him this morning. Garth will visit him tonight and the others have been keeping tab, too. Tough, my God! Five busted ribs and a cracked sternum. And damn near as much notoriety as you."

"How's Oscar handling that?"

"Like Oscar. Threw a water pitcher at one reporter, yesterday. Then he was nice as pie to one that came in later. Of course the second one was a woman."

"Makes a difference."

"For sure, with Mr. Thornstad. The nurses, though are asking for combat pay. So I hear."

They talked and planned for the latest and most important media intrusion. The main thing, here Marta was insistent, was the farm economy. The recent events in Black Loam County, tragic and heart wrenching happenings, were, each one, traceable to the one overpowering genesis, the plight of the family farm. Killings, suicides, enmities, all were relatively unknown in decades past. But the human spirit is not easily quenched. A rear guard action against the inevitable had taken these violent forms. And the future promised only more, not less, of the same.

"Think of your loss, and mine, in those terms, Bill. Think of Helen Rogers and the grandchildren, mine and so many others. Of Oscar Thornstad. Keep all of them in mind. You do and the right words will come. Automatically."

"I hope to God you're right."

Marta was vehement. "I know I'm right. First meeting of Harvest I attended I meant to just sit and listen. Too scared to say anything. Nothing prepared. But I found myself on my feet, sayin' things better than I could've planned. And the others listened with respect. The same thing'll happen to you."

And Marta proved correct. The interview was a smashing success. The anchorman, a nationally known figure, proved to be a man of some insight. He talked, earnestly, for more than an hour, with Bill and Marta, while the large network entourage made preparations. "It's just a strip of film, Mr. Adams," the anchorman reassured. "We'll get it right, the first time. If not, what the hell, we do it again."

Marta, he insisted, must be part of the feature. A local wheel of Harvest, she'd lend great authenticity to the story. The network people had done their research well, they were informed, to a point beyond even Marta's knowledge, of the power and scope of the fledgling farm organization. The anchorman had interviewed the national president of the group on two previous occasions.

Marta, with her penchant for farm kitchens, had hoped the film would be shot in the Adams' kitchen. Not possible, the kitchen was too small and modern. The living room served nicely. A half dozen farmers, all in field clothes, flanked Bill and Marta on the sofa and chairs as the equipment was set up. Perhaps for the best, reasoned Marta, the gothic bit has been overdone. This is the residence of a lawman, not a dirt farmer. Two of the county commissioners had been invited. They had declined to be interviewed. In a no win situation what could they possibly say that would not, in some sense, incriminate them?

Bill Adams did not freeze. In clear, direct words he told the story of George Rogers and Oscar Thornstad. He painted a stark, brief picture of the pressures building in the farm belt. More haltingly he spoke, in response to questions, of his own bereavement, the concurrence of this loss with the losses all around him. His allegiance had shifted, at long last, to the plight of the farmers, he could no longer carry out the duties of foreclosure enforcement. The quiet simplicity of the testimony was powerful.

Marta answered questions but spoke in a husky voice so soft that the interview was halted. She started again. In her own life, as a partner with her husband, as a widow, as a very potential member of the dispossessed, she had found no avenue of hope save Harvest.

Marta pulled no punches. Harvest was imperfect, she said. But the imperfections stemmed from growing pains, the members and leadership together floundered for solutions that had eluded the best brains of social structure and agricultural economics in the nation. She was asked the direct question, "What do you foresee happening if Harvest fails?" Marta did not flinch, looked directly into the camera eye.

"Harvest," she said, "is the last best hope for the future of the family farm as we have known it. Harvest must not fail. That is not the same as saying we will not fail. But if that happens we can say farewell, at last, to the ideals and hopes that were handed out with the old homestead grants. The dreams of the mid and late nineteenth century when the land was settled and made productive, will have vanished. One giant corporation will exist where a million farms are in place today, just as technology's engulfed the old one-sixties and two-forties and folded them into the big spreads that exist today. We've been able to live with expansion up till now. Beyond this point we're overwhelmed. History will have come full circle, there will be giant corporate farms and serfs, called employees, to farm them."

"An apocalyptic prospect," murmured the anchorman. He was getting better material than he had thought possible. Did the thoughts hold validity? He had no idea.

"Yes, isn't it?"

"Somehow, it doesn't seem like the kind of America I prefer for the future." He was prompting now she realized. But the fat was in the fire, there was no turning back.

"Talk to a hundred people. Anywhere, anytime. You might find that ninety-five agree with what I've said. And still, all this is happening."

"You sound like a prophet of doom."

"Naw." She laughed, easily. In the earnest conversation Marta had forgotten the camera and the bright lights. "I'm just a dirt farmer, struggling to stay alive, to remain on my land, mine and my brother's."

After the taping, the anchorman and crew relaxed with the locals over coffee and cake. Marta, always the hostess, even in another's house, had baked a huge Devils Food with lemon frosting at home and brought it with her. The crew feasted and praised the cake lavishly. "From a mix?" asked one. "You got to be kidding," lied Marta. She had not baked a cake from scratch in twenty years.

"A continuing story," intoned the anchorman, gravely. "Most of the great stories don't really reach a conclusion." He thanked them all for their splendid co-operation. "We may be back," he said. "I have a feeling for this land. I was born and raised in Nebraska, not a long ways from here."

In his hospital room, Oscar Thornstad watched the taped segment on the evening news. The stabbing pains of his upper torso had lessened to a dull ache. But he felt bound, a prisoner. All my life a free man, if a dumb bastard, he mused. Now I am forced to lie here, counting off the days like a convict, bound up by tape and bandages, bound by age and infirmity. But the old man was buoyed by the intense testimony on the screen.

"You're a gutsy guy, Bill," he muttered to the television. "I had you pegged wrong. I'll apologize the next time we talk. I ain't too proud to admit when I'm wrong. Christ, I've had enough practice." He grinned, there was fire, still, in the old war horse. "And you, Marty, God bless you. You tell it true, you prophesy the future. Is anyone out there listening? I mean, besides the old goats like me?"

Oscar ate his supper like a baby. The duty nurse, dumbfounded, took his pulse, twice, and checked the chart.

Marta didn't linger in town. She and Garth watched the broadcast in the barn, while the Surge machines pumped. The old black and white TV, brought to the farm by Garth from his old apartment in Pennsylvania, was grainy and flickering but the sound was clear enough. The segment, over five minutes of prime time, had been honed and edited to a degree but Marta found no fault with the final result. A picture emerged of an industry and way of life challenged as never before, in modern history, with the exception of the thirties. Then, hard times had been world wide, no one escaped. Land at less than one hundred dollars an acre, hogs at three cents a pound, oats at twenty cents a bushel. In the modern era inflation had driven land prices soaring, the interest costs beyond the ability to sustain. The unreal farm economy became the norm, production costs outracing the market value of the produce.

"You put the case for Harvest beautifully, Marty." Garth was unstinting in approval. "See. People are smarter than you think. I mean making you the mouthpiece for the county organization. You were just great."

"I was scared, Garth. So was Bill."

"Scared, confident, what's the difference? It didn't show, the message was delivered. And now that Mr. Adams has rejoined the human race, I would have to say the guy's O.K."

"He felt bad about the run-in with you and Jim Moenke. He really did, Garth."

"Well, hell," Garth laughed. He reached up and switched off the set. "Next time Jim and I go out trolling for scabs, maybe Adams can join us."

CHAPTER TWENTY-FIVE

Marta had gambled well. The broadcast was a sensation. Suddenly, almost overnight, Harvest occupied a niche of national awareness. The events in the Shawndo area could not be dismissed as the actions of a lunatic fringe of a depressed industry. From a bobtailed group of disgruntled farmers Harvest had emerged as the one clear voice speaking for a way of life, seeking desperately to hold on.

More national and regional exposure followed. Harvest became "hot" as the requests for interviews and background material poured in. Stories appeared on the two main protagonists, the widow and the widower, the dirt farmer and the displaced lawman Adams, who could abuse his constituency no longer. Marta had searched for a catalyst to turn the searchlight of truth on their problems. Now the light was nearly blinding. Harvest was on a roll, donations were bound to pick up. Days, she worked on the farm and did the chores with Garth. Inwardly she sought strength and balance. In the fields and in the barn her thoughts were clear.

There is a danger here, as well as opportunity, she reasoned. The message of Harvest, the plight of the family farm, has finally reached out across the land. But there was another side. Marta knew that both she and Bill Adams represented a new danger, the cult of individual notoriety, a celebrity greater than the larger issues. She'd made her splash, now she reflected, it's time to draw back. She had to run a farm. Bill Adams could go on the lecture circuit, eat the half cooked chicken.

Good reasoning. But things did not work out exactly as Marta hoped. Bill Adams withdrew into his shell. Basically a modest, almost bashful man, he couldn't handle the continuing pressure of publicity alone. When Marta could not be reached for advice or help, Adams tended to disappear. He broke appointments, canceled interviews. When Marta emerged, available for co-interviews, he was the same confident, intense man he'd been on the CBS news. No great surprise to Marta. She'd feared that Adams would be a reluctant hero. Now, she was caught in a bind. To help Harvest, to feed the fires of publicity so essential to the cause, she was forced to project herself, to bring far more attention to Marta Crawford than she wanted. A dilemma. Marta groped for answers in an area where she had no guideposts. She turned to Oscar.

The old man was near to bursting with restiveness, with anger at himself. The fire in his brain raced away. His bones knitted at a creeping pace; many of the vital signs remained fair to poor. All his life Oscar had been a sound sleeper, the deserved deliverance from the day's hard work. Now he slept very little, hardly more than an hour at a time, and the nights became long journeys, tough to get through, filled with disturbing remembrances of mistakes made, opportunities lost, neighbors and friends long since departed. His prognosis was a bit guarded. Oscar hoped for hospital release in three weeks. His doctor predicted, to Marta, more like two months and with skilled nursing care after that. At home, of course. No sane person in Black Loam County had any intention of attempting to install Oscar Thornstad in a nursing home.

"Hey, come on, Marty. You gonna fret yourself to pieces for nothing," he growled. "Ease up. Damn it, grin at me, you know you got a million dollar smile. Hell, get drunk if you feel so inclined."

"Well, I don't. And I'll thank you not to put such sinful ideas into my head."

"Sinful?" The old man's laugh was a testament to bitterness. "Don't play games with me, Marty. I've seen more black sins by more pious people in my time than you could ever believe. What's a snootful compared to turning women and kids into the street?" He leaned forward from the banked pillows, then winced in pain.

"Back off, Oscar," Marta was staggered by the vehemence of the man, his angry reaction to what would have been a kidding remark in the past. "I came here to visit you, you old coot. Not bury you."

"Not so far away as you think."

The hospital room was drab. An enterprising nurse or supervisor had installed flowered decals near the windows and light fixtures but the familiar white of plastered walls reflected antiseptic gloom. The small hospital was a community enterprise, run by a paid administrator, directed by a group of appointed local residents. A new wing, new labs and offices were desperately needed. The money was not available. The man should be in a double room for companionship, thought Marta. Still, what patient could put up with an old bear like Oscar?

She said, "Bill's getting jumpy. I'm sending him in to see you. He promised, maybe tomorrow."

"Well, he's taken his sweet time."

"Oscar, the man lost his wife, not two weeks ago. He's shook up. And he feels guilty. I mean your, accident. Bill figures it was his fault."

"How the hell can he think that? I got free will, for Christ's sake. He didn't push me."

"I know, I know. Still, he thinks he should have been more alert. Prevented you somehow."

"Aaah bullshit. I'll damn sure disabuse the man of that notion."

He brooded. "And don't worry, Marty. I'll get him calmed down. I may be on my back but I can make Bill Adams see the big picture, what we're all striving for."

"I hope so, honey."

"Don't honey me, hussy. I'll just brag him up about his TV appearance. Give him some background on the farm situation that he may not know. The man's a jewel, Marty, just needs a little polishing."

"It would be the greatest thing you could do for Harvest, Oscar. And for me."

They left it at that for the time being.

When Bill Adams visited the hospital the old hatchets were buried, old wounds healed. Oscar Thornstad felt, inwardly, as Marta had felt, that he was using the setting, the occasion, the flow of events to influence the future of Harvest. The old man felt no guilt about the tactic. First, his opinion of the ex sheriff had truly changed and, second, the ends of social and economic justice on the prairie justified nearly any means. The two men visited in a growing warmth of new friendship. Bill Adams relaxed, promised new commitment to the cause of rural survival. Oscar had for years felt an enmity near to hatred for the sheriff. Now, Adams' return to the fellowship of the local community would be made smoother by this new and unexpected alliance.

Marta heard of the successful visit as she prepared to leave the area on a three day trip. The state convention of Harvest was being held in St. Cloud. Previous conventions had taken place in the winter months but a streak of unusual weather had curtailed attendance. This year the final summer lull before harvest began seemed a better time. The elected delegates, and any other members who could make the trip, planned for the mid-week excursion. All told, forty-three members from Black Loam County attended all or part of the largest gathering of Harvest yet managed in the state.

Marta rode in a car with two farm couples, Mr. and Mrs. Bob Jasper and the Don Kliests. "A five passenger Olds," said Marta, with good humor. "If you didn't have a widow or a spinster along you couldn't make the numbers come out." The others hooted at her.

"Would you listen to the carefree single gal," said Liz Kliest. "We get to St. Cloud you can operate. Look who Cass and I are stuck with."

"Hell, you ain't stuck with nobody, Liz." Don Kliest winked at Bob Jasper and refused the bait. "Once we check in you just turn us loose. That old town might never be the same again."

Jasper agreed, heartily. This is going to be a good trip, thought Marta. No crepe hangers in the crowd. Farm folks are amazing. They walk, with grace and forbearance, through firestorms of drought, cold winters, depths of depression. Still, they can always smile and laugh, they can always find a bright side. They left the Shawndo area at ten A.M. on Wednesday. Garth wished them well. He and Marta were dairy people: he'd long since accepted that both of them couldn't be gone at the same time. The herd was producing well, new calves were favoring heifers two to one, always a good omen. But number seventeen had still not been replaced.

In a sense, Garth welcomed the time alone on the farm. The man of steel was experiencing a different phase, a new introspection had entered his life. He sought new directions. The end of his affair with Gail, unrewarding though the interlude had been, was forming, slowly, a mellower Garth Kyllo. He would stay away from the muni in Prairie City for a time. He was having second thoughts about Gloria, had absorbed too much idle gossip about her. He'd also curtail his contacts with Jim Moenke. The thought behind these changes was ill-formed but he sensed he'd been slipping away from the things he came back to regain, the basic elements of life. Too many diversions had been interfering.

Looking at his situation, Garth saw that the crops, after the crucible of drought, were fair to good, the cows doing well. Perhaps this winter, when things are quiet, he'd take a job in a factory if he could find one, to help them through until spring. Otherwise the winter might become a trap. Chores night and morning, booze and gambling in between. Garth's smile was cryptic. He wasn't about to become one of the guys who did their farming in town. Saloon farmers they call'em. And their animals and crops show the results. Marta had a lot of distractions these days. The Harvest convention, for instance. But nothing stood in her way of doing the job, here at home. Nothing.

Harvest had become big time. The leaders knew that the job at hand was now even tougher, preventing popularity from becoming a passing fad. Marta's days and nights in St. Cloud were packed with activity. Politicians who had disavowed Harvest in the past or, at best, ignored it, were, suddenly, available speakers. The congressmen lauded the actions of a grass roots organization that fought the good fight for price parity and a form of insurance against those foreclosures caused by vagaries of weather and markets. Republican and Democrat alike they pledged new help from Washington, D.C., a bare-knuckle battle for a better deal for the family farm.

The members of Harvest listened politely. The problem was, as always, to decide if they were hearing sincerity or merely the kind of posturing they'd seen so often before. The U.S. secretary of agriculture himself had hoped to attend the convention. He could not, finally, fit the trip into his schedule. But he sent warm wishes via closed circuit and answered questions from the group.

Banners throughout the big auditorium proclaimed deep feelings, "We HAD a Dream." "Farms, not Arms." "We pay taxes to the Enemy – the Government!" And, more simply, "Hear Our Prayers." Marta was asked to speak about the events at Shawndo. She had marshalled more poise and greater confidence than she ever had before. She spoke to a packed hall of her own situation, the double tragedy of George Rogers and Gerald Ryan, the resignation of Bill Adams. The story had become well known from the network telecast and other media exposure. Still, the events, in Marta's un-embellished style, took on a stark reality that stunned the crowd. They sat in silence until she had finished. After more than a minute had passed a thunderous ovation rose to the steel rafters. Marta, still on the platform, was shaken.

On the final evening of the convention the state vice president of Harvest, Lawrence Cahill, was elevated to the leadership for the following year. The retiring president was exactly that. Big Jess Pritchard, grain farmer from the Red River Valley, had sold out all his holdings. He was moving to Arizona for his health. The membership loved Big Jess, who had nurtured the organization through the birth pangs of the early years. He had watched as the organization faltered, stumbled and then grew stronger. Now it was time for Cahill to take command.

A new vice president for the group was needed. The state convention became almost a replay of the Black Loam County special meeting at Shawndo, merely on a larger scale. Marta's time had come. There was a surge beyond resistance to elevate the valiant widow to a post of leadership, next in succession to the actual state presidency. A tumultuous round of applause, deafening, invigorating, met her nomination. Two other farmers were placed in nomination, a poultry farmer from the southeast section of the state and a grain farmer from midstate. Both were good men. They didn't stand a chance. Marta was elected on a tremendous show of hands. The other candidates proposed a unanimous vote... the verdict was sealed.

Marta's rise made an amazing chronicle. From ordinary working membership just three weeks previously, Marta Crawford had become a symbol, the best known voice for agriculture in America. Journalists from the ag publications besieged her after the election. Marta put them off. She was bone weary. But by morning she was rested. She granted a lengthy interview at breakfast as she enjoyed her last meal in St. Cloud before heading home. The writers and broadcasters loved her. Marta dazzled the media with logic and her earthy language delighted everyone. She could be funny, sincere, poignant. Once again, as in the CBS interview, the word prophet surfaced. "More properly 'prophetess'", interjected one lady reporter. Either way, Marta didn't care for the label.

"If the sky is black in the afternoon, the humidity heavy and I say it looks like rain, does that make me some kind of forecaster?" she asked, earnestly. "My God, the handwriting is on the wall for the family farmers in this country. A kid in the third grade could see what's coming down as well as I can. They can't see it in Washington, D.C." She added, "So, what's new?" The reporters clung to each word. She had won them over with her candor and self deprecation. They promised to send her clippings from their printed stories, the radio and television people promised to visit the farm at Shawndo in the near future for follow-up.

The trip home was a celebration. Nothing in the farm picture had really changed but the euphoria of the state convention was heady inside the Oldsmobile. "Hope springs eternal," murmured Cass Jasper. Liz Kliest winked at Marta and the men nodded. But the remark was fitting. Harvest had gained new hope, new expectations All of them knew that the fulfillment of promises was far down the road. Cass is right, thought Marta. If we don't have hope we have nothing.

When the Olds arrived at Shawndo Marta was tested again. They stopped at the Crystal Cafe for coffee, though Marta was anxious to get home. But Jen had phoned to Don Kliest in St. Cloud, early in the morning. Then she'd put out the word.

An explosion of hand clapping greeted the group as they walked inside the old cafe. Nearly one hundred people had gathered for the surprise. The place was packed. Marta wept. She knew every face, each voice. She had never dreamed of such a welcome. I am blessed, again, she thought, this is just too much. Instinctively she searched the crowd for two faces she'd held dear. One was dead, one in the hospital. But Oscar had sent his greetings, the words from his bed were delivered by one of his nephews.

The usual cry went up. "Speech, speech." Glasses were pounded on the tables, a bedlam of noise erupted that Jen made no effort to control. The proprietor stood in her alcove by the range, smiling at the wall of sound.

I've talked so much this week, thought Marta. But this is different, this is home. A sudden realization struck her. None of the bankers were in the crowd... perhaps Jen had failed to invite them. Marta told them of the convention, of the new respect from officials, the new hopes and promises. "Take it all with a dose of salts," she advised. They howled, this was their Marta. "It's little more than a beginning," she went on. "But without Harvest, not even that much. All the big shots... did I pronounce that word right?"...laughter shook the cafe. "All the politicians now want to get aboard. Some of 'em we don't want, they've back-stabbed and lied too many times. But of course all that is up to you, not me. This is an organization of farmers, not blabber mouths like me."

Marta left them with that thought. Again the applause was deafening, her friends and neighbors couldn't get enough of her new prominence, a bit of fame that rubbed off, just a little, on each of them.

At the farm, Garth had heard the news. A huge grin split the lean face. He greeted his older sister with a mammoth hug that lifted her off the ground. The man was immensely proud, never more certain that he had turned his tortured life in the right direction.

CHAPTER TWENTY-SIX

The wound had long since been lanced, the poison, it seemed, was drained. A new Garth, tougher, leaner, wind-seared, heard the final words with a calmness near to indifference. I am astounded, he thought, that I can handle this bulletin without blowing it. A few months back he'd have been torn to bits, those days when he'd hoped for a different ending. But he'd made peace with the gods of inevitability. Perhaps it was the new life, the long hours in the fields, the return to the basics of dirt and growth and tending cows. Gail Samarro's voice on the phone was that of a stranger, one he had met in a distant city, flirted with, kissed and caught the next flight to somewhere.

Mid October. The corn harvest had begun, most of the soybeans had been combined and were stored in the bright new metal bin, the successor to the demolished granary. At nine in the evening Marta was upstairs, busy at her bedroom desk. Garth sipped a can of Grain Belt (he'd switched from Bud) and listened to the familiar voice.

"So," he drawled. "You're leaving tomorrow?"

"Bag and baggage, Garth. Kids, car and caboodle... the works."

"Happy?"

"I guess. As near as I can tell. I've kind of given up on happiness... the definition eludes me."

"Join the crowd."

"Anyway, I'm doing what I want to do. I suppose that has to be some kind of happiness."

"Like I felt when I left P.A." He lit a cigarette and pulled deeply, the nicotine warming him.

"I guess. Mama never told me it would be like this. Mixed emotions, you know."

"Well now, Mama, yours and mine, didn't know what a different world was waiting out there. I don't suppose you can do any better for your kids. And you're one peach of a mother."

"Oh hell, I try. What I'm saying is... I don't know. I'm happy to leave Shawndo. I hate to leave my friends."

"Um. Sure."

"And, God damn it... you."

"We've gone over that, Gail."

"I know!"

A sudden gust of wind rattled the kitchen window. Outside, the autumn wind sang dirges to the fading season and the temperature hovered at twenty-eight degrees. Perfect harvesting weather, the ground firm and dry, the cold wind drying the corn each day. A breezy fall was a harvester's dread... Garth knew the bromides. Cold, uncomfortable, bundled up against the elements. Tough on farmers, perfect for curing the grain. Garth shivered involuntarily, remembering twelve hours on the picker-sheller.

He had to say the words, make the break complete. "You joining Kenseth?"

"I'm going to work for him, yes."

"I mean otherwise."

"Yes. Otherwise too. You won't be invited to the wedding."

Garth chuckled.

"Actually I'd prefer to be invited. So I could stand you up."

"Bastard," she laughed, the sound as rich and throaty as ever. Gail, like Garth, was playing out the string. "Garth, I didn't have to make this call. But it didn't seem right, the other way."

"I know. It's a class act, baby. And class you never lacked."

"I wish you were right." The woman seemed tired now, unsure. "Class is character. I don't have that much, hon" – the endearment was a throwaway, he knew– "I'm just like everyone in this god-for-saken corner of the earth. What I have got is problems. That's what I'm taking a swing at with this decision."

"Sure. And you might come out smelling like a rose."

"Good bye, Garth. And thanks for everything. You've been a hell of a bright spot in my life this year."

"Yeah? Well, that's good. Best of everything. Give my love to the kids."

Garth nestled the phone, softly, into the cradle. He rose, stretched and walked to the refrigerator for a fresh Grain Belt. He sat again at the kitchen table and smoked a cigarette, face bleak, eyes crinkled to horizons beyond the plastered walls, the Marlboro Man in flannel shirt and faded denim. What a nowhere conversation, he thought, not even a chapter in my life. Just a couple of paragraphs that got sandwiched in between the real stuff.

Harvesting got underway. In the morning, first, as always, the milking and the chores. The wind still blew, a prairie nuisance the harvesters had learned to abide, just as they lived with harsh facts of life like minus thirty in January, sloggy wet springs and the anvil heat of July. Garth and Marta worked with a neighbor, John Harstad, and his son. The four alternated between the two farms daily as the fields ripened and the yellow ears, tip ends shrunken by the drought, reached a moisture point for safe storage. Some of the corn went to the Farmers Elevator for sale, cash flow was needed badly. The remainder of the crop went into separate bins and cribs and whatever space was available. Most of this, on the Crawford farm, would go to the dairy herd. Jon Harstad kept no milk cows. He had a few hogs and sheep but the bulk of his crop would be sealed for government loan.

We blast the government, mused Garth. We dodge their taxes as best we can, we curse their officials both elected and appointed, but we can never escape the long arm. Like a shadow cast by a plane in flight the dark presence of Washington is beyond escape. Would we fare better without that shadow or, as many believe, merely go busted sooner?

Oscar was right, always right and so disregarded. The wealth and forbearance of the taxpayers had been wasted on the few fortunate enough to garner the hundred grand and half million dollar subsidies. The pittance doled out to the small farmers were a band aid too tiny to cover the gaping wounds of markets and forces beyond the control, or even the understanding, of most. How many men like Oscar were needed and will never be placed in positions of influence, Garth wondered? The ag departments are choked with men and women long on seminars and conferences and short on common sense. The golden ears, test weight light, fed into the green implement, the shelled corn poured into the holding tank and was piped out to the wagons at the end of the field.

Today the four worked one of the Crawford fields. At noon they gathered around the kitchen table. Marta had fixed the meal before going to sleep the night before.

The corn harvest took eighteen working days for the two farms. The wind never let up and the stalks of corn gradually bent and tangled before the gusting onslaughts. Corn picking, always a draining task, became intolerable. The combine ground at a snail's pace across fields where the rows had been obliterated. On the final day, with less than two acres to go, the Harstad boy, absent from senior high for the harvest, lost two fingers of his right hand. The accident could not be blamed on the big picker-sheller. The picker, an ancient single row forced back into service because of the slow going, fought for days, like the larger machine, to clear the jungle of corn. As Billy Harstad pawed at the tangled stalks, the steel chains gripped him, pulling his arm into the rollers as the chains have done since the first mechanical marvel replaced the hand husking peg in the early part of the century.

Marta reeled at the sight, a red mist danced before her tired eyes. Her life dissolved into battles against sudden death on the land she loved. First Garth, then Oscar, now Billy; there could be no end in a way of life where danger never slept. Garth and Jon Harstad freed the boy, fixed a tourniquet upon the upper arm and stanched the flow of blood. A rush to the hospital at Prairie City, from there, by helicopter, to the Mayo Clinic where one of the fingers was reattached. The second finger too shredded to save. The final two acres had been left in the field for the cows to forage.

Days later, Garth met Jim Moenke for the first time in several weeks. While Garth had mellowed, the squat Moenke was still the same, swashbuckling through the Municipal Liquor Store in Prairie City, his voice a deep bellow in the smoky lounge.

Together the two old friends got sloshing drunk. A long dry spell, Garth rationalized, as the warm glow encased him. An early Thanksgiving you might say. Gloria was not on the scene. She had hung up her waitress uniform for a steady job at the creamery. Garth took the news with a large yawn.

But in the depths of his descent, Gail slipped back from the hidden recesses of his mind, a place from which she'd never vanish. "I thought I had it licked," he murmured, morosely, the oval face and dark eyes near to reality in the plastic booth they had often shared.

"Licked what?" The question from Moenke jolted Garth. "Licked who?"

"Oh shit, nothin' man. I was just squirreled out there for a minute. I'm O.K."

"Sure you are. And if there's some son of a bitch you can't lick, just let me know."

"I'll do that, buddy."

"Not talkin' about lickin' that half ass ex-sheriff are you?"

"Adams? Hell no, we're friends now." The news stunned Moenke.

"No shit?" Moenke puzzled the news. "Hey, yeah, I guess you are at that. The guy's sweet on your big sister, so I hear. Picked up that flash in the Crystal Cafe."

"You got big ears, James. Man can pick up most anything in a small town."

"Yeah, for sure. Any truth to it?" Moenke was unabashed.

"Hell, I don't know, Jim. I help Marta run the farm. I stay out of her private life." Garth was swept, suddenly, with a loneliness he had thought long put to rest. God, I hope James is right for once. Somebody in the old Kyllo clan ought to find a glimmer. No rainbow, that's asking too much. But a glimmer. This woman, his only sibling, who had wiped his running nose and protected him at school on his first days had become, in later life, his passport to an existence nearly forgotten in the brutal years of the steel mills. Garth's eyes were moist. He was remembering, he realized, through a haze of alcohol, a romantic version of hard cold facts. Balls, he thought, I'm plastered. Makes no difference. Drunk or sober the truth is real and Marty is the greatest I've ever known. We might, finally, lose the farm. I could handle that. For sure I could never deal with the loss of my sister. The lean man brooded into his drink and the smoky sound level of the lounge lowered as closing time drew near.

"Here's the thing," said Moenke. "I'm drunk and you're worse. You just ain't got my experience and you're too damn skinny."

Garth, his eyes red slits, allowed as how that was so.

"So," said Moenke, slowly, ponderously... the words came haltingly, one by one. "One more D.W.I. puts me out of business and you don't need your first one. Let's hail a cab."

"Cab? Cost a fortune."

"Naw. We split it. Fifteen miles to your spread, only eight to mine. The old lady has put up with me bringing home a buddy before. We sack out at home, I use the truck to drive you back to town in the morning, you collect your wagon and go home."

"James, you're a genius." Garth had worried about the flashing lights following him, the stop, the breathalyzer.

The muni manager had overheard. He called Junior Gherken. Gherken, crippled in a car accident years before , picked up a buck here and there doing local deliveries and had a rural Sunday paper route for the Pioneer Press newspaper. The "taxi," a full-size Chevy station wagon fitted with special controls, was waiting at the front door when the two weathered radicals returned from the ritual pit stop in the men's room.

For the first time since his return from the east, not counting his trip with Gail and the time spent in the hospital, Garth missed the morning chores. He pulled into the farm yard at eight-thirty. Marta, taking a leisurely breakfast in the kitchen, grinned wickedly at the hung-over wreck.

"Moenke, I presume?"

"Who else?"

"Well, I hope you guys didn't drink it all. You might want to go out again some night."

"Two chances, slim and none."

"I know the story." Marta rose and popped bread into the toaster. She poured a cup of hot coffee for Garth and smiled, fondly. "Hell," she said. "You got one coming now and then. But here's the thing. Can you do double duty for a few days?"

"Sure. Least I can do. What's up?"

"A trip. The famous ex-sheriff and myself are flying to Washington. Tomorrow."

"Washington, D.C.?"

"Naw. Washington, Idaho." Marta smoothed her shirt and front and looked, with disdain, on the soiled denim.

"I know," mocked Garth. "The old female complaint. You haven't got a thing to wear."

"Well, damn it. I haven't."

"Washington, huh?" Garth lit a cigarette, coming back to life. "Government stuff? connected with Harvest?"

"Sort of, I guess. I don't know the details but I've been picked to testify before some Senate committee, sub-committee, who the hell knows? On the farm problems. Bill, with his recent notoriety, will testify, I assume, from the viewpoint of a law man who had to come down on the slobs – against his will." The old realist returned. "None of it will do any good, I'm sure. Still ..."

"Yeah... still." Garth finished the toast and coffee and stubbed out his smoke. I'm getting to work. There's a million things to do around this place."

"Take it easy, hon."

"Aaah, I took it easy this morning." He reached for his mackinaw, hanging limp on a hook beside the sink.

"About those clothes for your trip... what the hell do I know? But make sure you pack a couple of frilly night gowns."

"Get to work... while you're still able."

CHAPTER TWENTY-SEVEN

In the days that followed Garth worked with a fury and persistence that dwarfed his efforts of the past. He spent long hours... surely the wrong time of the year for shingling... on the barn roof. A few leaks had shown up during the summer and the tornado had weakened the entire structure. Now he toughed it out, sawing, splicing, laying down new asphalt shingles, his face raw, hands reddened in a wind chill often far below zero. Day after bitter day, with Marta away on her hopeless pilgrimage, Garth drove himself, a catharsis to drive into submission once and for all the ghosts he had thought were conquered... before Gail's last hail and farewell.

The barn roof was only one project. The manure cleaner was down. New chain lengths and assorted hardware brackets were installed and the electric motor taken to a shop in Prairie City for repair. For days Garth forked and shoveled the aromatic refuse by hand, childhood memories floating back with each wheel-barrow load pushed out to the frozen pile in the barn yard. There were still some stumps and brambles to clear from the August storm and windows to glaze and repair in nearly every building including the house. The work was interminable in the time of year for taking it easy on the farm.

Garth didn't go near Prairie City. In the ten days Marta was gone he drove just once to Shawndo for groceries, cigarettes and two twelve packs of Old Milwaukee. Garth had a soft spot in his heart for breweries; he liked to help them all. In rough weather he took a meal at the Crystal Cafe and bestowed an early holiday bear hug on Jen that caused a mock fainting spell. Then he slid in to a wooden booth, opposite Oscar.

The old man had shrunk a bit more. The craggy features, wreathed in smoke, resembled more an icon than a living person. But the smile was still warm, the voice as rumbling as before. The man had become as close to Garth as his father ever was. They had helped each other in time of crisis... the ultimate bond. Now Oscar played out his final act with the grace that had fashioned all his days, true to his role, his heritage, sure of his lines.

The old man toyed with a slab of Jen's best apple pie. He did not, as many said, exist on cigarettes and snoose alone. But he'd always seemed removed from the physical realities imposed on lesser constitutions.

The two men tried their best to let the subject of Harvest lie dormant, pending Marta's and Bill's return. Their talk was humorous, of neighbors, crops and local sporting news from the high schools, low pressure subjects that didn't boil blood. Still, in a way, the old wars intruded.

"It's the matter of a marker for George's grave." Oscar worried the notion. It had been prying on his mind. "The man's laid to rest. We won't forget him and I hope the world, this little part of it at least, remembers him too."

"Helen is broke, for sure."

"Oh, Helen will get along. But yah, for an expense like this, she couldn't handle it. She shouldn't have to do it alone."

"And most everyone else in the same boat."

"I know... I know. Including me, but I'm better fixed than some. I'm going to start the ball rolling and see what happens. I can spare two bills."

Garth, for not the first time, was awed. Two hundred! He had a fair notion of Oscar's finances.

"You're a wonder, you old Norski. Put me down for fifty. I'll let Marty speak for herself."

The rock face softened, a trace of a grin appeared. "Smart. I think the last guy that spoke for that woman landed on his ass."

The deal had been blessed. Garth knew Oscar would see it through, no matter how long. Mike, George, Gerald Ryan... death reaches out in all directions and stone markers should record the days of anguish, if only for the sake of history. For this, Oscar Thornstad wouldn't hurry. He'd pressure no one, might even refuse donations that would be too much of a sacrifice. But he'd prevail.

The man had atrocious eating habits. He motioned Jen to the booth and ordered a second piece of pie. Garth laughed and jabbed at an old man who thumbed his nose at all the accepted precepts of health and longevity. Oscar lived by his own rules and, for the most part, found them fitting. He stood up to fate as he'd stood against the auctioneer's truck in a battle he couldn't win.

"Seen James Moenke lately?"

Garth chuckled. "More than too much on one night recently." He told Oscar of the monumental drunk and the punishing hangover. Oscar smiled.

"You try to keep up with that cowboy when it comes to drinking you'll sure as hell drown."

"I won't try it again. Count on it." Garth brooded. "I like what we did last summer. You know, pushing our little boycott. Never had a chance but, God, it felt good to try."

"The idea's sound, Garth."

"Yeah, I think so. But I'm going to cool it for awhile. Might be job hunting after New Years' to help out. I can't get too radical a rep."

"I know, buddy. You're boxed in."

The big front windows of the old cafe were, as always in cold damp weather, steamed over. Tiny drops of moisture formed on the sills, eroding further the chipped wood. The brave flowered curtains, Jen's lone artistic gesture, were bright and clean however, a defiant signal to a hostile environment, a crumbling economy.

But Harvest was unavoidable. "Not much in most of the papers," observed Oscar. "But the St. Paul daily did a fairly decent feature on the senate hearings. Seems as though our local pair drew some favorable reactions." The tone was impassive, the voice of a man let down too often.

"The piece was O.K.," agreed Garth. "Marta... what the hell can you say? And Bill Adams. Not fair to spring a man with principles on that crowd. Like interviewing a man from Mars."

Oscar nodded. "The man walked tall into that hearing room, a stranger in a strange land."

Three nights later the weather had cleared and deeper cold had settled on the prairie. Garth and Marta shared the old kitchen table, the cooking range augmenting the heat from the basement furnace. A feeling of peace was on them, the ten days apart had been their longest separation since Garth's return on that cold March day that seemed so long ago. They'd walked together, more than once, through the valley of the shadow; now they were, at least for the time, survivors. The days of winter crept in, another bleak year was drawing to a close.

The time was near to ten. Marta, bone tired, toyed with a cup of coffee. Garth popped a Schlitz, long legs stretched out in comfort beneath the table.

"So. Interesting trip?"

Marta could still grin. "Sure, an experience. The sight-seeing was grand. We'd like to go back some time in the early spring, see the cherry blossoms."

"Yeah, I been there. A pretty town. Of course you realize I'm asking you about the hearings."

"I know. I know. And I think you realize what word I'll use."

"Frustrating?"

"You got it." Marta rubbed her eyes. She wasn't sleepy, too tired for that, but her eyes were strained, dark shadows puffed beneath them. "Oh, we may have made some progress. I'm not real positive. But the senators are big shots, they think in terms of huge spreads, population shifts, retraining for the displaced... all that heavy think-tank bullshit that slides right over folks like us."

"Figures."

"We... Bill and I... tried to cut through all that, bring the picture down to gut level on one hand and the damage to a nation of a

170

disappearing small land owner class on the other. God, what a task."

Garth muttered, "Is there intelligent life along the Potomac?"

Marta laughed. "Very faint signs, hon. That's about all we could see."

Garth rummaged in the refrigerator for a fresh brew. He gazed at his sister, fondly.

"You're bushed, kid. No late-late show for you tonight. And no chores in the morning."

"Thanks Garth, you're a champ. Yah, I'm tired. But it's more than the trip." She looked around her, readjusting to the old familiar surroundings. "My life has disintegrated around me, Garth, the pieces are scattered, I can never put them together. Mike is long dead, George Rogers is dead and Oscar came near enough. I can't number Betty Adams among them, I didn't know her that well." Marta poured more coffee. "I wish I'd known Betty, had been close to her. But I didn't, so... " She looked into her brother's face and marveled at the love that had grown and strengthened between them.

"Garth, I'm going to marry Bill Adams. The Harvest woman will marry the enemy. The man was our enemy... once."

Garth took the news calmly. He winked.

"Sure, Marty. Good news."

"Maybe it had to be, Garth. Bill and I are both ships adrift." She laughed, a hollow sound. "I thought I was tough, hon, and damn it I am."

"Tough as nails."

"But I passed my limit. I've felt that, like Mike, I couldn't survive. But I can. Bill Adams has thrown me a lifeline."

"Seems to me that goes both ways. You've thrown him one, too."

"I hope so."

"What happens now?" Garth was unworried.

"We'll work things out, you and I. We can work out anything... 'cause we're family. I'll live in Prairie with Bill and commute, work the farm like always. But now you're the boss. Sink or swim, you're the man. We'll work out the details."

"Should be easy," said Garth. "Like falling off a shit spreader." The white teeth flashed and he flipped his brew. "We remember the math, kid. Something from nothing is still nothing."

"It might not always be that way. Besides, we may get some better representation in St. Paul. I've talked Bill into running for state senator next year. No cinches in politics, but Bill is on a roll with the public. He's a hero, which pays nothing. The salary of a state senator is pretty good for a part time job."

"The news continues to improve."

Marta rose and walked to the kitchen window, spreading the

curtains to look out at the frosty night. Prairie winter was in the air, nature was hunkered down against the onslaught to come.

Harvest season is over, she thought, the amber soybeans and the corn fill the bins, the silos are full. The moon was bright silver, brilliant in a cloudless eastern sky. Not a harvest moon... the word Harvest encompassed her... but a lovely light all the same. The harvest moon was long past for this season. Her new life would begin with the new year, would be well established before a harvest moon appeared again.

A Farm At Shawndo
WAS DESIGNED, EDITED AND TYPESET
AT
Lone Oak Press

The book was set via Microsoft Word for Windows on
a LaserMaster LX6 Typesetter. Fonts are from the
LaserMaster foundry.
Scanning was done on a Microtek 600Z
using Aldus PhotoStyler & OmniPage Professional